Jilly Cooper is a well-known journalist, writer and media superstar. The author of many number one bestselling novels, including *Riders*, *Rivals*, *Polo*, *The Man Who Made Husbands Jealous*, *Appassionata*, *Score!* and *Pandora*, she and her husband live in Gloucestershire.

Jilly Cooper was appointed OBE in the 2004 Queen's Birthday Honours List.

By Jilly Cooper

FICTION
Pandora
The Rutshire Chronicles:
Riders
Rivals
Polo
The Man Who Made Husbands Jealous
Appassionata
Score!

NON-FICTION
Animals in War
Class
How to Survive Christmas
Hotfoot to Zabriskie Point (with Patrick Lichfield)
Intelligent and Loyal
Jolly Marsupial
Jolly Super
Jolly Superlative
Jolly Super Too
Super Cooper
Super Jilly
Super Men and Super Women
The Common Years
Turn Right at the Spotted Dog
Work and Wedlock
Angels Rush In
Araminta's Wedding

CHILDREN'S BOOKS
Little Mabel
Little Mabel's Great Escape
Little Mabel Saves the Day
Little Mabel Wins

ROMANCE
Bella
Emily
Harriet
Imogen
Lisa and Co
Octavia
Prudence

ANTHOLOGIES
The British in Love
Violets and Vinegar

HARRIET

Jilly Cooper

CORGI BOOKS

HARRIET
A CORGI BOOK : 0 552 15251 X

Originally published in Great Britain by
Arlington Books Ltd

PRINTING HISTORY
Arlington Books edition published 1976
Corgi edition published 1977
Corgi edition reissued 2005

1 3 5 7 9 10 8 6 4 2

Set in 11/14pt Times by
Kestrel Data, Exeter, Devon.

Corgi Books are published by Transworld Publishers,
61–63 Uxbridge Road, London W5 5SA,
a division of The Random House Group Ltd,
in Australia by Random House Australia (Pty) Ltd,
20 Alfred Street, Milsons Point, Sydney, NSW 2061, Australia,
in New Zealand by Random House New Zealand Ltd,
18 Poland Road, Glenfield, Auckland 10, New Zealand
and in South Africa by Random House (Pty) Ltd,
Endulini, 5a Jubilee Road, Parktown 2193, South Africa.

Printed and bound in Great Britain by
Cox & Wyman Ltd, Reading, Berkshire.

Papers used by Transworld Publishers are natural, recyclable
products made from wood grown in sustainable forests.
The manufacturing processes conform to the environmental
regulations of the country of origin.

To my niece Amelia Sallit with love

HARRIET

Part One

Chapter One

It started to snow as Harriet was writing the last paragraph. Looking up she saw the flakes tumbling out of a sullen, pewter-grey sky, swirling and chasing each other, drifting into the branched arms of the trees. With a yelp of excitement she put down her pen and ran to the window. The flakes were small and compact. It was going to settle. Now they were belting down, and suddenly the towers of Oxford were encapsulated in a flurry of white flakes, as though someone had violently shaken a snow scene in a glass ball.

She went back to her essay, copying out the last two sentences with a flourish, then she wrote her name at the top of the first page: Harriet Poole, carefully closing up the Os, because she'd read somewhere that it was a sign of weak character to leave them open.

She had got up at six to finish her essay, having spent all week re-writing it. Anything to avoid the humiliation of last week's tutorial. Her tutor, Theo Dutton, who chain-smoked and showed no mercy, was famous for his blistering invective. When she had finished reading out last week's essay he had asked her three questions which entirely exposed the shallowness of her argument, then, tearing up the pages with long nicotined fingers, had dropped them disdainfully into the waste paper basket.

'That was junk,' he had said in his dry, precise voice, 'you merely copied out other people's ideas with varying degrees of accuracy. Read Shakespeare rather than books about Shakespeare. Look into your heart and write. You're trying too hard; relax; enjoy what you read or dislike it, but don't deaden it on paper.'

Her eyes had filled with tears. She had worked very hard. 'You're too sensitive, Harriet,' he had said, 'we'll have to raise your threshold of pain, won't we? A large dose of bullying each week until you build up an immunity.'

His hard, yellow eyes gleamed through his spectacles. He was smiling, but she wasn't sure if he was fooling or not. He always made her feel faintly sexy, but uneasy at the same time.

'Now,' he had said briskly, 'for next week, write an essay on which of Shakespeare's characters would be best in bed and why.'

Harriet flushed scarlet.

'But I can't . . .' she began, then bit her lip.

'Can't write from experience? Use your imagination then. Shakespeare didn't know what it was like to be a black general or a Danish prince, did he?'

'Hamlet wouldn't have been much good,' said Harriet. 'He'd have talked too much, and never

14

made up his mind to, until it was too late and one had gone off the boil.'

Theo had given a bark of laughter.

'That's more like it. Write something I might enjoy reading.'

Well, there was her essay, and it had taken her all week. She had read nothing but Shakespeare, and thought about nothing but sex. And she felt light-headed from exhaustion, a sense of achievement and the snow outside.

She was also starving. No-one was up. The land-lady and her husband liked to lie in on Saturday. Downstairs among the letters scattered on the floor lay one from her boyfriend, Geoffrey. Reading it, she wandered into the kitchen, her jeans, too long when she wasn't wearing heels, swishing on the linoleum.

'Dear Harriet,' wrote Geoffrey, on office writing paper, 'I am really fed up. I can't get down this weekend, but I must finish this report and hand it in to the MD on Monday.'

Then followed a lot of waffle about pressure of work, grabbing every opportunity in the present economic climate, and doing it for both their sakes.

'So pleased you have finally gone on the pill,' he ended up. (Harriet had a vision of herself poised like a ballerina on a tiny capsule.) 'I'm so fed up with being parked outside your bedroom every night like flowers in a hospital. I want you so much darling, I know I can make you happy. I'll be down next weekend, early Friday night. Meanwhile keep yourself on ice. Hugs and kisses and other things, love Geoffrey.'

Harriet felt a great wave of relief, then felt guilty. One really shouldn't contemplate losing one's virginity to someone one felt relieved one wasn't going to see. Virginity should be lost gloriously. Geoffrey wasn't glorious, just solid and very, very persistent.

Now that he wasn't coming down, she could lapse a bit, and not bother about dieting until Monday. She opened a tin of baked beans and put a slice of toast under the grill. After her tutorial with Theo, she could go to the library and get out a couple of trashy novels – she deserved a break after all that Shakespeare – and later go to the new Robert Redford film, and see it round twice, and eat a whole bar of Crunchie, and perhaps an ice-cream too. The weekend stretched out like the snow beginning to cover the lawn.

After eating every baked bean she felt fat, and decided to wash her hair in Theo Dutton's honour. There was no shower in the bathroom. It was either a question of scalding your head under the hot tap or freezing under the cold, which was much colder because of the snow.

As she alternately froze and scalded she pondered once more the problem of her virginity. All her friends were sleeping with their boyfriends, and she suspected that if she'd really fancied Geoffrey she'd have succumbed to him months ago. If Robert Redford, for example, came to Oxford in a play and bumped into her outside the theatre or met her at a party, she'd be his in a trice. She was conscious of so much love welling up inside her. If only she were beautiful and not so shy, she might attract some beautiful man to give it to. She couldn't be bothered putting conditioner on her hair after she'd washed it. Theo wasn't that attractive.

Dripping, she went into her room. Her papers and books were scattered all over the floor. She wished she were one of those people who could transform a room into a home with a few feminine touches. But she loved her room, messy as it was, and even if she didn't have a great love in her life, the days at Oxford had their own happiness. Theo Dutton, when he wasn't being vile, calling her his star pupil to another don who'd dropped in to borrow a book, a muddled feeling she had of the importance of intellectual things, music, writing books herself, being reviewed one dizzy day in the *Times Literary Supplement*, 'Miss Harriet Poole in her first novel shows sensitivity and remarkable maturity.'

The snow was covering the lawn and the red roofs now. Two children, shrieking with delight, were scraping it off the top of a car to make a snowball. On the ledge of the window lay a moth. Harriet picked it up – she had read somewhere that human hands burnt insects' feet like hot coals. It was too cold to put it outside. Running out of the room, she parked it gently in her landlady's maidenhair fern on the landing. At least it would have something to eat. She spent so much time worrying about dogs being put out on the motorway, and horses being sent to the slaughter house, and children in orphanages.

What on earth was she going to do when something really terrible happened to her – like one of her parents dying?

The snow had now nearly hidden a cluster of snowdrops that had courageously sprung out of the dark earth. Snow on snow, thought Harriet; perhaps she should write a poem about it. Crouching in front of the gas fire she got out a pen and began to scribble.

An hour later her hair was dry and she realized she was going to be late. She pulled on a red sweater because it brought some colour to her sallow cheeks, red tights and a grey skirt, which bagged slightly. She must get some new clothes, but her grant never went far enough.

She tried on a belt, then took it off because it emphasized her spare tyre. She really shouldn't have eaten all those baked beans; perhaps it was being on the pill for a week that made her feel so fat. The red tights had a ladder, but her black boots covered that. Her duffle coat had two buttons missing. The snow, like life, had caught her on the hop.

Aware that she might want to brood over Geoffrey's letter later, she put it with her essay in a blue folder. Outside the house, she caught her breath as the frozen wind cut through her like a knife. Her bicycle, its red paint peeling, lay against the ivied wall. The snow, now four inches deep, turned yellow where a dog had lifted its leg on her front wheel.

As she pedalled past the park snow was settling

in the dead leaves and hollows of the chestnut trees. In the churchyard the stone angels had white mobcaps on their heads. The frozen puddles didn't crack beneath her bicycle wheels. As she headed towards the Banbury Road, the snow stepped up the pace, exploding over her in rockets, filling up her spectacles, blinding her.

Grimly battling on, she thought about Geoffrey's letter. So pleased you're finally on the pill. Oh dear, but that was next week. Who knew but the world might end tonight? She turned a corner. Suddenly a dark blue car came out of a side road, swerved frantically, made a dizzy glide across the road, caught the wheel of her bicycle, and the next moment she was flying through the air on to the grass verge, her glasses knocked off, her possessions flying. The car skidded to a halt. The driver jumped out. He had dark gold hair, and his face was as white as the snow.

'Christ I'm sorry,' he said. 'I should have looked. Are you OK?'

Harriet sat on the verge, trembling and wondering if she was. The base of her spine felt agonizingly jolted. Her skirt was rucked up; her long red-stockinged legs in their black boots sprawled out like a colt; dark hair tumbled over her face.

'I'm all right,' she gasped. 'It was my fault. I should have rubbed the snow off my glasses. I couldn't see where I was going. I'm most terribly sorry.'

The words came out in a rush. Often, when she spoke, she had to hang on to a word to steady herself.

'No-one usually comes down this road,' he said.

'It's a short cut. I was going to a tutorial. Oh God, where are my glasses?'

'Here they are.' He picked them up and polished them for her. 'Are you sure you're all right? You've gone awfully white. Can you walk?'

He took her hands and pulled her gently to her feet, and, when she swayed slightly, put his arm round her. Harriet put on her spectacles and, looking at him, suddenly realized it was Simon Villiers and blushed scarlet.

'Where's my essay?' she muttered.

He retrieved it from a hollow in the verge.

'Pity you had it in a folder! The ink would have run in the snow. Been a marvellous excuse not to hand it in. Look, I really think I'd better take you to hospital.'

'I'm all right. I must go to my tutorial.'

Simon looked at her buckled bicycle. 'Well you won't get there on that,' he said ruefully. 'I'll get the garage to come and pick it up.'

There were flakes of snow gathering in his blond hair.

'What you need is a slug of brandy. I've got some in my digs. Come back, and I'll ring up and say you're ill.'

He helped her into his car.

'You don't have to bother, really you don't.'

'Shut up,' he said gently. 'Women are always being silly about inessentials.'

Inside the car he lit a cigarette and gave it to her. Harriet thought this was such a smooth gesture, she hadn't the heart to tell him she hardly smoked. The cigarette was very strong and made her cough. The heat was turned up overpoweringly, so was the wireless.

'Do you really have to go to this tutorial?' he asked, when he'd finally got the car out of the snow.

She nodded.

'Where is it?'

'Hallerton Street, No 44.'

'Theo Dutton?'

'You know him?'

'He tutored me my first year, until he realized I was past redemption. Not surprised he snapped you up; he always corners the pretty ones.'

He sat lazily beside her, driving with one hand. He was wearing dark grey trousers, a black shirt, and a pale blue velvet coat like Peter Rabbit. His eyes ran over her in an amused, speculative, slightly condescending way.

'I wish you'd take your glasses off again,' he said. 'Your eyes are far too sexy to be hidden. I must say it's a most unorthodox way to meet, but I'm very glad we have. What college are you at?'

'St Hilda's.'

She noticed he didn't introduce himself. He assumed rightly that everyone knew who he was.

'Why haven't we met before?'

'I've been working.'

'Theo keeping you to the grindstone?'

The car skidded slightly. Harriet jumped out of her skin. Simon laughed.

'Better keep my eyes on the road. Mind if I stop for petrol?'

As he got out to speak to the petrol pump attendant, Harriet surreptitiously turned the driving mirror and had a look at herself. Not too bad; thank God she'd washed her hair.

She couldn't believe it. Simon Villiers picking her up. She stole a quick glance at him, marvelling at the blond hair falling on the collar, the delicate aquiline features, the slightly cruel, beautifully shaped mouth, and tawny complexion without any trace of pink in it. Most amazing of all were his eyes, sleepy, and bluey-green with the dark lashes so thick and close together that they gave the illusion he was wearing eye-liner.

She was so dazed she forgot to put the mirror back and Simon nearly backed into a passing car.

'This journey's becoming pure Marx Brothers,' he said, replacing the mirror.

She didn't look at him, feeling that beastly blush staining her cheeks again.

'Come and have a drink after your tutorial.'

'Oh I don't . . . I mean you don't have . . .'

'There'll be other people there,' he said.

Oh God, she knew what they'd be like, models and actresses down from London. He read her thoughts.

'No-one very alarming. I'll look after you. Please,' his voice dropped, caressing and husky, 'let me make some reparation for nearly killing you.'

They drew up outside Theo's house.

'You'll come.'

22

'Yes, I'd like to.'

'Don't mention me to Theo. He'll give me a lousy press.'

As he drove off in a flurry of snow, she realized once again that he'd automatically assumed she knew where he lived.

Chapter Two

As she walked up the snowy path, her feet made no sound. The wonderful softening of the snow gave her a feeling of great irresponsibility, as though her reactions were blurred by alcohol. Hoods of white lay over the yew trees and turned the lavender bushes into white hedgehogs. Snakes of snow lay on the branches of the monkey puzzle.

Her brain was reeling, that she should have met Simon Villiers in this way. Ever since she'd seen him playing Brick in the OUDS production of *Cat on a Hot Tin Roof*, she'd known moments of exquisite unfaithfulness to Robert Redford. She knew Simon was a playboy with buckets of money and a frightful reputation. She knew that even her friends at St Hilda's, who happily slept with their boyfriends, still disapproved strongly of the Villiers Set. Harriet pretended to disapprove too, but she was secretly excited by their double-barrelled names, their fast cars, their frequent appearances in the gossip column, their ability to get chucked out of smart restaurants, their reputation for sexual ambiguity, and drugging and drinking.

'The downward path is easy, but there's no

turning back,' she muttered to herself as she pulled the doorbell. Theo Dutton's children fell on her.

'Hullo, Harriet. Harry ate a lamb for breakfast. It's a joke: Harriet a lamb for breakfast.'

'I've heard it before,' said Harriet.

'What time is it when an elephant sits on your fence?' said the eldest.

'I don't know,' said Harriet.

'Time to get a new fence,' the children exploded with laughter.

She often babysat when the Duttons went out.

'We've made a snowman in the garden. Come and look at it. What does it remind you of?'

'It looks like your father,' said Harriet.

'Waiting for the BBC to ring,' said the youngest.

Harriet giggled.

'Isn't the snow lovely?' she said.

'Will you take us tobogganing this afternoon? Daddy's working on a broadcast, which means he'll go to sleep.'

'And Mummy's got a cold.'

Three expectant faces gazed at her.

Euphoria at meeting Simon overwhelmed her.

'All right. I'll come and pick you up at 2.30,' she said.

'This is much better,' said Theo Dutton, lighting another cigarette.

Harriet watched the snow thickening on the roof opposite.

'The style leaves a lot to be desired. I want to

shake it and plump it up like a pillow, but your ideas are good. You've used your imagination.'

His shrewd, yellow eyes gleamed at her behind his spectacles. He tugged at his beard.

'You're very abstracted today,' he said. 'Someone's switched a light on inside you. What's happened? Boyfriend not coming down?'

Harriet laughed.

'Lack of sleep – and I just love the snow. I'm sorry if I seem a bit dopey. I got knocked off my bicycle on the way here. I didn't get hurt but it shook me a bit.'

She hoped she wouldn't be too terrified of the people in Simon's flat. She ought to go home and change into something better, but into what?

Theo looked at her speculatively, admiring the full breasts, the puppy plumpness, the long slim legs, the huge grey eyes with their heavy lids. One didn't normally realize the beauty of them hidden behind glasses. She was terribly shy, but through the shyness one could feel the vitality. She'll fall like a ripe plum any minute, he thought, with all the wistfulness of the happily married. There was nothing like a young, full-blooded girl suddenly introduced to the pleasure of the bed.

He sighed. Harriet wondered if she ought to rush out and blow the last of her month's allowance on a new sweater. It would do her good not to eat for a fortnight.

'This week,' said Theo Dutton, 'we'll look at the sonnets. "With this Key," said Wordsworth, "Shakespeare unlocked his heart." When my mistress walks, she treads on the ground, and don't forget it.'

At a quarter to twelve he got out the sherry bottle.

'There are two kinds of sherry in Oxford: one you cook with, the other you use for drinking. Usually the two get muddled, but not in my house. I think after this, you'd better go back to bed – alone.'

He poured the sherry into smeared glasses.

'I promised to take your children tobogganing,' said Harriet.

She came out of Theo's house to find a long, dark green car waiting for her. A man got out; he was smoking a cigarette and had auburn hair and the wild careering good looks of a red setter. Harriet recognized him immediately as one of Simon's cronies, Mark Macaulay.

'Simon sent me to fetch you,' he said. 'He thought you might get cold feet; as if anyone could get anything else in this bloody weather. Are you all right?' he added, as she got into the car. 'Simon said he sent you for six.'

Physically and mentally, thought Harriet.

'I'm a bit sore at the bottom of my spine,' she said.

'Your coccyx,' said Mark and laughed rather wildly. He already seemed a bit high.

'Are there lots of people there?' she said.

'About a couple of dozen, including one or two predatory ladies who won't be at all pleased that you've appeared on the scene.'

He shot her a sideways glance and laughed again.

Harriet felt nervous and excited at the same time. 'Do you think I ought to go?'

'It's more than my life's worth if you don't. Not that it's worth a lot anyway,' he said, taking a bottle of brandy out of the dashboard and taking a swig. 'I'm going down hill faster than a greased pig as it is.'

'I wish I could go home and change,' said Harriet.

'Don't change a thing. What Simon likes is novelty and you're certainly different.'

'He's only being kind because he knocked me off my bike.'

'Simon,' said Mark, 'never does anything to please anyone except himself.'

Chapter Three

Harriet had never seen anything like Simon's drawing room – with its shaggy fur rugs, huge tropical plants, emerald green silk curtains and roaring fire which flickered on the French paper-backs – mostly plays and pornography – in the bookshelves. Invitations were stacked like a pack of cards on the mantelpiece. Signed photographs of famous actors and actresses looked down from the black walls. Glamorous people prowled about the room like beasts in a jungle. Then, most glamorous of all Simon, his blue-green eyes glittering, came over to welcome them.

He removed Harriet's coat, then her scarf, then her spectacles.

'I don't want you to see my imperfections too clearly,' he said, kissing her on the cheek. 'Isn't she sweet?' he added to Mark.

'Yes,' said Mark. 'Much too sweet for you. That's worrying me.'

A handsome Indian strolled up to them.

'I wish you hadn't painted this room black,' he said petulantly. 'I don't show up against it.'

'Go and stand in the snow,' said Simon.

He gave Harriet a glass of ice-cold white wine, running his finger caressingly along her fingers as he did so.

'That should cool you up,' he said. 'How was Theo? Did he like your essay?'

'He seemed to – for once.'

'What was it about?'

'Which of Shakespeare's heroes was – well – the b-best in bed.'

'Bloody old letch excites himself that way. I suppose you're an authority on bed now?'

Harriet looked at her feet. There was a pause, then she glanced up at Simon and encountered a look that nearly took her skin off. Crimson, she turned to look out of the window.

'The snow's so beautiful, isn't it?' she said in a choked voice.

'We aim to please,' he said smiling at her. 'Sit down and enjoy the view. You don't need to meet any of these boring people.'

Harriet parked herself on a black velvet window seat, trying to merge into the green silk curtains. She had never seen so many exotic people, and the room smelt so exotic too. Not only must every pulse spot of each ravishing creature be throbbing with expensive scent, there was also the smell of the apple logs burning in the grate, a faint whiff of incense, and the heavy fragrance of a huge bunch of rainbow-coloured freesias massed in a blue bowl on the table. There was another, sweet, clinging smell she couldn't identify.

Suddenly there was a terrific pounding on the

door, and a handsome man with grey hair walked in. Harriet immediately recognized him as the leading actor at the playhouse this week.

'Simon darling, just knew this was your room. You can smell the stuff all the way down the street. You'll get busted if you're not careful. Hullo baby,' he added to a stunning blonde in a white silk shirt, and, taking a cigarette from her lips, inhaled deeply. When he breathed out about two years later, he turned to two elegant young men who were following him.

'They're both called Jeremy,' he said to Simon. 'And they're madly in love with each other, which makes things a bit complicated.'

The two young men giggled.

'Jeremy and Jeremy,' said the handsome actor. 'You haven't met Simon.'

'We've heard so much about you,' said the young men in chorus. 'Quite the rising star, aren't you?'

'Simon,' said a sulky-looking redhead with a mouth like a rubber tyre, 'can't we draw the curtains? All the plebs are looking in.'

'My friend here,' said Simon, giving Harriet a smile, 'enjoys the view, so we'll leave the curtains open.'

The redhead exchanged glances with the blonde in the white shirt.

'How's Borzoi, Simon?' said the actor taking another drag at the blonde's cigarette.

'Gone to the States,' said Simon.

'For long?'

31

'For good I hope,' said Simon, filling Harriet's glass.

The actor raised his well-plucked eyebrows.

'Like that, is it? Imagine she was a bit of a handful.'

'At least if she tries to come back, she's such a bitch she'll have to spend six months in quarantine,' said Simon.

Everyone laughed. More people arrived. Harriet watched the undercarriage of the gulls dark against the sky. The railings in the street were losing their shape now.

'I must do something about my hair,' said a wild-looking brunette.

'You could try brushing it,' said her boyfriend.

Simon, the actor and the two Jeremys started swapping such scurrilous stories of stars of stage and screen that everyone stopped their conversations to listen.

'Not boys, my dear, two girls at a time. His wife doesn't mind; she's got her own girlfriend anyway,' said the actor.

'I bet she minded her notices last week; they were ghastly,' said one of the Jeremys.

'Evidently in her costume she looks just like the Emperor Vespasian in drag,' said Simon. Harriet's eyes were out on stalks.

A rather ravaged beauty came through the door, wearing a fur coat and trousers. No-one took any notice, so she went out and came in again.

'Deirdre,' everyone shrieked.

'I'm exhausted,' she said. 'I haven't been to bed.'

'Darling,' said the actor, kissing her. 'I didn't recognize you with your clothes on.'

Someone put on a record.

'My very good friend the milkman says, that I am losing too much sleep,' sang Fats Waller.

Mark Macaulay came and sat down by Harriet, and filled up her glass.

'How's your coccyx?' he asked. 'I ought to work this afternoon, but I shan't.'

'What are you going to do after schools?' said Harriet.

'I thought of having a stab at a Dip.Ed.'

'I didn't know you wanted to teach, Markie,' shrieked Deirdre. 'You *hate* children.'

'I know, but a Dip.Ed'll give me another year to look around. They don't work one very hard, and by the end of another year, one might have decided what one wants to do.'

'I've got an interview with a military publisher next week,' said a boy in jeans with flowing blond hair. 'I expect they're awfully straight. Have you got a suit you can lend me?'

'Simon has,' said Mark. 'You'd better get a haircut too.'

The snow had deadened the roar of the traffic in the Turl to a dull murmur. A little bunch of protest marchers were struggling down the street with placards.

'The acne and anorak brigade,' said Mark. 'What are they banning this time, reds or fascists?'

'More jobs for teachers, I think,' said Harriet, trying to see without her glasses.

'Aren't they just like Good King Wenceslas and his page?' said Deirdre. 'Through the rude wind's loud lament and all that.'

'I'm sure Wenceslas had something going with his page boy,' said Simon.

'I wish I had principles,' said Mark, looking at the marchers.

'I like people better than principles,' said Simon, 'and I like people with no principles best of all.'

'Oscar Wilde,' muttered Harriet.

'Clever girl,' said Simon. 'Dorian Gray's my next part. OUDS are doing an adaptation.'

He'll be marvellous at it, thought Harriet, watching him move off to fill someone's drink. Even amidst the glittering menagerie of tigers he surrounded himself with, his beauty made him separate.

Two girls looked out of the window.

'That car's been parked there for ages,' they said, 'let's go down and write something awful all over it.'

They rushed out of the door, and a minute later their shrieks could be heard, as, lifting their slim legs up like Hackney ponies, they raced across the snow.

On the wall opposite was pinned a poster of a beautiful girl with long streaky hair and cheekbones you could balance a tray on.

'Who's that?' she said to Mark.

'Borzoi, Simon's ex,' he said.

'Why did they split up?'

'Inevitable, darling. They both spent far too much time arguing with the mirror which was the fairest of them both. Borzoi's doing better than Simon too,

34

at the moment, and that doesn't help. She's also extremely spoilt.'

He looked at Harriet in amusement. 'That's why he fancies you.'

'He couldn't.'

'Sure he does, and that's what's making Chloe so uptight.' He nodded his head in the direction of the sulky redhead who was flirting determinedly on the sofa with the handsome actor. 'She was convinced she was next in succession.'

Oh golly, thought Harriet, but the warm excited feeling inside her persisted.

Back came the two girls from the snow.

'I only got as far as "Bugg",' shrieked one, 'when a policeman came along.'

'Everything looks so white and virginal,' said the other, huddling by the fire.

'Don't know any virgins,' said the actor. 'Bit of a collector's item these days.'

'Moppet Wilson is,' said Deirdre. 'Never bares anything but her soul.'

'What's she saving it for?' said Mark.

'The man she marries. She thinks its something one gives him like a pair of cuff-links on one's wedding day.'

'I'd rather have cuff-links,' said Mark draining his glass.

'Virgins must be boring to go to bed with,' said Chloe, looking directly at Simon. 'They don't know first base from second.'

Harriet looked up. Simon was looking straight at her. He gave her his swift, wicked smile. He knows, she thought in panic, and felt herself going scarlet again. Oh why the hell had she worn red? She turned her burning face to cool it against the window pane.

'When I was a child I liked popping balloons, and fuchsia buds,' said Simon softly. 'I always like putting my finger through the paper on the top of the Maxwell House jar. I like virgins. You can break them in how you like, before they have time to learn any bad habits.'

There was a long pause. Harriet got up and stumbled to the lavatory. Her heart was thumping, but her thoughts had taken on a strange, sensual, dreamlike quality. In the bathroom was a bidet, which seemed the height of sophistication. She toned down her face with some of Simon's talcum powder.

As she came back into the room, the actor was leaving.

'Must go, darling. I've got a matinée. If I drink any more I'll fall off the stage. Come along Jeremy and Jeremy,' he added to the boys, who were feeding each other grapes.

'Do put in a good word for me to Boris,' said Simon casually. 'He was coming to see *Cat*, but he never made it. Tell him I'm doing Dorian Gray at the end of term.'

'Sure will, baby,' said the actor. 'We'll all have dinner one day next week.'

'He doesn't like the hours I keep. He suggests that you should marry me,' sang Fats Waller.

'Where shall we eat, Simon?' said Chloe. 'What about the Parisian.'

'I'm not forking out a tenner for a lot of old bones cooked in cream,' said Simon.

Chloe glared at him.

'I must go,' said Harriet hastily.

'We're just going to eat,' said Simon.

She didn't want to eat. She knew at last she had come face to face with someone so fascinating that, if she allowed him to do so, he would absorb her whole being. She felt on the verge of some terrible crisis. She wanted to be alone and think.

'I promised to take Theo's children tobogganing.'

'Oh come on,' said Simon. 'They won't mind.'

'I promised.'

'All right then, as long as you come back later.'

'You'll be fed up with people by then.'

'Only of certain people. *We* haven't begun yet.'

He put her coat on, and as he flipped her hair over the collar he let his hand slide caressingly down its newly washed length.

She jumped away nervously.

'I'll drive you back,' he said.

'No,' she stammered. 'I'd rather walk.'

But as she moved away down the path, he caught the two ends of her red scarf and pulled her back till they were only a few inches apart.

'Promise you'll come back?'

She nodded. She could see the scattering of freckles on the bridge of his nose. The bluey-green eyes were almost on a level with hers. He had hardly to bend his head to kiss her. He tasted of white wine and French cigarettes. She felt her stomach go

37

liquid, her knees disappear, as all the books said they would and they never had with Geoffrey.

Breaking away from him, she ran down the street, not even feeling the icy winds now. As she rounded the corner, she surprised two undergraduates with placards by bursting out laughing.

Chapter Four

Her manic high spirits infected the children. They drove up to Hinksey Hill yelling Knick Knack Paddy Wack at the top of their voices, and screamed with delight as the red and silver toboggan hissed down the silent hillside, throwing them into the drifts and folds in the snow. Then they got up and, panting, pulled the toboggan to the top of the hill, hurling snowballs at one another, the Duttons' cairn snapping at the snow with ivory teeth, until they were all soaked through but warm inside.

Simon Villiers kissed me, she wanted to shout to the white hilltops, and happiness kept bubbling up inside her as she hugged the children more tightly. They were reluctant to let her go.

'Stay to tea,' they pleaded. 'There'll be crumpets and chocolate cake and *Doctor Who*.'

'Harriet obviously has other plans,' said Theo Dutton, who opened the front door to them. 'Be careful, my sweet. Read your sonnets. Try to shun the heaven, if it's only going to lead to hell.'

Was it so obvious to everyone, wondered Harriet, as she galloped back to her digs through the snow. She passed the Robert Redford film without a twinge of regret. She'd got the real thing ahead of her.

Back in her room, she examined the picture of Geoffrey, smiling self-consciously and clutching a tennis racket. And that photograph makes him better looking than he really is, she thought. She glanced too, at the photograph of her elder sister Susie, looking ravishing on her wedding day and hanging on Peter Neave's arm. That was one of Harriet's problems, always being compared with a slim, beautiful sister who never got spots, and who had the kind of self control that never took too many potatoes, or betrayed too much interest in a man until she knew that he was hooked. Harriet knew how Susie had churned inside over the rich and glamorous Peter Neave, how she had waited all day biting her nails for him to ring, and when he finally did, had had the nerve to say, 'No I can't tonight, or tomorrow, or the next night, and I'm away this weekend,' playing hard to get for the next few weeks until she'd literally brought Peter Neave to his knees with a proposal of marriage. How could one ever believe one was attractive when one ate too many cream buns and lived in Susie's shadow, and frightened men off by getting too keen too quickly? She must try and be sensible about Simon.

What could she wear? Her grey shirt had a mark on the front; the maroon sweater had lost its elasticity in the wash so the polo neck looked like a surgical collar; she'd sweated lighter rings under the arms of her brown dress when she'd been nervous at a party. Her jeans were clean but they covered her legs, which were her best thing, and they were so tight they would leave marks all over her body when she took them off. But she was *not* going to take them off, she said to herself furiously. Soon there were clothes lying all over the floor. The water only ran to a tepid bath. She was in such a state she washed her face twice, cut herself three times shaving her legs, and then got back into the bath to wash between her toes in case Simon was the sort of man who kissed one all over. Then she rubbed her landlady's handcream all over her body and smothered herself in French Fern talcum powder.

In the bedroom, she examined herself naked in the mirror. Were the goods good enough? Her bust was much too big. But men didn't seem to mind that. Her legs were all right except for the bleeding, but everywhere else was a bit voluptuous. She took the mirror off the wall and, holding it above herself, lay down on the bed. Would she pass muster at this angle? Her stomach looked flatter anyway, and her hair fanned out nicely. Stop it, she said to herself furiously, you're only going to have a drink with him.

There was a knock on the door. She jumped up guiltily, grabbing a towel.

'Going out, dear?' said the landlady, Mrs Glass. 'There's a nice piece of hot gammon if you fancy it.'

Mrs Glass often grumbled how much her lodgers cost her, but she prefered the ones that stayed in. Miss Poole was a nice, quiet girl, and sweet natured too, if she wasn't so dreadfully untidy.

'Your poor mother wouldn't want you to starve

41

yourself,' said Mrs Glass, who thought everyone under eleven stone needed feeding up.

'I'm going to a party,' said Harriet. 'I'll probably stay the night with a girlfriend, so don't worry if I don't come back.' The glib way she could lie.

'Quite right not to trust young gentlemen driving on these roads,' said Mrs Glass. 'Do you good to get out and enjoy yourself for a change.'

'I'll have a real tidy out tomorrow,' said Harriet, wincing as she put deodorant under her arms. Her leg was still bleeding; it must be all that excitement pulsating through her veins.

She put on a pair of black lace pants and a black bra with a red ribbon she had bought in anticipation of Geoffrey. The pants hardly covered her at all and the red ribbon was too much, so she tore it off.

There was her black sweater all the time under the bed. She could wear it with her red skirt. It was getting late. What happened if Simon got bored of waiting and went out?

For once, her hair obeyed her. She splashed a bottle of scent, a Christmas present from Susie, all over her. She hoped it didn't clash with the French Fern. How did French ferns differ from English, she wondered. Perhaps they were more sophisticated.

She galloped back along the streets. It was very cold now and the street lights gave the snow a curious pale radiance. Her breath crystallized in little clouds before her. The white nights, she said to herself; she was Anna Karenina smothered in furs hurrying to meet Vronsky, Natasha quivering with guilty expectation waiting for Anatole.

She felt more and more sick with nerves. Perhaps her mouth tasted awful; she stopped at the news-agents to buy some chewing gum. The windows of Simon's digs were black. He's gone, she thought in panic; one of those dazzling creatures has spirited him away. No, a thin beam of light trickled through the green silk curtains. A group of people were coming out. Oh, those echoing self-confident voices!

'I do think it's anti-social of Simon to throw us out when it's so cold. Chloe is going to be simply livid,' said one of the girls, scooping up a snowball and throwing it at one of the boys, as they all went screaming off into the night. Harriet threw away her chewing gum, it made no sound as it landed in the snow. The door was still open as she went up the path. Simon emerged from the darkness, his hair gleaming white in the street lamp.

'I thought you'd done a bunk,' he said.

'I got soaked. I had to change.'

He put his hand out and touched her cheek.

'You're frozen. Come in.'

Only three people were left in the drawing room. Deirdre, who was putting on lipstick, a blond man who was rooting around the drinks tray to find himself some more wine, and Chloe who sat on the sofa, huddled like a sparrow on the telegraph wires on a cold day.

'Oh poor thing,' thought Harriet. 'I'd mind losing Simon.'

'Come on chaps,' said Simon removing the bottle from the blond man, 'chucking-out time.'

Harriet went over to the fire. She felt miserably

embarrassed. Chloe looked mutinous. Simon got her blond, squashy fur coat out of the bedroom and held it out for her.

'Come on, darling,' he said firmly. 'Beat it.'

Two angry spots of colour burnt on her cheeks. She snatched the coat from him and put it on herself.

'You're a bastard, Simon,' she hissed. 'And *you* won't escape unscathed either,' she added to Harriet, and, with a sob, ran out of the room down the stairs.

'We might all meet at Serena's party later,' said Deirdre, kissing Simon on the cheek. 'She is expecting you, Simon.'

'Not tonight, darling. Tell Serena I had a previous . . .' He shot a glance at Harriet. 'No, a *subsequent* engagement. Now good night, darlings.' And he shut the door on them.

He turned and shot Harriet that swift, devastating smile.

'One has to be brutal occasionally to get what one wants in life.'

'She was awfully upset,' said Harriet.

'She'll recover,' said Simon.

He chucked some logs on the fire, covering the flame and throwing the room into semi-darkness, and gave her a drink, the cold condensing on the outside of the glass. She held onto it to stop her hands shaking and took a huge gulp; it was a long time since the baked beans.

Simon disappeared into another room. She felt as though she was alone in some deserted woodland house, and that Indians or some invaders were slowly creeping through the undergrowth towards her – but she didn't know when or from where they were going to attack. Simon returned with the remains of a quiche on a plate.

'We never did have any lunch. Do you want some?'

She shook her head.

Simon helped himself to a slice.

'You're all right after the crash, are you?' he said with his mouth full.

'Just a few bruises, that's all.'

'I must look at them later.'

Her heart thumped madly; the firelight flickered on his face. She jumped as a log fell out of the grate.

'Relax,' said Simon. 'I've never seen anyone as terrified as you. What put that scared look in your eyes? Were you raped as a child? Did you have strict parents? Were you bullied at school?' He was making fun at her now, but his voice was like a caress.

She took another gulp of wine. Having eaten the inside of the quiche Simon was about to throw the pastry into the fire.

'We could give it to the birds,' said Harriet.

'We could, I suppose.' He opened the window, letting in a draught of icy air; the snow gleamed like a pearl. Simon put a record on the gramophone. It was a Mozart piano concerto.

'You still look sad,' said Simon.

'I was thinking . . . about Chloe.'

'Not worth it. She's the most frightful scrubber. I

only took her out a couple of times. She's one of those girls like scrambled egg, amazingly easy to make, but impossible to get off the pan afterwards.'

Harriet giggled.

'That's better,' said Simon, 'now come and sit on the sofa. No, next to me, not six feet away.'

She was still trembling, but the excitement was beginning to take over. He picked up her hand and kissed it.

'I thought you were terribly good in *Cat on a Hot Tin Roof*,' she said brightly.

'I know I was,' said Simon. 'So we've exhausted that subject.'

His hand on the back of the dark green velvet sofa was edging towards her hair, but he didn't touch her. His timing was so good, he held off until she was in a panic that he was never going to. It was terribly hot in the room, she could feel the sweat trickling between her breasts.

'You're so pretty,' he was saying in a low husky voice, and then he kissed her. At first she kept her arms clamped down by her side, but suddenly like the reflex action when one's knee is tapped, they shot up and coiled themselves round Simon's neck, and she was kissing him back with all her might, and his hands were on the move all over her body. Hastily she pulled in her spare tyre.

'I mustn't.'

'You must, you must.'

'You'll think I'm too easy.'

'I don't. I just think you're overdressed, that's all,' and he took off her earrings and put them side by

46

side on the table. Then took off her shoes, and took the telephone off the hook.

She sat back waiting for an attack on another front.

'You've got such a lovely body,' he said, filling both their glasses.

'One should really take lessons at prep school in undoing bras. Oh, I see; it does up at the front,' he said a minute later.

His hands were warm on her bare back. He kissed her eyes, her hair, her mouth; she'd never dreamed he'd be so tender.

'No,' she gasped, leaping up as his fingers edged inside her waistband.

How could she explain she wouldn't be easy like this, if she didn't find him so overwhelmingly attractive?

'Sweetheart, stop fighting it,' he whispered. 'I refuse to be put outside the bedroom every night, like flowers in a hospital.'

Harriet gasped. 'You've read Geoffrey's letter!'

'I picked it up in the snow. I'm glad he's glad you've gone on the pill, but I'm even gladder.'

'You shouldn't read other people's letters,' she said furiously.

'One must, just to find out all the nice things they're saying about one. Tell me about Geoffrey. What does he do?'

'He's a marine biologist.'

'Oh well, we can't all be perfect.'

'He's clever,' said Harriet defensively. 'He's just come down from Plymouth.'

'One can't come down from Plymouth. One can only go up,' said Simon. He was attacking her waist-band again.

'It's too soon,' she muttered. 'I don't even know you.'

'You talk too much,' he said. 'I've never heard so much fuss about something that's so nice.' He started to pull off her sweater and she was enveloped in a fuzz of black wool.

'It's got buttons at the back,' she squealed, as he nearly removed her ears.

'Don't be frightened,' he said, when she was finally freed, and he pulled her down on the floor beside him. The applewood of the logs mingled with a trace of his lavender aftershave, and the animal smell of the white fire rug which scratched against her back. She had no will power. It's going to happen she thought in panic.

'Will it hurt?'

'You'll be so excited by the time I've got you revved up, you won't feel a thing,' he whispered.

In a few minutes the Mozart concerto jigged jollily to its ending, and the only sounds in the room were her gasps for breath and the soft crackling of the fire.

Later they went into the bedroom, and once in the night she got up to go to the loo, and gazed at herself in the bathroom mirror, searching for lines of depravity. She looked rather disappointingly the same except that her face was flushed, her eyes glazed. She wondered why she didn't feel more guilty, then realized it was because she loved him.

Chapter Five

'That was so gorgeous,' she said next morning when they woke up.

He grinned. 'You'll find it a perfect hobby, darling, and so cheap. I say,' he added, 'what's your name?'

She gave a gurgle of laughter.

'Harriet,' she said. 'Harriet Poole.'

'I've never had a Harriet before.' He lay back and laughed, 'Oh I'm just wild about Harriet,' and then he pulled her down on top of him.

For the next fortnight she had to keep pinching herself. Simon Villiers was her lover; the impossible had been achieved. They hardly got out of bed, except for the occasional excursion to the Randolph for breakfast, or an excursion to Hinksey Hill to see what making love was like in the snow. Harriet found it extremely cold, and nearly died of a heart attack when a cow looked over the fence and mooed at her.

Never in her life had she been so happy. Willingly she cooked for Simon, ironed his shirts rather badly, ran his errands, and submitted rapturously over and over again to his love-making.

'You really do ad-dore it, don't you?' he drawled in amazement.

The snow seemed here to stay. The ploughs came and scattered salt and sand on the roads, but the houses and the parks were still blanketed in whiteness. Harriet was doing absolutely no work. Simon had forbidden her to wear her glasses, so work gave her a headache anyway. She rang both Theo Dutton and Geoffrey and told them she'd got 'flu. The weight fell off her; she lost over a stone living on wine and love.

Never had she met anyone so witty, so glamorous, so glorious as Simon. Only one thing nagged her, at this supreme moment in her life: she felt unable to describe him adequately in her diary. There was an elusiveness about his character that she couldn't pin down; he seemed permanently to be playing someone other than himself, and watching himself doing it at the same time. Although books filled his flat, he never appeared to read, except theatre reviews in the paper or the odd stage magazine. When he watched television he was far more interested in the techniques of the actors and actresses, and in who was playing whom, than in the story.

It was only in the third week things started to go wrong. Simon had an audition in London with Buxton Philips. Not realizing it was early closing day, Harriet arrived too late to get his grey velvet suit out of the cleaners. She was shattered at the storm of abuse that broke over her when she got home.

'But you've got hundreds of beautiful suits,' she stammered.

'Yes,' hissed Simon, 'but I wanted to wear this one,' and he walked out of the house without even saying goodbye.

Harriet was supposed to be writing her essay on the sonnets, but she couldn't stop crying. In the end she gave up working, wrote a poem to Simon, and spent hours making a moussaka, which she knew he liked.

He came back from London on the last train, if anything in a worse mood than when he left.

'How did it go?' she said nervously.

'Bloody terrible! Buxton Philips didn't show up.'

'Oh no,' wailed Harriet. How could anyone stand up Simon?

'All I saw was some old bitch of a secretary. "Ay'm sorry, Mr Villiers, but it's always wise to ring Mr Philips in the mornin' to check he's able to make it, he's *so* busy."'

'Oh poor Simon.' She got up and put her arms round him, but she could sense his detachment.

'Fix me a drink,' he said, pacing up and down the room. 'In a few years' time, that bastard'll be crawling to me. "Ay'm sorry, Mr Philips, Mr Villiers is far too busy to see you." He'll regret this.'

'Of course he will,' said Harriet soothingly. 'You're going to be a big star, Simon. Everyone says so.'

She handed him a drink.

'I missed you so much, I've even written you a poem,' she said blushing. 'I've never written anyone a poem before.'

She handed it to him.

Simon skimmed through it, his lips curling.

'"Our love is like a rainbow arched in shuddering orgasm against the sky",' he read out in a deliberately melodramatic voice. '"Orgasm" in the singular? I *must* be slipping.'

Harriet flushed and bit her lip.

'I also found this lovely sonnet, which describes exactly how I feel about you,' she said hastily, handing him the volume of Shakespeare.

'Harriet de-ah,' sighed Simon, as he glanced at it, 'if you knew the number of women who've quoted that poem at me! You're in danger of getting soppy, sweetheart. I don't mind women being romantic, but I can't stand soppiness.'

She tried once again.

'I've made some moussaka for supper,' she said.

'I'm bored with moussaka,' said Simon.

She was still crying when he came to bed. 'What's the matter?' he said. 'I love you,' said Harriet, in a choked voice. 'Well, if you love me,' said Simon softly, 'you must like the whip.'

He woke up next morning in a better mood, and they made love, sat drinking coffee and reading the papers in bed until lunchtime. Harriet had forgotten the insults of last night, aware only of a swooning relief that everything was all right again. Her euphoria was short-lived. She was looking at the horoscopes.

'It says I'm going to have a good day for romance,' she giggled. 'Perhaps I shall meet a tall dark stranger. I always dreamed I'd fall in love with someone tall and dark. Funny you should be small and blond.'

'I am *not* small,' said Simon icily.

She knew by the idle drumming of his fingers on the bedside table that there'd be trouble, that he'd bide his time and then retaliate without scruple. He started to read a piece about some famous actor's sex life. When he came to the end he said:

'That's why I want to make it up the top. Apart from telling Buxton Philips to get stuffed, just think of the birds one could pull. Once you become a big star, you can virtually have any woman you want.'

There was a pause. Harriet felt faint at the thought of Simon having another woman. A great tear fell onto the paper she was reading, followed by another, and another.

'What's eating *you*?' said Simon.

She got clumsily out of bed; not wearing her spectacles and blinded by tears, she bumped into a table, knocking off a little Rockingham dalmatian that she knew Borzoi had given Simon. It smashed beyond redemption. Harriet was appalled.

'I'll buy you another, Simon, truly I will.'

'As it cost about £80, I think that's extremely unlikely,' he snapped. 'For God's sake stop snivelling. It's bad enough you breaking it, without making that Godawful din. I'm hungry. Go and put on the moussaka, and then have a bath, but don't forget to leave the water in.'

Harriet lay in the bath, trying not to cry and wondering what it wouuld be like to be married to Simon. 'Harriet Villiers' had a splendid seventeenth

53

century ring. Could she cope with being the wife of a superstar? Some stage marriages she knew lasted for ever. She wouldn't be a drag on him; when he was away acting, she'd have her poems and novels to write; she might even write a play for him.

She could just see the first night notices:

'Simon Villiers's wife is not beautiful in the classical sense, but there is an appealing sensitivity, a radiance about this brilliant young playwright.' Unthinkingly she pulled out the plug.

Simon walked into the bathroom, yawning, hair ruffled, to find Harriet sitting in an empty bath, dreamily gazing into space.

'I thought I told you to leave the fucking water in.'

Harriet flushed unbecomingly.

'Oh God, I'm frightfully sorry. Perhaps there's some hot left.'

There wasn't.

Even worse, she went into the kitchen and found that, although she'd turned on the oven, she'd put the moussaka into the cupboard instead, so when Simon came in, shuddering with cold and ill-temper, there was nothing to eat. The row that followed left her reeling. He really let her have it. She had no defences against the savageness of his tongue.

Once more she went and sobbed in the bedroom, and she heard the front door slam. Hours later when he came back she had cried herself to sleep. He woke her up.

'You're too sensitive, Harriet baby. You over-react all the time. Poor little baby,' he said gently, 'poor, poor little baby. Did you think I wasn't coming back?' Never had he made love to her so tenderly.

Chapter Six

Harriet woke up feeling absurdly happy. True love could only be forged on rows like that. It was the first of March, her meagre allowance had come through. She got up, leaving Simon asleep. She cashed a cheque at the bank, and bought croissants and orange juice. In spite of a bitter east wind, the snow was melting, dripping off the houses, turning brown and stacked in great piles along the road.

It would be spring soon. She imagined herself and Simon wandering through the parks with the blossom out, or punting under long green willows, and dancing till dawn at a Commem ball. All great love affairs had their teething troubles.

When she got back to Simon's rooms, she took his mail into his room. He was still half asleep, so she went to the kitchen and made coffee and heated up the croissants. She was worried about a large spot that was swelling up on the side of her nose. However much make-up she put over it, it shone through like a beacon; she must start eating properly.

When she took breakfast into his room, he had woken up and was in excellent form.

'Buxton Philips's written me a letter saying he's

sorry, he's coming down to Oxford to take me out to lunch,' he said, draining a glass of orange juice.

'Oh darling, that's wonderful,' said Harriet.

Simon drew back the curtains. Harriet sat down on the bed, with the spot side furthest away from him, pouring out coffee.

'I think you'd better start packing, darling,' he said, liberally buttering a croissant.

'Oh God, is your mother coming to stay?'

He shook his head, his face curiously bland. 'I just think it's time you moved out.'

She looked at him bewildered, the colour draining from her face.

'But, why? Was it because I smashed your dog, and let out your bath water, and forgot about your suit, and the moussaka? I'm sorry, I will try to concentrate more.'

'Darling, it isn't that,' he said, thickly spreading marmalade. 'It's just that all good things come to an end. You should live a little, learn a bit more about life, play the field.'

'But I'm not like that. I'm a one-man girl.'

Simon shrugged his shoulders.

'W-when will I see you,' she was trembling violently now.

'You're making this very difficult for me,' he said gently.

She sat down.

'Mind my shirts,' said Simon hastily, removing the shirts she had ironed from the chair.

She stared at him. 'What did I do wrong?'

'Oh, for Christ's sake, you didn't do anything wrong.'

It must be a bad dream, it must be. She felt her happiness melting round her like the snow.

'Why can't I see you any more?'

'Darling, for everything there is a reason. You're a lovely warm crazy girl, and we've had a ball together. Now I've broken you in nicely, you'll be a joy for the next guy, but it's time for us both to move on.'

'But I love you,' she stammered.

He sighed. 'That's your problem, sweetheart. I never said I loved you. I never pretended this was going to last.'

Her face had a look of pathos and stricken dignity.

'I don't believe it,' she whispered.

Simon was not finding this as easy as he had expected, rather unpleasant in fact. Oh God, why did women get so keen on one? He was nibbling the skin round his thumb nail. He seemed to Harriet to have shrunk in size; there was something about his eyes like an animal at bay.

She licked her dry lips. 'Will you find someone else?'

'Of course I'll find someone else,' he snapped, anger with himself making him crueller towards her. 'Borzoi's coming back. I got a letter from her this morning.'

'And so I get d-dumped like an unwanted dog on the motorway.'

Slowly it was dawning on her that his future didn't contain her.

He tried another tack. 'You're too good for me, Harriet.'

'I'm not,' she said helplessly.

'Yes, you are, I need a tough cookie like Borzoi.'

The sun, which hadn't been seen for ages, suddenly appeared at the window, high-lighting the chaos of the room – the unmade bed, Harriet's clothes strewn over every chair, the brimming ash-trays.

'Cheer up,' said Simon. 'At least it's a lovely day. Come on, lovie, get your things together; we haven't got much time.'

As he threw records, scarves, papers, make-up into her suitcase, she felt he was getting out an india rubber and carefully erasing every trace of her from his life. He was hard put to contain his elation. Even his goodbye was absent-minded. He patted her on the bottom and told her to behave herself. She could almost hear his sigh of relief as he shut the door and rushed back to tidy up for Borzoi.

She went straight home and dumped her suitcase. For a minute she lay on her bed and listened to the clocks striking all over Oxford. Only eleven o'clock. A whole day to be got through, a whole lifetime without Simon stretching ahead. She got up, turned on the gas and knelt down beside it; after ten seconds the meter ran out.

Mrs Glass came in and started to shout at her for the rent, then she saw Harriet's face and stopped. 'White as a corpse, poor little thing,' she told her husband afterwards. ''Er sins must have catched up with 'er.'

Harriet got up and went out and walked round the town, the slush leaking into her boots. She didn't notice the cold even in her thin coat. She had nothing of Simon's. He had written her no letters, given her no presents. How crazy she had been, how presumptuous to think for a moment she could hold him. It was like trying to catch the sun with a fishing net. She walked three times round the same churchyard, then took a bus to Headington, looking at the trees, their branches shiny from the melting snow. She got off the bus and began to walk again, thinking over and over again of the times Simon and she had spent together, illuminated now in the light. Never again would she tremble at his touch, or talk to him or gaze at him. All she would hear was stupid people yapping about his latest exploits, that he'd landed a part in a play, that he was back with Borzoi.

It couldn't be true. Borzoi would come back, Simon would realize they couldn't make a go of it, and send for Harriet again. Wading through the cold grey slush, she walked back to her digs and fell shuddering into bed.

Everyone said, 'I told you so.' Geoffrey was magnanimous, then irritated that she wouldn't snap out of it, then furious that Simon had succeeded where he had failed, and made violent attempts to get her into bed. Her girlfriends, who had all been jealous of her and Simon, were secretly pleased it was over. Theo Dutton was vitriolic about the badness of her essay.

The child looked in terrible shape. She was obviously having some kind of crisis.

'Come on,' he said. 'Who is it?'

'No-one, nothing,' she muttered. 'Simon Villiers.'

'Oh dear, oh dear. He was the nasty bug all my girl students caught last summer. I thought he'd gone out of fashion now. I must say I'm disappointed in you, Harriet. I thought you had better taste. He was one of the worst students I've ever had; his mind is earth-shatteringly banal.'

Then, like Mrs Glass, he saw the stricken look on her face and realized he was on the wrong tack.

For days she didn't eat, wandering round Oxford getting thinner and thinner, gazing for hours at the river, wondering whether to jump, hanging around Simon's digs at a respectable distance hoping to catch a glimpse of him. Mostly she saw him come out and sit in his car, impatiently drumming his fingers on the steering wheel, revving up the car, lighting cigarette after cigarette. Then Borzoi would come spilling out, spraying on scent, trailing coloured scarves, her gorgeous streaky gold hair tumbling over her face. And they would drive off arguing furiously.

Chapter Seven

It was only after a month that Harriet started to worry – but it was a worry that was nothing compared with losing Simon. Another week slipped by, then one evening she washed her hair and put on a black dress of Susie's that she'd never been able to get into before, but which now hung off her, and went to see Simon. She waited in the cold till Borzoi had gone out, almost biting her lip through as she watched Simon kiss her in the doorway. Then Borzoi drove off with a roar, and Simon went back into the house. He took a long time to answer the doorbell. For a minute she gazed at him close up; he was after all only a face. How could he have caused her so much unhappiness? Then suddenly all the old longing came flooding back.

'Hullo,' he said, hardly seeming to recognize her. 'Oh it's you,' he added politely. 'What can I do for you?'

'Can I come in?'

He looked at his watch. 'I'm going out in a second.'

'I don't want to hassle you, but it's important.'

'Oh dear,' he sighed. 'Well, you'd better come in.'

The room was in chaos. There were ashtrays full of stubs everywhere and finger-smeared tumblers, and cups full of old wet coffee grounds. Clothes, everything from fur coats to party dresses, lay piled high on every chair.

'Tidiness has never been Borzoi's strong point,' said Simon, picking some dead flowers out of their vase and throwing them dripping into the ashes of the fireplace. 'Thank God the char's coming in the morning.'

He put a cigarette in his mouth – not offering her one.

'Well,' he said, noticing her red-rimmed eyes. 'How are things? You've lost a lot of weight. Been dieting?'

Harriet took a deep breath. 'Simon, I'm pregnant.'

The match flared. Simon breathed in deeply. The end of the cigarette glowed. He threw the match into the fire.

'Are you sure?'

'Yes, I had the results of the test yesterday.'

'But you were on the pill.'

'I know; but I'd only just started taking it, and the night we first w-went to bed together, I was in such a state beforehand I think I may have forgotten to take it.'

'Bloody little fool,' said Simon, but not unkindly. 'Are you sure it's mine?'

She looked up horrified, her eyes full of tears.

'Oh yes, there's never been anyone else.'

'What about Jeremy or Gordon, or whatever he was called.'

'Geoffrey? Oh no, I couldn't. I didn't . . .'

She started to cry.

'Oh dear, oh dear,' said Simon. She was aware only of the terrible boredom in his voice. She might have been some mild inconvenience, a button off his shirt, a pair of dark glasses left in a taxi.

He went into the kitchen and put the kettle on.

'Well, you'd better go to London as soon as possible, and see Dr Wallace.'

'What for?'

'To get rid of it of course.'

'B-but I couldn't.'

'It's not dangerous any more, darling. You don't want to listen to any of those old wives' tales. Dr Wallace is a pro. They just suck it out with a Hoover these days.'

Harriet winced.

'Borzoi's been to him twice,' said Simon. 'So have Chloe and Deirdre and Anne-Marie and Henrietta. Honestly, he ought to give me a discount the number of birds I've sent to him.'

'But I don't want . . .' Harriet began.

'You might feel a bit depressed afterwards, but it's the end of term next week, so you can go home and recuperate.'

'But it'll be so expensive. I don't want to rip you off.'

'Oh don't worry about that, darling; I'll treat you. I'm not that much of a sod. Do you mind Nescafé? Borzoi insists on making real coffee, but it's so disgusting, and I can never get the coffee grounds out of my teeth.'

He poured boiling water into two cups and handed one to her.

'If you like,' he went on, putting two saccharine into his cup, 'I'll ring old Wallace now, and fix you up an appointment. The old bags on the switchboard give people they don't know rather a hard time.'

The scalding coffee burnt her throat but seemed to give her strength.

'Would you mind terribly if I kept it?'

'Oh be realistic, angel. You of *all* people are simply not cut out to be a one-parent family. I know people keep their babies, but they have a bloody awful time, unless they're rich enough to afford a lover and a nanny.'

Harriet sat in Dr Wallace's waiting-room feeling sick, thumbing feverishly through the same magazine, watching girls go in and out. Some looked pale and terrified like herself, others obviously old timers, chatted together and might have been waiting for an appointment at the hairdresser's. Two models embraced in the doorway.

'Fanny darling!'

'Maggie!'

'Friday morning – see if you can get booked in at the same time, and we can go in together.'

Dr Wallace was smooth, very suntanned from skiing and showed a lot of white cuff.

'You're certain you don't want to get married and have the child, Miss Poole? This is a big step you're taking.'

'He doesn't want to marry me,' whispered Harriet, unable to meet the doctor's eyes. 'But he's perfectly happy to pay. I've got a letter from him here.'

Dr Wallace smiled as he looked at Simon's royal blue writing paper.

'Oh dear! Mr Villiers again; quite a lad, isn't he? One of our best customers.'

Harriet went white. 'Fond of him, were you? Shame, shame, boy's got a lot of charm, but not ideal husband material, I wouldn't say. You're very young, plenty more fish in the sea. Not much fun bringing up a baby on your own, pity to ruin a promising academic career.'

'I know,' said Harriet listlessly.

'Just got to get another doctor to sign the form. Will first thing Friday morning be all right for you? You'll be out in the evening. There, there; don't cry, it'll be soon over.'

Her last hope was her parents. She caught a train down to the country. As she arrived one of her mother's bridge parties was just breaking up. Middle-aged women, buoyed up by a couple of gin and tonics were yelling goodbye to each other, banging car doors and driving off.

Harriet noticed as she slunk up the path that the noisiest of all was Lady Neave, Susie's mother-in-law.

'Goodbye, Alison,' she was saying, clashing her cheek against Harriet's mother's cheek with infinite condescension. 'Great fun! We're all meeting at Audrey's next week, aren't we, Audrey? *Hullo,*' she added, suddenly seeing Harriet. 'Are you down for the weekend? You must go over and see Peter and Susie. The new wallpaper in the drawing room is such a success.'

What a gauche child thought Lady Neave, as she drove the Humber off in a series of jerks, narrowly missing the blue gates at the bottom of the drive. One could hardly believe she came from the same family as Susie, who although not quite what the Neaves would have liked for their only son, knew her place and was shaping up as a nice little wife.

Mrs Poole, having made her farewells, found Harriet slumped in a chair in the kitchen, the cat purring on her knee. Why must the child look such a fright, she thought, that awful duffle coat with all the buttons missing, no make-up, hair unkempt. She was just like her father, always grubbing round in his silly old museum.

'I wish you'd warned me,' she said. 'I've only got sausages for supper. Are you staying the night?'

'Yes please,' said Harriet.

'That'll be nice – just the two of us.'

'Where's Daddy?'

'Away; gone to one of his dreary ceramics conferences.'

Harriet's heart sank. Her father was the only person she could talk to.

Her mother put some sausages on to fry, and started washing up.

'These bridge fours have become a regular thing,' she said, plunging glasses into soapy water. 'Elizabeth Neave's really a wonderful girl.'

How could anyone over forty be described as a girl? thought Harriet.

'She's really bullying me to get a washing-up machine; she says they're such a boon when one's entertaining.'

Harriet looked at the rubber gloves whisking round the hot suds – like surgeon's hands, she thought in horror, sucking a baby out like a Hoover. The smell of frying sausages was making her sick. Out in the garden the wind was whirling pink almond blossom off the trees.

Look at her just mooning out of the window, thought Mrs Poole. Susie would have picked up a tea-towel and been drying up by now.

'How's the 'varsity?' she said. 'You look very peaky. Have you been working too hard?'

Harriet turned round:

'I'm pregnant,' she said.

'What?'

'Pregnant.'

The rubber hands stopped, then suddenly started washing very fast.

'How do you know?'

'I had a test.'

'It's Geoffrey,' said her mother in a shrill voice, 'I never liked that boy.'

'No it isn't. It's someone else.'

'You little tart,' hissed her mother.

Then it all came flooding out, the hysterics, the tears, the after all we've done for yous, the way we've scrimped and saved to send you to university. 'I knew this would happen with all those

Bohemians with their long hair and petitions, and free love,' shouted her mother. 'It's all your father's fault. He wanted you to go so badly. Where did we go wrong with you? What will the Neaves say?'

On and on, round and round, repeating the same arguments with relentless monotony.

Harriet sat down. The cat, no respecter of crisis, rubbed against her legs, and then jumped onto her knee purring like a kettle drum.

'Could you please turn those sausages off?' said Harriet, suddenly overwhelmed with nausea.

'What are you going to do about it?' said her mother. 'I suppose the young man's ditched you.'

'He doesn't want to marry me, if that's what you mean.'

'He may have to,' said her mother ominously.

'Oh, Mummy, it's the twentieth century,' said Harriet. 'Look, it meant something to me, but it didn't mean anything to him. He doesn't love me, but at least he's given me the money for an abortion.'

Her mother took the cheque. Her expression had the same truculent relief of people who have waited half an hour in the cold, and who at last see a bus rounding the corner.

'Banks at Coutts, does he? Fancies himself I suppose. Isn't it against the law?'

'Not any more,' said Harriet. 'I went to a doctor this morning in London. It's all above board; they'll do it on Friday.'

'It seems the best course,' said her mother somewhat mollified. 'The young man does seem to have his wits about him.'

Harriet took a deep breath.

'Do you really want me to go ahead with it? Wouldn't it be better to keep the baby?'

Her mother looked appalled, as though the bus had turned out to be 'Private' after all.

'What ever for? Where could you keep it?'

It was as though she was talking about a pet elephant, thought Harriet.

'You can't have it here,' her mother went on. 'Think what people would say – the Neaves for example. It's not fair on Susie and Peter. Where would you live? You haven't got any money.'

'You thought it was all right when Amanda Sutcliffe had a baby,' said Harriet.

'Everyone knows Amanda Sutcliffe's a bit potty. Those sort of girls are expected to get themselves into trouble. It seems callous, I know, but with your 'varsity career and all that the only answer seems to be to get rid of it.'

'It isn't an "it", it's a her or a him; it's your grandchild,' said Harriet in desperation. 'You always wanted grandchildren.'

'But in the proper way,' said her mother, starting to cry. 'What would everyone say?'

'What does it matter?' said Harriet, and, rushing out of the room, ran upstairs to her own room and threw herself down on the bed.

Later her mother came up and sat on the bed and stroked her hair.

'I'm sorry I shouted at you, darling. It's just the shock. You must realize you can't just have a baby. It's a serious responsibility; having it's only the beginning. A child needs a stable family, parents, financial support. Once Friday's over, you'll be able to carry on with your life. You know how heartbroken Daddy will be if you don't get a degree. You need a holiday. We might all go to the Lakes this vac. I know you've always wanted to see Wordsworth's cottage.' She was smoothing her shoulder lightly but firmly now as though she were making pastry. Harriet found it dimly touching that her mother was trying to be nice, but only dimly. Since Simon had gone she found it very difficult to react to anything normally. She came down and watched television with her mother, who later said she was tired and went to bed. Harriet sat dry-eyed and stared at the horror movie which was about a huge tarantula spider. She hardly realized that the spider had been replaced by a vicar talking about resignation:

'For everything there is a season,' he began in his thin reedy voice.

And it reminded her so much of Simon that tears suddenly spurted out of her eyes. Growing inside her was the only thing of Simon's she had left. It was at that moment she decided to keep the baby.

Part Two

Chapter Eight

Mrs Hastings closed the box file with a snap.

'I'm afraid I've nothing for you, Miss Poole,' she said.

Harriet felt desperation sweeping over her.

'But there must be something!' she said. 'I'll do any kind of work, as long as it's living in.'

'You said that last time, Miss Poole, before you took that post with Mr Widnell.'

'I know I did. I'm sorry.'

Mrs Hastings examined her long red nails, as though she'd just enjoyed tearing some animal apart.

'I should have thought a girl with your background, Miss Poole, would know how to keep a man like Mr Widnell at a distance. But I suppose keeping men at a distance isn't quite your forte, is it?'

Harriet clenched her hands together. She could feel the sweat rising on her forehead. Keep calm, she told herself. Don't shout at her – it won't do any good.

'You must have something,' she repeated. 'I mean we won't survive unless I get a job.'

Mrs Hastings's neon smile flashed on again. 'You

should have thought about that before you left Mr Widnell in such a hurry. Come back on Monday.'

Harriet was about to plead with her when the telephone rang. Mrs Hastings picked it up.

'Mr Erskine? Oh, not again! All right, put him through.' Her voice turned to honey. 'Hullo, Mr Erskine. How's it all going?'

There was a pause. 'None of them will do? But I must have sent nearly a dozen girls along to see you. Well, yes . . . I fully appreciate your going to France tomorrow, Mr Erskine, but what can I do? I've sent all my best girls along . . . What about my worst girls? We don't have any of that sort on our books!'

Suddenly, her eyes lit on Harriet. 'Just a minute, Mr Erskine.' Her tone became conciliating. 'How would you feel about a girl who's – I might say – rather tragically placed?'

Harriet squirmed with mortification.

'What sort of circumstances?'

The red-nailed hand rearranged the cacti on the desk. 'Well, I have a Miss Poole on my books who has a young baby . . . no, quite by chance she's not married. You'll see her?' The neon smile was really flashing now. 'Marvellous! You'll find her a charming person. Very quiet and refined, not at all the type you'd expect. She drives a car, cooks, she's got a degree in English, lots of experience with children.'

She waved away Harriet's exclamation of protest.

'All right, Mr Erskine, I'll pop her in a taxi right away.'

She put down the receiver.

'Well, Miss Poole, you're in luck. That was Cory Erskine.'

'The writer?'

Mrs Hastings nodded.

'I love his books,' said Harriet.

'He's obviously better at writing than getting it together with people,' said Mrs Hastings. 'His marriage has just come unstuck.'

'Unstuck?' said Harriet in amazement. 'But he's married to Noel Balfour, isn't he? They're always being held up as a model couple. She keeps being interviewed in magazines on how to keep one's husband happy.'

'No-one,' said Mrs Hastings sourly, 'could keep Mr Erskine happy. He's one of the most difficult men I've ever had to deal with. You won't get the job but, if by some miracle he does offer it to you, mind you take it. People in your position can't afford to be choosy. And do smarten yourself up before you go round there, and try to be a little bit more positive. His address is Number Nine, Chiltern Street.'

How can you smarten yourself up, thought Harriet dolefully, as she frantically combed her hair, when you've run out of cleansing cream, deodorant and eye make-up. When you can't afford to get your shoes mended, and you've taken the sheen out of your hair washing it in soap powder.

Chapter Nine

Number Nine stood out from the other houses in Chiltern Street, because it was painted cobalt blue with an emerald green door. Quaking with nerves, Harriet gave her last pound in the world to the driver and rang the bell. After some delay the door was answered by a tall angry looking man in a black polo-necked sweater.

'Yes?' he said unhelpfully.

'Mr Erskine? I've come from the agency about the job.'

'Come in. I'm on the telephone.'

She followed him upstairs into a large, untidy room. Books covered the walls, littered a very large desk, and were strewn all over the rose-coloured carpet.

'I won't be long,' he said.

Lighting a cigarette, he picked up the telephone.

'Oscar? You're still there? Look, I don't give a damn if the Yanks do pull out, we'll raise the cash some other way, but I'm not writing another major character into the script!'

Poor Oscar, thought Harriet sitting down in a

lemon yellow chair, hoping her laddered tights didn't show too much.

Then she studied some photographs on a side table. Two were of very beautiful children, a boy and a girl, with long blonde hair and dark slanting eyes. Another photograph was of a racehorse. Cory Erskine, she remembered, had once been famous as an amateur jockey. The fourth was of Noel Balfour, herself, in a bikini, looking not unlike a sleek and beautiful racehorse – long-legged, full bodied, with the fine head, tawny eyes, classical features and wide sensual mouth that were so familiar to cinema audiences all over the world.

And what of the man Noel Balfour had been allegedly happily married to for so long? Harriet turned back to look at Cory Erskine, examining the aloof, closed face with its deadpan features, high cheekbones and slanting, watchful eyes. He looks like a Red Indian, she thought, inscrutable and not very civilized at that.

As he came to the end of his conversation, a shaft of winter sunshine came through the window, lighting up the unhealthy pallor of his face, the heavy lines around the mouth, the grey flecks in the long, dark hair.

'Sorry about that,' he said, putting down the receiver. He picked up a half empty whisky bottle. 'Have a drink?'

Harriet shook her head. She hadn't eaten since yesterday lunchtime, and a drink the size of the one Cory Erskine was pouring into his own glass would put her out like a light.

When he offered her his cigarette case, however, she couldn't resist taking one, although she knew one wasn't supposed to smoke at interviews. Her hand shook so badly when he gave her a light that he had to steady it with his own hand.

He straightened up and looked at her for a minute. 'You're in pretty bad shape, aren't you?' he said abruptly. 'How long is it since you had the baby?'

'Three months,' said Harriet. 'I wasn't awfully well afterwards; but I'm fine now.'

'Who's the father?'

Harriet blushed.

'You can tell me,' he said. 'I don't make a habit of rushing round on roller skates with a megaphone, as soon as anyone tells me anything.'

'He was an undergraduate,' said Harriet, 'called Simon Villiers.'

Even after so long, the mention of his name made her mouth go dry, her throat tighten.

Cory Erskine looked up.

'Simon Villiers? Good-looking boy, blond? Loaded with money? Doesn't he want to go on the stage?'

Harriet started shaking. 'You know him?'

'I've met him. I had to give a couple of lectures on drama at Oxford last summer. Simon Villiers was allotted to look after me.'

'How was he?' asked Harriet in a strangled voice.

'Extremely pleased with himself. Don't you see him now? Doesn't he help you?'

'He gave me a lot of money to have a proper abortion, but I funked it so I bought some contact lenses instead and kept the baby.'

'Does he know you've had it?'

'I wrote and told him. He didn't answer. I think he's probably abroad. He wasn't in love with me.'

'Won't your parents help?' he asked.

'Only if I have William – that's the baby – adopted, and I can't bear to do that.'

'Where's he now?'

'I've left him with a friend – but only for the afternoon.'

Her stomach started rumbling with hunger. She felt at a distinct disadvantage in his lemon yellow chair, her bottom much lower than her legs.

Cory Erskine shook the ice round in his whisky. 'And you want to look after my children?'

Harriet nodded, trying desperately not to appear too eager. He pointed to the photographs on the table.

'Jonah and Chattie, aged eight and five. Contrary to all the rubbish you've read in the papers about Noel's and my married bliss, they've had a very rough time. Ever since Jonah was born, Noel's been making her mind up whether or not to leave me. The children have been used as pawns. Now she's finally decided she wants to marry Ronnie Acland.' His voice hardened. 'And we're getting a divorce.'

'I'm abroad a lot. The children live up in Yorkshire in my old family home. Noel has never got on with any of the nannies. As a result, they've had a succession of people looking after them. They desperately need someone kind, loving, responsible and permanent to give them security.'

He looked at Harriet, taking in the pitiful thinness,

the long legs sprawled like a colt's, the lank dark hair drawn back in a crumpled black ribbon, the irregular features, sallow skin, huge frightened eyes, full trembling mouth.

'Have you any idea what you'll be in for?' he said. 'It's a dead-end part of the world. Nothing ever happens there. All the locals ever talk about is hunting. I go up to work there because it's more peaceful than London. Could you throw yourself into looking after two children? Because if you can't, there's not much point your coming. How old are you?'

'Nearly twenty,' said Harriet.

'But Mrs Hastings said you've got a degree.'

'No, I dropped out when I got pregnant.'

'But you do have experience with children?'

'I've looked after friends' children a lot.'

'But I gathered you'd had a job, or was that just part of Mrs Hastings's meticulous inaccuracy? How long did it last?'

Harriet shuffled her feet. 'Only one night,' she said in a low voice. 'It was a housekeeping job for a man in the country.'

'And?'

'He . . . he tried to rape me the first night.'

Cory Erskine raised an eyebrow. 'Quick work! How did he manage that?'

'He came into my bedroom j-just after I'd turned out my light and . . .'

'And you didn't feel it worth your while to capitulate. Very admirable.'

Harriet flushed angrily. If she had expected

82

sympathy, she was quite wrong. Cory Erskine's face was without expression.

'And the baby,' he went on. 'Is he good? Does he cry much?'

Harriet took a deep breath. She might as well be honest, as she obviously wasn't going to get the job.

'Yes, he does; but I think babies are barometers. They reflect the mood of the person looking after them. I mean,' she floundered on, 'if I were happier and less worried, he might be, too. It's just that I haven't been very happy lately.'

Cory Erskine didn't appear to be listening. He was examining the page in his typewriter. He turned it back, and typed in a couple of words with one finger.

Bastard! thought Harriet. How dare he be so callous!

'Well, if he cries that's your problem,' he said without looking up. 'We'll put you both at the far end of the house, and then no-one but you will hear him.'

Harriet gave a gasp.

'You can cook and drive a car?' he went on.

She nodded.

'Good. You don't have to do everything. There's a housekeeper, Mrs Bottomley. She's been with our family for years, but she's getting on and the children exhaust her. Jonah's a weekly boarder at a prep school, and Chattie goes to day school. You'd have to look after them when they're at home, ferry them to and from school, see to their clothes, cook for them, etc. I'm going to France for at least a month from tomorrow, but when I come back, I'm coming up North to finish a couple of scripts.'

'Do you mean you're really going to hire me?' asked Harriet in a bewildered voice.

He nodded. 'I only hope you won't be horribly bored.'

'Bored?' said Harriet slowly. 'That's like asking a drowning man if he'd be bored by a lifebelt.'

It was the first time Cory Erskine had smiled, and Harriet could suddenly see why Noel Balfour had once found him so attractive.

'I suggest you travel up on Sunday,' he said. 'There's a good train at twelve o'clock. I'll arrange to have you met at Leeds. Now, if you'll forgive me, I've a lot of last-minute things to do.'

'I can't begin to thank you,' she stammered. 'I'll do everything I can to make them happy.' As she stood up, she swayed and had to clutch at the edge of the desk to stop herself falling.

'You'd better start eating properly,' he said, getting out his cheque book. 'Twenty pounds for travelling, twenty-five pounds in advance for your first week's salary.' He handed her a cheque for forty-five pounds.

Harriet found herself fighting back the tears. 'I'm sorry,' she said, turning her head away. 'I'm just not used to getting breaks. You can't give me that much money.'

'I want you to look after my children properly, not just moon around the house. Now, I don't anticipate Mrs Bottomley will try and rape you, so I'll see you again towards the end of February. You'll probably find it easier to settle in without my poking my nose in all the time.'

After she'd gone, still stammering her thanks, he sat down to work again. Then, a minute later, he got up and looked out of the window. Harriet was walking down the road. He watched her take the cheque out of her bag, examine it in amazement, hold it up to the light, then give a little skip of joy, so that she nearly cannoned into a passer-by.

Before she rounded the corner, she turned round to look up at the window, and waved at him timidly. He waved back.

I'm a bloody idiot, he told himself. I could have got any Nanny in London and I end up with a waif with a baby – which means four children to look after instead of two!

He looked at the photograph of his wife and his face hardened. He poured himself another stiff whisky before settling down.

Chapter Ten

Once the euphoria of landing the job had worn off, Harriet grew more and more apprehensive. She had difficulty enough looking after one baby. What right had she to take on two children, who were probably spoilt and certainly disturbed?

I won't be able to cope, she kept telling herself as the train rattled through the Midlands the following Sunday. Each mile, too, was taking her further and further away from Simon, and the remote possibility that one day she might bump into him in London.

As promised, a car met her at Leeds station and once they were on the road, William, who had yelled most of the journey, fell into a deep sleep, giving the exhausted Harriet a chance to look at the passing countryside. It did nothing to raise her flagging spirits.

The black begrimed outskirts of Leeds soon gave way to fields and woodland then to wilder and bleaker country: khaki hillsides, stone walls, rusty bracken, with the moors stretching above, dark demon-haunted, Heathcliffe land. Harriet shivered and hugged William closer. No wonder Noel Balfour had run away from such savage desolation.

They drove through a straggling village of little grey houses and then the road started climbing steeply upwards.

'There's Erskine's place, up yonder ont' hill,' said the driver. 'The Wilderness, they call it. Wouldn't like to live there myself, but these stage folks have funny notions. I suppose you get used to anything if you have to.'

The big grey house lay in a fold of the moors, about half a mile from a winding river. Surrounding it was a jungle of neglected garden. Pine trees rose like sentinels at the back.

Harriet knocked nervously at the huge studded door, which was opened by a middle-aged woman with piled-up reddish hair and a disapproving dough-like face. She gave Harriet a hostile stare, but seemed far more interested in stopping a large tabby cat from escaping.

'Ambrose! Come here, you devil!' She just managed to catch the cat by the tail and pull him squawking into the house.

'Miss Poole?' she said icily, very much on her dignity. 'I'm Mrs Bottomley.'

'How do you do?' said Harriet, trying to shake hands and clutch William and the luggage at the same time.

As she walked into the hall, two children rushed down the stairs, dragging a black labrador, and stopped dead in their tracks, gazing at her with dark, heavily lashed and not altogether friendly eyes.

'Jonah and Charlotte,' said Mrs Bottomley, 'this is Miss Poole.'

'How do you do?' said Harriet nervously. 'This is William.'

'Did you have a good journey?' said the little girl in a formal voice. 'We're so recited to see you. Ambrose is on heat; that's why he's not allowed out. We thought he was a "he" when daddy bought him.'

Mrs Bottomley picked up one of her suitcases.

'I'll show you to your room,' she said coldly, starting up the stairs.

'Watch the string,' said Harriet in anguish, but it was too late. The string snapped and the contents of the suitcase – all the dirty laundry – her own and William's that she hadn't had time to wash before she left – cascaded onto the floor with a crash.

The children shrieked with laughter. Chattie went into hysterics of excitement. Nothing could have broken the ice more completely as they rushed round putting things back.

Mrs Bottomley, frostier than ever, led Harriet along a winding passage to her room. The house, in contrast to its grim exterior, was positively sybaritic inside. Whoever had chosen the moss-thick carpets, the watered silk wallpapers, the brilliantly clashing curtains, had had an inspired eye for colour, if no regard for expense.

There were also looking glasses everywhere, in the hall, on the stairs and at the end of the landing. Harriet tried not to look at her worried, white-faced reflection.

'What a lovely house, and how beautifully you keep it,' she said, making a feeble attempt to remove the rigid expression of disapproval from Mrs Bottomley's face. The housekeeper ignored her.

'You're in here,' she said, showing Harriet into a little grey and white room with yellow curtains and yellow flowered four-poster bed. 'The child can sleep next door,' she added coldly. It was as though she couldn't bear to acknowledge William's existence.

'Chattie and Jonah are at the far end of the passage, but there's a device you switch on, so you can hear if they wake in the night. I'll see them to bed tonight. Your supper will be ready in an hour.'

All this time she had not looked Harriet in the face. Oh dear, sighed Harriet, she really does resent my coming here.

Later, feeling more and more depressed, Harriet found a place laid for one in the huge green Victorian dining-room.

She looked at Mrs Bottomley timidly:

'Won't you come and eat in here with me?' she asked.

'I have my meals in my own part of the house. I hope that will be all,' said Mrs Bottomley.

But as she stalked majestically towards the door, she heard a muffled sob and, looking round, she saw that Harriet's face had disintegrated into a quivering chaos of misery, as she fished out her handkerchief.

Mrs Bottomley's heart melted. She padded across the room and put an arm round Harriet's shoulders.

'There, there, my lamb, don't cry. You'll get used to it all in no time. I know it seems an out-of-the-way place for a young girl, but the children have been so excited, especially with you bringing the baby, and you'll be company for me. I get lonely of an evening.'

Harriet wiped her eyes. 'You don't mind about William, and me not being married?' she said.

'Never gave it a thought,' lied Mrs Bottomley, who had been boasting in the village that she'd soon put the hussy in her place.

'You come and eat in the kitchen with me. You'll feel better when you've got something inside you. We'll have a drop of sherry to cheer ourselves up.'

From then on Harriet and Mrs Bottomley were firm friends. The housekeeper bossed her, fussed over her, bullied her to eat, and gave her endless advice on how to look after the children.

Chapter Eleven

Even so Harriet often wondered afterwards how she survived those first few weeks looking after Cory Erskine's children. The day seemed neverending, rising at six, feeding and bathing William, getting Chattie off to school, by which time William's next feed would be due. Then there was endless washing and ironing, shopping, rooms to be tidied, meals to be cooked, beds to be made.

Night after night, she cried herself to sleep out of sheer exhaustion, to be woken a couple of hours later by William howling because his teeth were hurting.

Hard work alone she could have coped with. It was just the endless demands on her cheerfulness and good temper. Chattie, incapable of playing by herself, wanted constantly to be amused or comforted. She adored the baby and was a perfect menace, feeding him indigestible foods which made him sick, going into his room and waking him just after he'd fallen asleep.

Jonah, Harriet found even more of a problem than Chattie. He was obviously deeply unhappy and, when he came home at weekends, Harriet did her best to amuse him.

In between bouts of moodiness, he was very good company, but Harriet could never tell what he was thinking behind the aloof Red Indian mask he had inherited from his father. Often he didn't speak for hours and, although he never mentioned his mother, Harriet noticed that he always hung around when the post was due, and was hard put to conceal his disappointment when no letters arrived.

Cory wrote to them regularly, long letters full of drawings and wild, unexpectedly zany humour. Noel Balfour patently didn't believe in correspondence. Only one postcard arrived from her in five weeks, and that was postmarked Africa and addressed to Cory. On the front was a picture of a team of huge muscular Africans playing football. On the back she had written, 'Had them all except the goalkeeper, darling.'

Mrs Bottomley's face shut like a steel trap when she saw the postcard, but Harriet, although dying to know more about Cory Erskine's relationship with his wife, was sensible enough not to ask questions. She felt that Mrs Bottomley would tell her in her own good time. She was right.

They were sitting before supper one evening towards the end of February in the small den off the dining room. Above the fire hung a huge, nude painting of Noel Balfour. She's so beautiful, thought Harriet, I can't imagine any man not wanting her.

'Who did it?' she asked.

Mrs Bottomley puffed out her cheeks and went red in the face with disapproval, but the desire to gossip was too much for her.

'Master Kit did, and he never should have done, neither.'

'Who's he?'

'Mr Cory's younger brother.'

'Goodness,' said Harriet. 'That's a bit close to home. It's awfully good.'

'So it should be,' said Mrs Bottomley glaring at the lounging, opulent figure of Noel Balfour. 'He took long enough over it. Mr Cory was abroad at the time, and Master Kit rolls up cool as a cucumber. "Ay've come to paint the magnificent scenery, Mrs B." he says, but there was a wicked glint in his eyes. I knew he was up to no good.'

'What's he like?' said Harriet. 'Like Mr Erskine?'

'Chalk and cheese,' said Mrs Bottomley, helping herself to another glass of sherry. 'He's handsome is Master Kit. Tall and golden as one of them sunflowers, and enough charm to bring roses out of the ground in winter. But he always brings trouble. Drove his poor mother mad with worry. Magnificent scenery, indeed. He never moved out of Mrs Erskine's bedroom, and she lying there totally nude, as though butter wouldn't melt in her mouth, and the central heating turned up so high, you'd think it was a heatwave. And it wasn't just painting they got up to, neither.'

'Whatever did Mr Erskine say when he got home?' said Harriet in awe. 'He must have hit the roof.'

''E did,' said Mrs Bottomley. 'You should have heard them. Mr Cory, very controlled as always, but very sarcastic, and Mrs E. in hysterics. You could hear her shouting all over the house: "Well, at least I kept it in the family, this time"!'

There was a pause before Mrs Bottomley said, in a confidential voice, 'You see Harriet, Master Kit wasn't the first by a long way. Ever since Master Jonah was born, it's been one young gentleman after another.'

'But why does Mr Erskine put up with it?' said Harriet. 'He doesn't strike me as being the permissive type.'

Mrs Bottomley shook her head.

'He isn't,' she said glumly. 'He's tough in most ways, but where she's concerned, he's as weak as water. He loves her.'

'But how's he got the strength to divorce her now?'

Mrs Bottomley shrugged her plump shoulders. 'Happen he won't. She claims she wants to marry this Ronnie Acland, but I reckon Mr Cory will take her back in the end. She likes being married to him. It gives her respectability, and he makes a lot of money. She's extravagant, you know, wants the best of everything – and she likes having power over him, knowing he's still under her spell.'

Harriet understood so well how Cory felt. Now that she no longer worried about being able to keep William or where the next penny was coming from, all her thoughts centred on Simon.

Her longing for him grew no less with time. It hungered in her, night and day, engulfing her senses and her reason in an aching void. She tried to fill the void with hard work, to stupefy the ache by watching endless television, and reading long into the night, but her loneliness deepened round her as though she were alone in a huge cave.

Later that evening, after Mrs Bottomley had gone up to bed, the telephone rang. Harriet answered it.

'Mr Erskine calling from Dublin,' said the operator. 'Will you accept the call?'

'Yes,' said Harriet, wondering what Cory was doing in Ireland.

'Hullo, hullo, Cory. Can I speak to Cory, please?' It was a man's voice – slow, lazy, expensive, very attractive.

'He's not here,' said Harriet.

'Hell, I thought he'd be back,' said the voice. 'Where is he?'

'In Antibes still. Can I help?'

'Not really, darling, unless you can lend me a couple of grand. I've found a horse Cory's got to buy.'

'Do you want to ring him?' said Harriet. 'I've got the number. Who is it?'

The voice laughed. 'Kit Erskine, registered black sheep. Hasn't Botters been telling you horrible stories about me?'

'Oh no, not at all.' Even though he was miles away at the other end of a telephone, Harriet could feel herself blushing.

'Of course she has. Don't believe a word. It's all true.'

Harriet giggled.

'And you must be Harriet?' he went on. 'The distressed gentlefuck.'

'What do you mean?' said Harriet furiously, immediately on the defensive. 'How do you know?'

'Cory told me or, rather, he issued king-sized ultimatums that I was to keep my thieving hands to myself where you're concerned. Is that your little baby making that horrible noise?'

'His teeth are hurting,' said Harriet.

'Why doesn't he go to the dentist? Any news of Noel?'

Harriet, rather indiscreetly she felt afterwards, told him about the postcard of the African footballers.

Kit laughed. 'Funny how she likes to keep an eye on Cory, and on me, too, for that matter. In fact, she's had her eye on so many men in her time, I'm surprised she hasn't developed the most awful squint. Everyone's laying bets whether Cory'll divorce her or not.'

'I think I'd better go and look after the baby,' said Harriet, feeling suddenly that she shouldn't be discussing her employer.

'Don't go,' said Kit. 'Are you as sexy as your voice is? What do you look like?'

'Scrawny and sallow-skinned,' said Harriet.

'Just my type,' said Kit. 'I've a portrait to paint up North next month. I'll come over and case the joint. Don't go shacking up with any of the local gentry before I arrive.'

Bitter, bitter, sweet, thought Harriet afterwards. Bitter because, in his gaiety, panache and directness

96

of approach, he reminded her so much of Simon; sweet because, even over the telephone, it was nice to be chatted up once more.

Later still that night, Ambrose the cat decided to have her kittens at the bottom of the huge four-poster quadruple bed in Cory and Noel's bedroom. At six o'clock in the morning, having finally installed her, tired but contented, in clean straw in the kitchen with five kittens, Harriet finally fell into bed.

It seemed only a few minutes later that she was woken up by Chattie's voice telling her very smugly it was half past nine.

'Oh, my god!' said Harriet, leaping out of bed. 'And it would be Mrs Bottomley's day off.'

Frenziedly pulling on her clothes, not even bothering to wash, she rushed downstairs, fed Chattie and Jonah bread and marmalade, packed Jonah's suitcase for the week, put William bawling and unfed into the car in his carry cot, and set off to drop the children at school.

It had frozen the night before and the road was like a skating rink. Harriet tried hard to concentrate on driving, but was distracted by Jonah fiddling with the door handle. The next moment, his hand slipped and the door swung open, nearly taking him with it. Narrowly missing an oncoming car, Harriet pulled him back, locked the door and gave him a ringing slap on his bare leg.

'Don't ever do that again!' she shouted.

Jonah said nothing, gazing in front of him, colour slowly draining out of his cheeks, as the red finger marks grew on his thigh.

Chattie, of course, was delighted. 'Naughty, naughty Jonah,' she chanted.

'Shut up, Chattie!' snapped Harriet, turning the car into Jonah's school gates.

Jonah grabbed his small suitcase and jumped out of the car.

'Goodbye, darling,' said Harriet her anger evaporating. 'Pick you up on Friday evening.'

Jonah was white with rage.

'Don't call me darling!' he said in a trembling voice. 'I hate you! I *hate* you! I wish you'd never come. I'm going to tell my father to send you away.'

On the verge of tears, Harriet dropped Chattie off at her school. William was bellowing his lungs out with hunger all the way home.

'William! Please!' she said, her voice rising in desperation. 'It won't be long.'

While she was heating up milk for a bottle she very hurriedly washed some of William's clothes and put them into the spin dryer.

Suddenly the telephone rang. William redoubled his howls. At the same moment, the milk boiled over and as she rushed to retrieve it, she realized she'd forgotten to put a bucket underneath the spin dryer.

'Oh, my God!' she screamed hysterically, as soapy water belched forth round her feet. 'Oh, shut up! Shut up, William!'

'You appear to be in some difficulty,' said a dry voice behind her. Aghast, she swung round. Standing in the doorway stood Cory Erskine.

His reactions were incredibly quick. In a second,

as Harriet gaped at him, he had turned off the spin dryer and removed the milk from the boil.

'There's enough milk left for one bottle,' he said. 'I'll get the telephone.'

Oh, God, thought Harriet wretchedly, I've really done it now. He couldn't have come back at a worse moment!

'It's Jonah ringing,' said Cory. 'He wants you.'

'Where's he ringing from?'

'From a call box. Take it upstairs. When he's through, tell him it might be diplomatic if he went back to school. Give the baby to me. I'll feed him.'

Jonah had rung up to apologize. His voice sounded high and strained. 'I just rang to say I don't want you to go away. I won't complain to my father about you, and I'm s-sorry, Harriet.'

She felt a great lump in her throat.

'It's all right, darling,' she said. 'It's lovely of you to ring. I'm sorry, too.'

Returning to the kitchen, she found William had fallen asleep halfway through his bottle, his mouth open, his long lashes sweeping down over his cheeks.

'He's a beautiful child,' said Cory, handing him back to her. 'What was Jonah on about?'

'We had a row this morning. He was apologizing.'

Cory grunted. 'That child's got far better manners than either of his parents. Wonder where he gets them from. How's Chattie?'

'Fine, in tearing spirits. I'm so sorry you had such an awful homecoming,' said Harriet. 'I'm afraid we all overslept, and things got a bit chaotic. Would you like some breakfast?'

Cory shook his head. 'I'm going to follow William's example and get some sleep. I've been driving all night.'

He looked absolutely played out – deathly pale, unshaven, his eyes bloodshot and heavily shadowed.

An appalling thought struck Harriet. 'Oh, you can't go to bed yet. Ambrose had her kittens last night in your bed and I haven't changed the sheets!'

He must loathe coming back here, she thought, as she made up the huge double bed in the room he had once shared with Noel Balfour. It was such an ultra-feminine room. Everything stagily erotic – the thick, white carpets, the rose-strewn wallpaper, the huge canopied four-poster, the pink frills frothing round the dressing table – must remind him so poignantly of her.

But if Cory minded, he gave no indication. 'It's going to snow,' he said, gazing out of the window.

As Harriet put on the pillow cases, pink from her exertions, she realized he was watching her, and was suddenly conscious that she hadn't even had time to wash her face that morning, and was wearing an old red sweater, drastically shrunk in the wash.

'You look better,' he said. 'You've put on weight.'

'Mrs Bottomley keeps feeding me up on suet puddings,' said Harriet, blushing.

Cory surfaced about seven, and came into the kitchen, Chattie hanging on one hand, a large glass of whisky in the other. Chattie was also clutching a six-foot tiger balloon.

'Look what Daddy brought me,' she said. She turned to Cory. 'Harriet overslept this morning and made me late for band, so I had to play the triangle instead of the tangerine.'

'Tambourine,' said Cory. 'And don't sneak.'

Chattie ran to the window.

'Look how deep the snow is! Can't I stay up for supper?'

'No,' said Cory. 'You can show me Ambrose's kittens, and then you're going to bed.'

'How are you getting on at school?' he went on. 'Have you got a best friend yet?'

'Everyone wants to be my best friend,' said Chattie. 'But they've got to learn to share me.'

At that moment Mrs Bottomley walked in from her day off, weighed down with carrier bags, her maroon wool coat and felt hat trimmed with a bird's body covered in snowflakes.

'Mr Cory,' she squawked. 'You 'ave given me a turn; you should 'ave warned us. If I'd known, I'd 'ave opened up the front room. Still it's *very* nice to see you.'

And he really was nice to *her* thought Harriet, taking her parcels, and teasing her about buying up the whole of Marshalls and Snelgrove, asking after her rheumatism.

'Mustn't grumble,' said Mrs Bottomley. 'Having Harriet here's made a difference. Saves me a lot of work, 'aving a young pair of legs running about the house.'

Cory glanced at Harriet's legs.

'Pleased with her, are you?' he said.

'Well I'm not saying she isn't a bit dreamy at times, but we've had some laughs, and she's a hard worker,' said Mrs Bottomley, unpinning her hat. 'Which is more than I can say for some of those hoity-toity misses in the past. And how was Antibes?' she added, pronouncing it Anti-bees.

For a second Cory's eyes met Harriet's.

Then he said gravely, 'Anti-bees was very exhausting.'

'You look peaky, I must say,' said Mrs Bottomley, 'as though you'd walked all the way home. Must be all that foreign food – frogs legs and ratty twee – you need feeding up.'

Harriet was determined to redeem the morning's disastrous homecoming by cooking Cory a magnificent dinner, but it was not to be. She went into the garden to shake the water out of a lettuce, and stood transfixed. The pine trees now carried armfuls of gleaming white blossom, urns filled with snow were casting long blue shadows across the lawn, flakes soft as tiny feathers poured out of the sky.

Memories of the first time she'd met Simon came flooding back. Oh, God, she thought, in an agony of despair, when will I ever see him? She didn't know how long she stood there – five, ten minutes – but, suddenly, she realized she was frozen.

When she got back to the kitchen she gave a shriek. Tadpole, Cory's labrador, had the steak on the floor, Ambrose was sitting unrepentant on the kitchen table, tabby cheeks bulging with the last of the prawns and the sauce had curdled past redemption on the stove.

102

At that moment, Cory walked in. 'For Christ sake, what's the matter now?'

Trembling, Harriet pointed at Ambrose and Tadpole. 'The snow was so beautiful, I forgot I'd left the steak and the prawns on the table.'

Again Cory surprised her. It was the first time she'd heard him laugh and, after a few seconds, she began to giggle.

'There's nothing in here,' he said, looking in the fridge. 'We'd better go out.'

'Oh, God, I'm so sorry.'

'Stop apologizing and go and do your face.'

'But you can't take me!'

'Why not? Mrs Bottomley'll babysit.'

'But, but . . .' Harriet began a stream of feverish excuses.

Cory interrupted her. 'I don't mind hysterics, nor having my dinner ruined, but I can't stand being argued with. Go and get ready.'

He took her to a restaurant down the valley. Harriet, appalled by the prices on the menu, chose an omelette.

'Don't be silly,' he said irritably. 'What do you really want to eat?'

'It's all so expensive!'

'You should see the prices in Paris. Anyway I've just had a large advance so you might as well take advantage of it.'

At first, he kept the conversation on a strictly impersonal level, telling her about his trip to France, and the black mare, Python, he had just bought on Kit's recommendation, who was being flown over next week. 'If she's any good I'll just have time to get her fit for the point-to-point in April.'

By the time coffee arrived, wine had considerably loosened Harriet's tongue.

'Well,' said Cory, re-filling her glass, 'how's it working out, looking after the children?'

Harriet smiled nervously. 'Fine, I'm awfully happy here.'

He didn't smile back. 'I've been watching you for the past two hours. You still give the impression of a girl who cries herself to sleep every night.'

'Black or white coffee?' asked Harriet, confused.

'Black, please, and don't change the subject. Sure, you think you're fine. You've filled out, you've got some colour in your cheeks, but your eyes are still haunted; you get flustered far too quickly. And you've torn that paper napkin you've been clutching into shreds.'

'I'm OK,' she muttered. Then added in a trembling voice, 'Are you trying to say you want me to go?'

If she had looked up then she would have seen his face soften.

'You don't know me very well yet,' he said gently. 'If I wanted you to go, I'd tell you straight. Tomorrow you're going to see my doctor for some tranquillizers and sleeping pills. You'll only need them for a few weeks. I don't want you cracking up, that's all. Now, I suppose you'd prefer I talked on impersonal subjects. How did you meet Simon Villiers?'

Harriet choked over her coffee, then shrugged her shoulders. She so badly needed to talk to someone.

'I met him at Oxford. It was snowing like today. Simon drove round a corner and knocked me off my bicycle. Of course, I knew who he was. Everyone knew about the Villiers set – all night parties, fast cars, models down from London. I wasn't hurt, but he insisted on my going back to his rooms. There was a party on. Later he kicked everyone out. When we woke up next morning, he asked me what my name was. You're not shocked?'

Cory lit a cigar. 'Not unduly.'

'It was the first time I'd been to bed with anyone. It was like stumbling into Paradise.' She looked at her hands. 'I thought it would last for ever. Then one morning we were drinking coffee and he suddenly announced I'd have to move out as his regular girlfriend was coming back that day. I was so stunned, when I found I was pregnant, it seemed un-important compared with losing Simon. The reason I kept William really was because he was the only thing of Simon's I had.'

She looked at Cory with huge, troubled, slate-grey eyes.

He smiled. 'Do you think Jonah's happy at school?'

She was intensely grateful that he realized she didn't want to talk about herself any more.

Chapter Twelve

Life became much easier for Harriet after Cory Erskine arrived. It was having a man to make decisions, to shoulder responsibilities, to shut up the children when they became too obstreperous and, most of all, to talk to.

Cory was, in fact, not easy to live with – aloof, peremptory, exacting, often extremely bad-tempered. But in a good mood, Harriet found him lovely company, amusing, never pulling intellectual rank on her, an inspired listener. Yet as weeks passed, she didn't feel she knew him any better.

He was very unpredictable. Some days he would bombard her with questions, what did she feel about this, how would she react to that. On other days he was so abstracted she might not have been there, or he would suddenly get bored with a conversation and walk out leaving her mouthing like a goldfish in mid-sentence.

He also kept the most erratic hours, working most of the night. Often when she got up because William was crying she would hear the faint clack of the typewriter against the gramophone pouring out Verdi or Wagner. Then he would appear at breakfast looking terrible, read the paper, drink several cups of impossibly strong black coffee, and go out and ride across the moors for a couple of hours.

After that he generally snatched a few hours' sleep on the sofa in his study (Harriet had a feeling he couldn't bear sleeping alone in the huge mausoleum of a double bed), and emerged at teatime absolutely ravenous, and often as not wolf all the sandwiches Harriet had made for the children's tea.

He was also drinking too much. Every day Mrs Bottomley, her mouth disappearing with disapproval, would come out of his room with an empty whisky bottle.

He was obviously miserably unhappy. The drinking to drive out the despair would plunge him next day into black depression, which made him irritable and arbitrary. While he was working he hated interruptions. The children had to be kept out of his way. The telephone rang all the time for him, and he went spare if Harriet didn't catch it on the third or fourth ring. Always she had to make the same excuse: 'I'm afraid Mr Erskine's working. If you leave your number I'll ask him to ring you back,' which he so seldom did that Harriet was on the end of a lot of abuse from people – mostly women – who rang a second and third time and were convinced Harriet hadn't passed on the message. He also made notes, as thoughts struck him, on bits of paper and telephone directories all over the house; and after the day, when she had to go through four dustbins to find the magazine Cory had scribbled a few lines of script on the back of, she learnt not to throw anything away again without asking him.

One afternoon in early March, however, Cory was sitting in the kitchen eating raisins absent-mindedly out of a packet and reading one of Jonah's comics. William sat propped up on a red rug spread out on the flagstone floor, beating a saucepan aimlessly with a wooden spoon, gurgling happily and gazing at the gleaming copper pans that hung from the walls. Harriet, who'd that morning read an article in a magazine about the dangers of an all-tinned-food diet for babies, was rather dispiritedly sieving cabbage and carrots, when the telephone rang. Glad of any diversion, Harriet crossed the room to answer it, but it stopped on the third ring, then just as she got back to her carrots, it started again, rang three times and stopped. Then it started again and this time kept on ringing:

Sighing, Harriet put down the sieve again.

'Don't answer it,' snapped Cory. He had gone very pale. 'It's only someone playing silly games.'

Then it stopped, then started the three rings stop, three rings stop formula again. Then kept on ringing for about three minutes. Harriet noticed the way his hands gripped that comic.

'I'm going out,' said Cory. 'And don't answer the telephone.'

Next minute she heard the front door slam.

The ringing kept on. It must be the secret code of someone he doesn't want to talk to, thought Harriet. It was getting on her nerves. She'd run out of bread, so she decided to walk William in his pram down to the village and get some. She enjoyed shopping; she was beginning to know all the shop people who made a tremendous fuss of William.

It was a cold, cheerless day. The only colour came from the rusty bracken and even that lay flattened by the recent snow. The village was deserted except for a few scuttling, purple-faced women in head-scarves. Harriet came out of the bakers, warming her hands on a hot french loaf, and went into the supermarket opposite. She immediately noticed one customer, a girl with bright orange curls, wearing an emerald green coat with a mock fur collar and cuffs, stiletto-heeled green boots, and huge dark glasses. Taking tins down from the shelves she was attempting to lob them into the wire basket she had placed in the middle of the floor.

'Loves me,' she muttered as a tin of lemon meringue pie filling reached its destination safely, 'Loves me not,' as she missed with a bag of lentils, 'Loves me not, oh hell,' she added as she also missed with a tin of dog food. A child with very dissipated blue eyes, and a pudding basin haircut was systematically filling the pockets of his waisted blue coat with packets of fruit gums. The shopkeeper, who was trying to find a packet of washing-up-machine powder for another customer, was looking extremely disapproving.

The girl in dark glasses looked up and peered at Harriet.

'Hullo!' she said to Harriet, 'You must be Cory Erskine's nanny. I'm Sammy Sutcliffe; I look after Elizabeth Pemberton's kids across the valley;

they're more or less the same age as Chattie and Jonah; we ought to get them together.'

'Oh that would be lovely,' said Harriet, suddenly craving companionship her own age.

'We've been skiing, or I'd have come over before,' said the girl.

'You look terribly brown,' said Harriet.

'Yes,' said the girl, 'but it only goes down to my collar bones. Stripped off, I look like a toffee apple.'

She giggled and took off her glasses to show large, rather bloodshot, green eyes framed by heavily blacked lashes.

'They're to hide my hangover, not to keep out the sun,' she said. 'You never see the sun in this backwater.'

She put the lentils, which were spilling out of their packet, back on the shelf, took another packet and moved towards the cash desk.

'And put those sweets back, you little monster,' she screeched at the small boy, who was busy now appropriating tubes of Smarties. 'You've got the morals of an alley cat. He's a little bugger our Georgie,' she added to Harriet. 'Just like his Dad, except his Dad pinches bottoms rather than sweets.'

Outside she admired William.

'What a little duck,' she said. 'You must be knackered looking after three of them. Why don't you bring Chattie and William over to tea tomorrow and I'll fill you in on all the local scandal?'

'Gosh, thanks awfully,' said Harriet.

'Ours is the big house stood back from the river on the Skipton Road, just beyond the village,' said

Sammy. 'You'll recognize it by the sound of crashing crockery. Don't be alarmed. It'll only be my boss hurling the Spode at her hubby. Actually I think Cory's coming to dinner tonight. She rather fancies him, my boss. Can't say I blame her. I think he's lovely too – looks straight through one in such a god-damned sexy way.'

Cory got home about eight. He looked terrible. He's been in the pub, thought Harriet. She accosted him with a list of telephone messages.

'Mrs Kent-Wright rang. Could you open a fête in May, and if not could you find one of your show business friends to do it?'

'No,' said Cory. 'I couldn't.'

'A lady from *Woman's Monthly* wants to come and interview you next Wednesday at seven.'

'No,' said Cory, 'ring and say I can't.'

'And Elizabeth Pemberton rang to say they're wearing black ties this evening.'

'Oh, Christ,' said Cory bounding upstairs. 'I'd forgotten. Bring me a drink up in my dressing room, would you?'

In twenty minutes he was gone, leaving the bathroom awash, five towels at high tide, and his five o'clock shadow in the basin.

Through her two-Mogadon-induced slumber Harriet heard ringing and ringing. Don't answer she thought, it's someone trying to get through with a secret code. She pulled the blanket over her head. The ringing went on. It was the doorbell. Cory had a key. Who the hell could it be calling at that hour? Burglars, she thought in terror, then realized they'd hardly be ringing the bell. It must be some maniac off the moor, bent on rape. Wearing only her short scarlet nightgown, her hair falling in tangled curls down her back, she turned on all the lights, and nervously crept downstairs. Tadpole emerged, frowsty and bug-eyed, from the kitchen, and thumped his tail.

'You're a fine watch dog,' she said. The ringing went on. The chain was on the door. She opened it an inch.

'Who is it?' she said nervously.

'It's me, Cory.'

'Oh God, I'm sorry,' she said undoing the chain. 'I thought you had a key.'

He stood in the doorway, swaying slightly. He was deathly pale; there was a cut on his forehead where the blood had dried; his tie was crooked, his hair ruffled. He looked at her intently, trying to focus but squinting slightly like a Siamese cat.

'What have you done to your head?' she said, thinking irrationally of Elizabeth Pemberton's flying Spode saucers. 'Are you all right?'

'I am,' he said in a blurred voice. 'The car's a write off.'

He walked into the house unsteadily, heading towards the drawing room.

'Oh my God,' said Harriet running after him. 'You poor thing, sit down at once.' She dived under the table, pulling her nightgown as far as it would go over her bottom, to put on the lights by the fire. 'I'm so terribly sorry. Shall I ring for the doctor?'

'I'm perfectly all right,' said Cory. 'I ran out of fags on the way home, which didn't help.' He took a cigarette with a shaking hand out of the green jade box on the table. Harriet found a match and lit it for him.

'I'll get you a cup of strong, sweet tea,' she said.

'You can fix me a drink,' said Cory.

He's had far too much, thought Harriet. 'You might be concussed,' she said aloud.

'I'm OK,' he said irritably. 'I walked all the way home from the other side of the village, following the white lines in the middle of the road admittedly; so I've had plenty of time to work up a thirst. So if you please . . .'

Harriet poured him a large whisky and soda. He drained half of it in one gulp.

'Why didn't you ring me?' said Harriet, 'I'd have come and collected you.'

'I'd spent my last 10p in the pub this afternoon,' he said. 'And that reminds me, I took a quid out of the housekeeping. Do you want a drink?'

Harriet looked at the clock. It was three in the morning. She'd have to get William up in three and a half hours.

'Go on,' said Cory.

She poured herself a small glass of white wine.

Tadpole scratched at the fur rug in front of the fire, circled twice, then sat down as near the dying embers as possible.

'Are you sure you don't want a cup of tea?'

'I just want someone to talk to for a few minutes.'

Harriet curled up on the sofa, trying not to yawn,

tucking her long legs under her. She hadn't shaved them for months, not that Cory would notice in the state he was in.

'Was it a good evening?' she said politely.

'Bloody awful. "Just a few friends", said Elizabeth, and I arrive an hour late to find three couples and a battle-scarred thirty-five-year-old with a "for hire" sign on her forehead lined up specifically for me. She was called Geraldine or Jennifer or something. We were put next door to each other at dinner, with everyone surreptitiously watching to see how we were hitting it off, just like mating dogs.'

'Was she very beautiful?' said Harriet.

'Very – but she laughed too much, and asked too many questions about the ages of my children, and the script I'm writing at the moment, and didn't I adore ballet, because she simply adores it. I was lumbered with her after dinner too, and out of the back of my head, I could see Elizabeth mouthing to all her friends, "It's going frightfully well." "Frightful" just about summed it up. Then at midnight she asked me if I'd terribly mind running Jennifer or Geraldine back to her cottage in Gargrave.'

The pale mask of his face was expressionless. He finished his drink and put his glass very carefully down on the table.

'So I ran her home, and she gave me all the old crap about dropping out of London and leaving her stockbroker husband because he didn't want children, and anyway he was knocking off his secretary, and how much more genuine and sincere people are in the North. And tomorrow I shall get a bollocking.'

'Who from?' said Harriet.

'Elizabeth. For behaving badly.'

'What ever did you do?'

'Didn't try and pull Geraldine or Jennifer.'

'Mary Whitehouse would have been proud of you,' said Harriet.

'I know,' said Cory, 'it's a great source of consolation to me. Fix me another drink, there's a good girl.'

'Did she terribly want you to?'

'She wanted me to try. She's frightened of the future and she wants someone to blot out the loneliness and to describe as "the man in her life". She even put more scent on in the car going home, very secretively so I wasn't supposed to notice. She waited when we got to the house, wriggling down in the seat with her head tilted back but I need that sort of complication like a hole in the head, so I got out and opened the door for her, and she started to cry and fled up the path, and then the poor cow couldn't find her latch key until she'd turned her bag out. And I felt such a sod. Some sort of instinct of self-preservation made me put on a safety belt for the first time in years, and I drove off down the Fairmile slap into a tree. Hostesses can't resist a spare man.' He was rambling now. 'They're gold dust round here, a going spare man, a going-to-sleep-in-the-spare-room-every-night man. I got very used to spare rooms when I was married to Noel.'

His long eyelashes lifted, and his dark eyes

frowned at her as though she was the one who had hurt him.

He must be pissed out of his mind, thought Harriet; it's the first time he's mentioned Noel since the interview.

'They want to get their own back on her for pinching their husbands,' he went on.

'Did she pinch them?' said Harriet.

'The ones she wanted, she did, and the wives of the ones she didn't were in a way more piqued that their husbands should be slavering over Noel and her not taking a blind bit of notice of them.'

He picked up Jonah's homework composition book which was lying on the table. 'People in India have no food,' he read out, 'and they often go to bed with no supper.' He laughed. 'And all the old harridan puts at the bottom of the page is "Try and write more clearly, and write out the word Tomorrow three times".'

He picked up a pencil:

'Tomorrow and tomorrow and tomorrow,' he said, writing with great care, 'creeps on this petty pace from . . .'

'Oh you mustn't,' cried Harriet in horror. 'Jonah's teacher will murder him.'

'I pay the fees,' said Cory. 'If Miss Bickersteth wishes to flip her lid she can ring up and complain to me. People in India have no food,' he repeated slowly, 'and they often go to bed with no supper. People in Yorkshire have a great deal too much to drink, and often also go to bed with no supper.

Please get me another drink,' he said, 'and don't tell me I've had enough. I know I have.'

'You look absolutely exhausted,' said Harriet. 'You're the one who should be taking sleeping pills and eating regular meals.'

'Stop trying to mother me,' said Cory.

Harriet handed him a drink.

'It's a bloody weak one,' he grumbled.

Their hands touched. 'You're cold,' he said.

'I've got a warm heart,' said Harriet, flustered and wincing at the cliché. Cory didn't notice.

'My wife has hot little hands,' said Cory, 'but her heart is as cold as the grave. She's a nymphomaniac. I suppose you've heard that.'

'Well, something of the sort.'

'She's also the most beautiful woman I've ever seen.'

'I know,' said Harriet.

'Do you think the children look like her?'

'No,' lied Harriet. 'Much more like you.'

'Today's our wedding anniversary,' said Cory.

'Oh God,' said Harriet, stricken. 'How awful for you. I am sorry.'

'You really are, aren't you?' said Cory. 'All that messing around with three rings on the telephone was her trying to get through. It was our secret code.'

'You'll find someone else soon,' said Harriet unconvincingly.

'Easy lays aren't the problem,' he said. 'It's like pigs in clover working in the movie business; always plenty of pretty girls hanging about. Then you wake up in the morning, and it's the wrong head on the pillow beside you, and you can't get them out quick enough.'

He put his head in his hands, feeling gingerly at the bump on his forehead.

'I could have Noel back tomorrow if I wanted, but it's like being an alcoholic, one drink and I'd be lost.'

'It's that bit about shunning "the heaven that leads men to this hell",' said Harriet. She felt she was having a very adult conversation.

'That's right,' said Cory. 'If she came back she'd be all over me the first week or two. Then she'd get bored and start looking for distractions. I couldn't even work properly when she was around. If she was at home she wanted constant attention. If she was out, I couldn't concentrate for worrying where she was. Show business's happiest couple indeed!'

He laughed, but the laugh had a break in it. She could see the chasm of his despair.

'Today's our tenth wedding anniversary,' he went on, his voice slurring. 'The bloody bitch was the beat of my heart for ten years. Being married to her meant drifting along from day to day on the edge of despair. Do you know what I did this afternoon? I went out and sent her six dozen roses. Imagine the smirk on her face when she gets them. My lost love is so utterly, utterly lost, but just the same I did it. All tough guys are hopeless sentimentalists. Jesus I'm wallowing in self-pity. I'm sorry.'

He was shivering now. I must get him into bed, thought Harriet.

He shot her a sideways glance. 'I'm keeping you up,' he said.

'No, no,' she said, gritting her teeth to hide a yawn.

She heard a faint wail from upstairs. 'I'll just go and see who that is.'

'Sometimes they go to bed with no supper,' muttered Cory.

Upstairs Chattie was lying out of bed, Ambrose curled up in her arms, her long white legs sticking out. Harriet tucked her up and replaced her blankets. William was sleeping peacefully too, and when she got downstairs she found Cory asleep as well, his elegant narrow-hipped length sprawled across the sofa, his half-smoked cigarette in his hand. She put it out, loosened his tie and took his shoes off, then got the duvet and a blanket from his bedroom and covered him up.

'It's you and me babe,' she said to Tadpole, and suddenly felt very responsible and grown up, as she looked down at Cory's face. In sleep it had lost all its anguish.

Chapter Thirteen

The next day was catastrophic. After two hours sleep, Harriet was walking round like a zombie. Matters grew worse as William regurgitated sieved carrot and cabbage over everything, the washing machine gave up the ghost, and in the usual rat race of rounding up homework books, pinnies and gymshoes, she realized there wasn't any dinner-money left for Chattie in the housekeeping. Mrs Bottomley was away for the night and therefore not available for a touch. After rifling every pocket in her wardrobe, the only solution was to wake Cory – who was not best pleased at being roused from a heavy slumber to one of the worst hangovers in recorded history. His temper was not improved by the embarrassment of finding himself still in evening clothes and lying on the sofa.

'Why the hell can't you organize the bloody house-keeping?' he howled.

It was hardly the moment, Harriet decided, to remind him that he had filched the last of it him-self.

When she got back from driving Chattie to school, he had changed into day clothes, was trying to keep down a glass of alkaseltzer, and in the sort of picky mood that soon reduced her to screaming hysteria.

How was he to find a pair of socks, he demanded, when the hot cupboard looked as though a bomb had hit it. Why didn't she ever put anything back where she'd found it? Was it really necessary to have toys lying all over the hall, nappies dripping over the kitchen?

'The washing machine's broken,' protested Harriet.

'Well, get it mended,' said Cory.

For something to do she busied herself opening a tin of dog food.

'There are already three tins, two of them with mould on, open in the fridge,' said Cory.

Chattie had demanded coca-cola for breakfast and Harriet had been too bombed to refuse her. Cory now picked up Chattie's half-full mug.

'Do you really want to ruin the children's teeth? Shouldn't they have milk occasionally?' he asked.

'They usually do,' said Harriet through gritted teeth.

Before he could think of a crushing reply, she turned on the waste disposal to remove the remains of Chattie's Weetabix.

'For God's sake turn that thing off,' yelled Cory, clutching his head.

'What?' said Harriet, pretending not to hear.

The next moment he stalked out of the room.

Pig, pig, pig, she said to herself, keeps me up till three o'clock in the morning, banging on about his bloody wife, and then expects peak efficiency. And

121

to relieve her feelings she went upstairs and cleaned the bath with his flannel.

By lunchtime she felt contrite. He really had looked very ill. He ought to eat something. She took great pains making a mushroom omelette, and taking it with a glass of freshly squeezed orange juice up to his study.

His hangover obviously hadn't improved.

'I didn't ask for anything to eat,' he said. 'I'm not hungry. Please take it away.'

'You ought to have something, just to blot up the alcohol,' she said brightly, putting the tray down amid a pile of papers.

Then she saw the expression on his face, and bolted out of the room before he could throw the tray at her. She and Tadpole shared the omelette.

'It would have been wasted on *him*,' she said to Tadpole who chewed it up with great, greedy, crocodile jaws. At least she, Chattie and William were going out to tea, so they'd be out of Cory's hair.

She was just getting ready when the telephone rang. Even running down the landing, clutching a protesting, half-dressed William, she couldn't reach it before Cory. He came out of his study, looking bootfaced.

'It's Elizabeth Pemberton's nanny,' he said. 'For you.'

Muttering apologies, Harriet fled downstairs to answer it.

'We've got problems,' said Sammy cheerfully. 'Elizabeth says she's got one of her ancient aunts whose just lost her husband coming over – at least that's *her* story. I've never known anyone change the sheets and have a bath in the middle of the day for an ancient aunt. Anyway she wants us all out of the way. She thinks it would inhibit poor "Aunt Barbara" to have all the kids hanging around. Can we come over to you instead?'

'Yes, of course,' said Harriet, wondering what the hell Cory would say.

Sammy arrived with Georgie, looking very done-up in a tight navy blue sweater, with *Come and Get Me* printed across her jacked-up bosom, drainpipe jeans, blue and yellow glove socks and impossibly high-heeled sandals.

'I do like your walking shoes,' said Harriet, giggling.

'Elizabeth hates them,' said Sammy. 'They make holes in the parquet.'

She reeked of cheap scent.

'It's called *Seduction*,' she said. 'Worn specially in Cory's honour. Is he here?' She looked round expectantly, patting her hair.

'He's working,' said Harriet, 'and not at his most sunny.'

'Hungover up to his teeth, I shouldn't wonder,' said Sammy. 'Elizabeth said he was as high as a kite when he arrived last night.'

Tadpole shambled in, wagging his tail, and promptly goosed Sammy.

'Good old Tadpole,' she said patting him. 'Never forgets a crutch.'

Chattie bore Georgie upstairs.

'There's a Shirley Temperature film on television,' she said.

'Well don't disturb Daddy, whatever you do,' said Harriet.

'Do you mind if I bath William?' said Harriet. 'I didn't get around to it earlier.'

'Do you mind if I borrow a razor and shave my legs?' said Sammy. 'I'm going out with a new guy tonight, and one should always be prepared.'

'This is a much nicer room than mine,' said Sammy, lounging on Harriet's yellow counterpane, painting her toe nails with Harriet's nail polish. 'Noel spent fortunes having it done up in the faint hope it might help her to keep a nanny longer than three weeks. Admittedly she threw all the pretty ones out because she was convinced they were after Cory.'

Her spikily mascara'd eyes softened as they lighted on William, splashing around in the water, chuckling with laughter, and waving his arms about.

'Don't you love him? Look at his lovely fat wrists,' she said. 'The folds always look as though they've got elastic bands on. I envy you really. I got knocked up last year, but it was too much hassle, so I got rid of it. You're very brave to keep him. I wouldn't have the courage.'

Harriet dripped water from a flannel onto William's round belly.

'The unmarried mothers' home wasn't much fun; all those films on VD and drugs, and having to sew for charity and go to church,' she said. 'And it was awful in hospital. All the fathers coming to see the mothers, holding their hands and admiring the babies. One girl had a lover and a husband rolling up at different times; both were convinced they were the father. No-one came to see me. But it was all worth it in the end.'

'What was the father like – no good?'

Harriet swallowed. 'That's him by the bed,' she said.

'Crikey,' said Sammy gaping at the photograph. 'Wouldn't kick *him* out of bed. Not surprised you fell for him.' She looked at Harriet with new respect. Obviously there was more behind that uptight, rather shy exterior than met the eye. 'Never mind, you've got Cory,' she said. 'I wouldn't mind sharing a house with him.'

'And Mrs Bottomley,' said Harriet.

Sammy grinned. 'Can't say I'd fancy a threesome with her.'

She started a second coat of polish.

'I must say it's nice being here again. I got quite friendly with their last but one nanny. She liked Cory but couldn't stand Noel. Noel treated her like dirt, always trying to get her to bring up breakfast in bed, and lay out her clothes, and comb out her wigs for her. Can you believe it, she needed a nanny more than the children did. She's a friend of Elizabeth's,' she went on, 'or rather they both pretend to be, lots of kissing and darlings when they meet, and bitchy as hell behind each other's backs. Elizabeth doesn't need a nanny either. She just wants one for status, and to take the children off her hands when she wants to see one of her boyfriends. Honestly she's had more pricks than a second-hand dart board.'

Harriet laughed, but felt the conversation was getting a bit indiscreet.

'Are you going out with anyone nice tonight?' she said.

'Smashing! He's a Finn. His firm have sent him over here to build a factory outside Leeds. He's got a lovely accent and an island all of his own. I said I thought all Finns were very drunken and uncouth. He said Finns ain't what they used to be. I thought that was quite witty.'

Harriet sprinkled William with talcum powder, trying not to feel envious. It was such a long time since she'd had a date. In the same magazine that she had read about sieving carrots and cabbage had been a piece on bringing up children. 'All babies need the love of a father and a mother,' it had said, 'a background of security and a happy home.'

Oh dear, perhaps she ought to start looking for a father for William.

'Where does one meet people round here?' she said.

'Darling,' said Sammy. 'On the other side of the valley is Wakeley, with discos and bright lights and rich industrialists with loads of bread just waiting to spend it on you and me. There's even a singles bar just opened called the Loose Box. It's always packed with the most dishy single guys, people who've come up North on conferences and who've got nothing to do in the evenings. I picked up my Finn there. I'll take you there one evening next week.'

Harriet cuddled William, feeling his small solid weight against her left shoulder, his fat hands clutching her hair, thinking how gorgeous he smelt. The Loose Box sounded rather too advanced for her.

The telephone went.

'I'll take him,' said Sammy, holding her arms out to William.

It was a Senora di Cuizano ringing from Rome. It was imperative to talk to Cory, she said. Harriet wasn't risking it.

'I'm afraid he's awfully busy at the moment. Can he ring you back?'

The Senora sounded extremely put out. Perhaps she ought to tell Cory? Then she heard the front door bang. He'd probably gone out to get some cigarettes. She went into the kitchen to get tea. Sammy came down and sat in the rocking chair, hiding behind her hair, then peeping out making William crow with laughter.

Ten minutes later she heard the front door open; he must have just gone down to the stables.

'I wonder what Chattie and Georgie are up to,' said Sammy, making no attempt to move.

'I'll just make the tea,' said Harriet, 'and I'll go up and see.'

'Oh look – walnut cake,' said Sammy, 'how lovely. Elizabeth's so mean we're never allowed anything like that for tea and when you consider the amount they spend on drink, and pouring oats down their horses. It must be quite a nice life being Elizabeth's horse.'

'Cory's nice that way,' said Harriet. 'He's not

interested in how much money I spend. He's nice anyway,' she said, 'when he's not being nasty.'

She had spoken too soon. At that moment Cory threw open the door.

'Harriet,' he roared, 'will you get those bloody children out of my hair. Can't you manage to control them for five minutes. That infernal Georgie's been smoking my cigars, and sprayed water all over my script, and Chattie's scribbled over the walls.'

Sammy giggled.

'Oh God,' stammered Harriet. 'I'm sorry. I'll remove them at once. I thought they were watching television.'

'Who was that on the telephone?' said Cory.

'A Senora di Cuizano rang from Rome.'

'And what did you say to her?' said Cory, his voice suddenly dangerously quiet.

'I – er – said you were busy.'

'Jesus Christ,' said Cory. 'Don't you realize that was Zefferelli's PA? I've been trying to get hold of her all day. You've probably just lost me half a million bucks.'

Harriet fled upstairs and met Chattie and Georgie coming down.

'I don't like Daddy,' said Chattie, sniffing.

'Makes two of us,' muttered Harriet.

Georgie was looking very green.

'Where does Dracula stay in New York?' he said.

'I don't know,' snapped Harriet.

'The Vampire State Building,' said Georgie, and was violently sick all the way down the stairs.

*   *   *

Later she was telling Chattie a bedtime story.

'Who's been sleeping in *my* bed?' she said in mother bear's medium sized voice.

'Why don't Mummy and Daddy bear say, "Who's been sleeping in *our* bed",' said Chattie. 'Mummy and Daddy used to sleep in the same bed, although they don't now. They might again one day, I suppose.'

'And little baby bear said, "Who's been sleeping in my bed",' said Harriet, in a high voice.

'My mother's very famous,' said Chattie. 'She looks like a princess all the time. Georgie says his mother doesn't look like a princess first thing in the morning, only when she goes out. People are always asking for my mother's naughty-graph.'

Harriet decided she'd heard quite enough about Noel Balfour in the last twenty-four hours.

'And Goldilocks looked up and saw the little baby bear, and screamed and screamed.'

'Is Drackela in real life?' said Chattie.

'Oh Chattie,' wailed Harriet, 'can't you concentrate for one minute?'

Cory appeared in the doorway.

'Hullo, Daddy,' said Chattie.

Harriet refused to look up; her lips tightened; she was fed up with Cory.

'That's enough stories for one night,' said Cory.

Harriet got up, and walked straight past him.

She heard Chattie shrieking with giggles as he kissed her good night.

Downstairs, the tea things were still waiting to be cleared away. Harriet groaned. She felt absolutely knackered. Dispiritedly she started loading the washing-up machine.

Cory walked in and opened the fridge.

'I'm starving,' he said.

Serve you right, thought Harriet, you should have eaten that omelette.

He opened his mouth to speak, once again she turned on the waste disposal. For a minute they glared at each other, then he laughed.

'Turn that bloody thing off. I'm going out to get some curry.'

Harriet's mouth watered.

'There's a movie I want to watch later,' said Cory.

'Really,' said Harriet, crashing pans.

'Will you *please* stop sulking,' said Cory. 'I'm sorry I kept you up half the night. I don't remember what I said, but I must have bored the pants off you.'

Didn't have any on, anyway, thought Harriet.

'I'm sorry I've shouted at you and bullied you all day,' he went on. 'It was entirely my fault. I was feeling guilty about wasting a whole work day yesterday, and then being in no condition to do any work today. You're a good girl. I've put on a bath for you, so go and have a long soak – by which time I'll be back with the curry.'

Totally disarmed, Harriet gave a grudging smile. One had to admit that Cory had his moments.

She was just getting into her bath when she heard crying. It was William. She'd only just put him to bed. She wrapped a towel round her and went into his room. Immediately, he stopped crying and cooed and gurgled at her. His nappy was quite dry, but as soon as she'd tucked him up, and turned off the light he started yelling again.

She was just about to go back into the room when Cory came down the passage with his car keys.

'Leave this to me,' he said. In amazement Harriet watched him go over to William's carry cot, wrap his arms into his shawl, winding it up tightly like an Indian papoose.

'They like to feel secure,' he said to Harriet.

William opened his mouth to bellow indignantly.

'And you can shut up,' said Cory sharply. 'Give your poor mother a bit of peace.'

William was so surprised he shut his mouth and didn't make another sound.

Out on the landing, Harriet blinked at him.

'You're absolutely brilliant with babies,' she said.

'Noel was never the maternal type,' said Cory. 'So I've had plenty of practice.'

They had a nice, relaxed evening, drinking red wine, sluttishly eating curry off their knees in the drawing room, and throwing the bones into the fire. Harriet enjoyed the film, but, as Cory was an expert on movies, was determined not to appear too enthusiastic.

'It's quite good,' she said. 'Although some of the dialogue's a bit dated. Who wrote it?'

'I did,' said Cory.

Harriet was so glad the room was lit by the fire and Cory couldn't see how much she was blushing.

'Have some meat and mushroom, it's quite good too. I wrote it,' he went on, 'with a Hollywood Pro called Billy Blake. It's the last time I'll ever collaborate with anyone. It shortened my life, but I learnt a lot.'

'What was she like?' said Harriet, as the heroine took off her dress.

'Thick,' said Cory.

'And him,' said Harriet, as the hero hurled her on to the bed.

'Nice fag – lives with a hairdresser.'

'Golly,' said Harriet, 'I never knew that. If you know all these people, why don't you ever ask them up here?'

'Film people are all right to work with,' said Cory. 'But I don't want to go into their houses, and I don't want them here, talking the same old shop, movies, movies, movies. And I don't like the way they live, eating out every night in order to be seen. If you hang around with them you start believing you're a star, everyone treats you like a star, and doesn't act normally towards you, and you start thinking that's the way people really behave, and you lose touch with reality – which is lethal for writers.'

He threw a chicken bone at the fire, it missed, and Tadpole pounced on it.

'No, darling,' said Harriet, retrieving it from him, 'It'll splinter in your throat.'

Cory emptied the bottle between their two glasses.

'The script I'm doing now's a bastard,' he said. 'It's about the French Civil War in the seventeenth century.'

'The *Fronde*,' said Harriet.

'That's right. It needs so much research.'

He picked up two biographies of French seventeenth-century aristocrats, which were lying on the table.

'Instead of stuffing your head with novels, you could flip through these and see if you could find anything filmable.'

Harriet wiped her chicken-greasy fingers on Tadpole's coat and took the books. 'I could certainly try,' she said.

Cory's glass was empty. 'Shall I get another bottle?' she said.

'Nope,' said Cory. 'That's my lot for tonight. I'm not risking hangovers like yesterday any more. I'm turning over a new leaf. Bed by midnight, no booze before seven o'clock in the evening, riding before breakfast. Don't want to die young, I've decided.'

'I'll cook you breakfast,' said Harriet.

'That's going too far,' said Cory nervously. 'How did you get on with Sammy?'

Harriet giggled. 'She's staggeringly indiscreet.'

'I hope you never discuss me the same way,' said Cory.

'I s-said you were absolutely marvellous,' said Harriet, her words coming out in a rush. 'Then you spoilt it by coming in and shouting about that telephone call from Italy. She's going to take me to the Loose Box one evening to pick up rich Finns.'

'Not sure that's a very good idea. From all I've heard about that dive, "Loose" is the operative word.'

He picked up a handout from Jonah's school that

had been lying under the big biographies. 'What's all this?'

'The Parents' Association on the warpath again,' said Harriet. 'They want money for the new building, so they're holding a Parents' dance. Tickets are £3.50 and for that you get dinner, and a glass of wine. You should go. You might meet Mrs Right.'

'Not if I'm going on the wagon,' said Cory. 'I can't allow myself lapses like that.'

Chapter Fourteen

Cory kept his word. He cut down smoking and drinking to a minimum and although occasionally she heard the gramophone playing long into the night, he was usually in bed by midnight.

Most evenings he would come downstairs and talk to her while she was giving William his last feed. They spent a lot of time together, gossiping, reading, playing records, and talking about Cory's script. Harriet was enjoying the research she was doing for him; it was the first time she'd used her brain since Oxford. She also found she was taking more trouble with her appearance. She was tired of saving up money for her and William's future. She wanted to buy some new clothes.

There were also two new additions to the household: Python, a little black mare who arrived from Ireland – Cory was delighted with her and immediately began getting her fit for the point-to-point – and Tarbaby, a lamb with a sooty face, whose mother had died on the moors, and who Harriet was trying to bring up with a bottle.

'Just like having twins in the house,' said Cory, as

he watched her make up bottles for the lamb and William.

One Monday towards the end of March she was cooking breakfast and getting Jonah and Chattie off to school when Cory walked in. She still couldn't get used to seeing him up so early.

He threw a pair of underpants down on the kitchen table.

'I know you think I'm too thin, but this is ridiculous. These pants belong to Jonah.'

Harriet went pink. 'I'm sorry, I get muddled. I'm just putting eggs on for Chattie and Jonah. Do you want one?'

Cory grimaced.

'It'd be so good for you,' she said.

'All right. I suppose so.'

He sat down and picked up the paper.

'I haven't finished my general knowledge homework,' said Jonah, rushing in, one sock up and one sock down, hair unbrushed, waving an exercise book.

'Who was Florence Nightingale?' he said.

'She was a lesbian,' said Cory, not looking up.

'How do you spell that?' said Jonah.

'You can't put that,' said Harriet. 'Just say she was a very famous nurse, who looked after wounded soldiers in the Crimea.'

'She was a lesbian,' said Cory.

'Can I have sandwiches today?' said Chattie. 'We always have mince and nude-les on Monday, it's disgusting.'

'You'll eat what you're given,' said Cory.

'What has a bottom at the top?' said Chattie.

136

'I really don't know,' said Harriet.

'Legs,' said Chattie, flicking up her skirt, showing her bottom in scarlet pants and going off into fits of laughter.

'Oh shut up, Chattie,' said Jonah. 'I'm trying to concentrate. Why is a Black Maria called a Black Maria?'

'She was a large black lady who lived in Boston,' said Cory, 'who helped the police arrest drunken sailors. She kept a brothel.'

'What's that?' said Jonah.

'Better call it a house of ill-fame,' said Harriet. 'Oh God, the toast's burning.'

She rescued it from the grill, and cut three pieces into strips, then unthinkingly cut the tops off three eggs, and handed them out to Cory, Jonah and Chattie.

'Toast soldiers,' said Cory, 'and no-one's taken the top off my egg for years either.'

Harriet blushed: 'Sheer habit,' she said.

'What's a house of ill-fame?' said Chattie.

Harriet dropped off Jonah and then Chattie.

'Don't forget to feed Tarbaby,' shouted Chattie, disappearing into a chattering sea of little girls.

As Harriet walked out of the playground, she met a distraught-looking woman trying to manage three rather scruffy children, and a large grey and black speckled dog, who was tugging on a piece of string. Harriet made clicking noises of approval. The dog bounded towards her pulling its owner with it.

'What a darling dog,' said Harriet, as the dog put

his paws on her shoulders and started to lick her face. 'Oh isn't he lovely?'

'We can't bear to look at him,' said his owner. 'Come on Spotty.' She half-heartedly tried to pull the dog away.

'Why ever not?' said Harriet.

'I've got to take him to the dogs' home, after I've dropped this lot.'

The children started to cry. 'I can't afford to keep him,' went on the mother. 'I've got a job, and he howls something terrible when I go out, so the landlady says he's got to go. They'll find a home for him.'

'But they may not,' said Harriet. 'They put them down after seven days, if they can't. Oh dear, I wish we could have him.'

Spotty lay his cheek against hers and thumped his plumed tail.

'What kind is he?' she said.

'A setter, I think,' said the owner, sensing weakness. 'He's only a puppy.'

Harriet melted. 'Hang on,' she said, 'I'll go and ring my boss.'

Cory had started work and was not in the mood for interruptions.

'Er-Mr Erskine, I mean Cory, there's this absolutely sweet puppy here.'

'Well,' said Cory unhelpfully.

'He's got to be put down unless they can find a home for him. He's so sweet.'

'Harriet,' said Cory wearily, 'you have enough trouble coping with William, Chattie, Jonah and me, not to mention Tadpole and Tarbaby. We haven't got rid of any of Ambrose's kittens yet and now you want to introduce a puppy. Why don't you ring up the zoo and ask them to send all the animals up here for a holiday? Telephone Battersea Dogs' Home, and tell them we keep open house.'

'I'm sorry,' said Harriet, chastened.

'What's his name?' said Cory.

'Spotty,' said Harriet, 'and he's a setter.'

There was a long pause.

'Well, you'd better think up a new name before you get him home,' said Cory and rang off.

Harriet couldn't believe her ears.

'We *will* look after him,' she said to the woman, 'and he'll have another dog to play with.'

She was worried Spotty's owner might burst into tears, but she seemed absolutely delighted, and later, as Harriet drove off with the dog, she saw her chattering very animatedly to a couple of friends. Not so Spotty, who howled lustily for his mistress for a couple of miles then got into the front seat beside Harriet, and finally collapsed moaning piteously all over the gear lever, his head on her lap.

'I must think of a name for you,' she said, as they got home. She opened the AA book and plonked her finger down blindly. It landed on Sevenoaks.

'Hullo, Sevenoaks,' said Harriet. 'You've got a cattle market on Monday, two three star hotels and you're twenty-five miles from London.'

'Harriet,' said Cory, as Sevenoaks charged round the drawing room, trailing standard lamp wires like goose grass, 'That is not a puppy – nor is it a setter.'

'Come here,' said Harriet, trying to catch him as he whisked past.

'He's fully grown,' said Cory. 'At least two and virtually untrainable.'

Sevenoaks rolled his eyes, charged past Cory, and shot upstairs, followed by Tadpole, who was thoroughly overexcited. Sevenoaks had already received a bloody nose from Ambrose, a very frosty response from Mrs Bottomley, and tried to eat one of Cory's riding boots. Now he could be heard drinking out of the lavatory. Next he came crashing downstairs, followed once more by Tadpole, and collapsed panting frenziedly at Harriet's feet. She looked up at Cory with starry eyes.

'Look how he's settled down,' she said. 'He knows he's going to be really happy here.'

All in all, however, Sevenoaks couldn't be described as one hundred per cent a success. Whenever he wasn't trying to escape to the bitches in the village, he was fornicating with Tadpole in the front garden, digging holes in the lawn, chewing everything in sight, or stretching out on sofas and beds with huge muddy paws.

The great love of his life, however, was Harriet. He seemed to realize that she had rescued him from death's door. He welcomed her noisily whenever she returned, howled the house down if she went out and had a growling match with Cory every night because Cory refused to let him sleep on Harriet's bed.

The following Wednesday was another day of

disasters. Cory was having trouble with his script and was not in the best temper anyway, particularly as William was teething and spent the day screaming his head off, and Sevenoaks had chewed up Cory's only French dictionary. Harriet botched up Chattie's lamb chops by burning them under the grill while she was filling in a How Seductive Are You quiz in a women's magazine, and she'd just finished pouring milk into William and Tarbaby's bottles when Ambrose came weaving along and knocked the whole lot onto the floor. She was also in a highly nervous state, having at last promised Sammy she would accompany her to the Loose Box that evening.

It was half past seven by the time she'd cleared up and got everyone to bed. There was no time to have a bath; she only managed to scrape a flannel over her face and under her armpits, pour on a great deal of scent and rub in cologne in an attempt to resuscitate her dirty hair.

At five minutes to eight the doorbell went. Sammy was early. Harriet rushed downstairs with only one eye made up, aware that she looked terrible. Cory met her on the landing.

'Going out?' he said.

'Yes,' she said defensively. 'It's my night off.'

She opened the front door to two earnest-looking women with wind-swept grey hair. One was clutching a notebook, the other a rather ancient camera.

'I'm sorry we're late,' said the woman with a notebook. 'It's a very difficult place to find at night.'

141

Chattie wandered down the stairs in her night-gown. Visitors always meant a possibility of staying up late.

'And who are you, young lady?' said the woman with the camera.

'I'm Chattie. I had a pretty dress on today.'

'And I'm Carol Chamberlain,' said the woman with the notebook. 'We've come all the way from London to interview your Daddy.'

'Come into the drawing room and I'll get you a whisky and tonic,' said Chattie.

Harriet went green, fled upstairs and knocked on Cory's door.

He didn't answer. She knocked again.

'Yes,' he said, looking up, drumming his fingers with irritation.

'I don't know how to tell you this.'

'Oh God,' he said, with infinite weariness. 'What the hell have you done now? Have all Sevenoaks' relations arrived?'

Harriet turned pale.

'I-um-I'm afraid I forgot to put off *Woman's Monthly*. They've come all the way from London. They're waiting downstairs.'

'Was he absolutely insane with rage?' said Sammy, who always enjoyed stories of other people's disasters. It was a source of slight irritation to her that Harriet got on so well with Cory.

'Absolutely insane,' said Harriet miserably. 'I may well have joined the great unemployed by tomorrow.'

They were tarting up in the Ladies of the Loose Box. Crowds of girls around them were back-combing like maniacs. One girl was rouging her navel.

Harriet was fiddling with her sweater.

'Do you think it looks better outside my jeans?' she said to Sammy.

'No,' said Sammy. 'Doesn't give you any shape. Let's see what it looks like tucked in. No, that looks even worse. Leave it hanging out. You look absolutely fantastic,' she added with all the complacency of someone looking infinitely better.

She was poured into black velvet trousers and a low-cut black sweater, her splendid white bosom spilled over the top like an ice-cream over a cone. She was also wearing black polish on her toes and fingernails, and a black rose in her newly dyed mahogany curls.

No-one's going to want to talk to me, thought Harriet as they went into the arena. All around her people were circling and picking each other up. Some of the girls were ravishingly pretty. It could only have been a spirit of adventure, not a shortage of men, that led them to this place.

Sammy was already leering at a handsome blond German in a blue suit.

'I'd just love a sweet Cinzano,' she said fluttering long green eyelashes at him.

The German fought his way to the bar to get her one. The next moment a pallid youth had sidled up to her.

'I work in films,' he said, which he patently didn't.

143

'Really,' said Sammy. 'I'm a model actually.'

Harriet had completely forgotten the hassle of hunting for men. She kept trying to meet men's eyes, but hers kept slithering away. Don't leave me, she pleaded silently to Sammy. But Sammy was on the hunt like Sevenoaks after a bitch, and nothing could deter her from her quarry.

'It's always been my ambition to go to Bayreuth,' she was saying to the handsome German.

The worst part of the evening for Harriet was that she wasn't a free agent. She couldn't split because Sammy was driving and she hadn't brought enough money for a taxi.

Sammy having downed eight sweet Cinzanos was well away with the German, and seemed to be having an equally devastating effect on his friend, who had spectacles, a nudging grin and a pot belly.

'Come over here, Harriet,' said Sammy. 'You must meet Claus.'

She pushed the fat, nudging grinning German forward.

'Harriet's frightfully clever and amusing,' she added.

Harriet became completely paralysed and could think of nothing to say except that the weather had been very cold lately.

'Ah but the freezing North brings forth the most lovely ladies,' said the fat little German with heavy gallantry. He was in Yorkshire, he told Harriet, for a textile conference and had lost 10 kilos since Christmas. Harriet didn't know if that were good or bad.

'Isn't he a scream?' said Sammy.

She pulled Harriet aside.

'They want to take us to The Black Tulip,' she said. 'It's a fantastic place; you have dinner and dance, and there's a terrific group playing.'

'It's going to make us frightfully late, isn't it?' said Harriet dubiously.

'Oh come on,' said Sammy, drink beginning to make her punchy. 'No-one's ever taken me to a place like that before. It's the chance of a lifetime.'

Oh God, thought Harriet, I mustn't be a spoil-sport.

The Black Tulip was even worse than the Loose Box. Harriet found her smile getting stiffer and stiffer as she toyed with an avocado pear.

'First I cut out all carbohydrates,' said the little fat German.

Opposite them Sammy and the handsome German couldn't keep their hands off each other. They were both getting tighter and tighter. Harriet wondered who the hell was going to drive her home.

'Then I gave up bread and potatoes,' said the fat German.

He must have been huge before he lost all that weight, thought Harriet, as she rode round the dance floor on his stomach. She suddenly longed to be home with Cory and William and the children. What would happen if William woke up? Mrs Bottomley slept like the dead. Cory'd go spare if he had to get up and feed him. She wondered how long he'd taken to get rid of *Woman's Monthly*.

'A new penny for your thoughts, Samantha,' said the handsome German.

145

'They're worth a bloody sight more than that,' said Sammy.

They all laughed immoderately.

'I also cut out all puddings and cakes,' said the fat German.

'I get no kick from champagne,' sang the lead singer. 'Pure alcohol gives me no thrill at all.'

You can say that again, thought Harriet.

Sammy was leaning forward, the fat little German gazing hungrily at her bosom.

'Shall we go for a drive on the moor?' he said.

'No,' said Harriet, violently. 'You all can,' she added. 'But could you drop me off first?'

'We're all going back to Heinrich's hotel for a little drink,' said Sammy, getting rather unsteadily to her feet.

'I must get back in case William wakes,' said Harriet desperately.

After some argument, Sammy relented. 'We'll get you a cab,' she said. 'Claus can pay. The only one going at this hour is driven by the local under-taker.'

Harriet felt as cheerful as a corpse, as she bowled home under a starless sky. She couldn't stop crying; she had no sex appeal any more, the world was coming to an end, she'd never find a father for William.

As she put the key at the door, Sevenoaks, who usually slept through everything, let out a series of deep baritone barks, then, realizing it was her, started to sing with delight at the top of his voice, searching round for something to bring her.

'Oh please, Sevenoaks, lower your voice,' she pleaded.

But as she crept upstairs, Cory came out of the bathroom with a towel round his waist, his black hair wet from the bath, his skin still yellow-brown from last summer.

'Did *Woman's Monthly* stay for hours?' she said.

'Hours,' said Cory, 'I had to throw them out. It must have been pre-menstrual tension I was suffering from before they arrived.'

Harriet was feeling too depressed to even giggle.

'I'm terribly sorry,' she said.

Sevenoaks sauntered into Cory's room and heaved himself up onto Cory's bed.

'Get him off,' snapped Cory. 'That dog's got to go. He's been whining ever since you went out. Where have you been anyway?' he said in a gentler tone, noticing her red-rimmed eyes.

'To the Loose Box, with Sammy. We met some Germans, one was quite good-looking, the other one was awful. The good-looking one fancied Sammy, so did the awful one, but he had to put up with me. I tried to get out and find some people of my own age, but I don't think they liked me very much.' And with a sob she fled to her room.

When she turned down the counterpane and got into bed, she found her electric blanket switched on, and a note pinned to the pillow.

'Dear Harriet,' it said.

'Doesn't matter what *He* says, we think you're smashing, and so does he really, love from Tadpole, Ambrose (Miss) and Sevenoaks.'

Harriet gave a gurgle of laughter. Suddenly the whole evening didn't seem to matter very much any more. She lay in bed and thought about Cory. She felt like a child joining up numbers to discover what a picture was; she felt she hadn't managed to join up any of Cory's numbers at all.

Chapter Fifteen

Harriet was ironing in the kitchen when a car drew up.

'Come on, let's hide,' whispered Chattie. 'It's awful old Arabella. She only turns up when Daddy's at home.'

'We can't,' protested Harriet, watching a tall girl get out of the car. 'She's seen us.'

'Anyone at home?' came a debutante quack from the hall.

The girl who strode into the kitchen was in her late twenties, very handsome, high complexioned, athletically built, with flicked-up light brown hair drawn back from her forehead.

'Hullo, Chattie,' she said breezily. 'How are you?' But before Chattie could answer she turned to Harriet. 'And you must be the new nanny. I'm Arabella Ryder-Ross. Cory's spoken about me, I expect.' But before Harriet could answer the girl turned to William, who was aimlessly beating the side of his chair with a wooden spoon.

'What a darling baba. Not another of Noel's cast-offs?'

'No, he's mine,' said Harriet.

'Oh?' said Arabella. It was strange how someone could get four syllables out of that word.

'Doesn't your husband mind you taking a job?'

'I'm not married.'

'Oh, how amazingly brave of you.' Arabella paused and looked at William again. 'I must say Cory's a saint, the lame ducks he takes under his wing.'

'One, two, four, five. Bugger it. I've left out three,' said Chattie, who was counting Ambrose's kittens.

Harriet tried not to giggle. Arabella looked appalled.

'Chattie, don't use language like that. Run along and play. I want to talk to Nanny.'

'She's not called Nanny, she's Harriet, and I don't want to play, thank you,' said Chattie. Then a foxy expression came over the child's face. 'Would you like a sweetie, Arabella?'

'Aren't you going to offer Nanny one?'

'It's my last,' said Chattie. 'And I want you to have it.'

'That's very kind of you, Chattie,' said Arabella, popping the sweet into her mouth. 'I get on so well with children,' she added to Harriet. 'People are always saying I'd make a wonderful mother.'

At that moment Cory wandered in and Arabella flushed an unbecoming shade of puce.

'Hullo, Arabella,' he said. 'You look very brown.'

'It fades so quickly. You should have seen me last week. I've just got back from St Moritz, or I'd have been over before. We're having a little party next Friday.'

Cory frowned. 'I think something's happening.'

'Well, we'll have it on Saturday then.'

How could she be so unsubtle? thought Harriet.

'No, Friday's all right,' said Cory. 'I've just re-membered. It's Harriet's birthday. It'll do her good to meet some new people. Yes, we'd like to come.'

Harriet didn't dare look at Arabella's face.

'Did you like that sweet, Arabella?' said Chattie.

'Yes thank you, darling.'

Chattie gave a naughty giggle.

'Tadpole didn't. He spat it out three times.'

Harriet scolded Chattie when Arabella had gone, but the child shrugged her shoulders.

'I hate her, and Mummy says she's after Daddy. I hope she doesn't get him,' she added gloomily. 'She never gives us presents; she says we're spoilt.'

'She's got a point there,' said Harriet.

'She's just told Daddy he ought to give you the push, because we're so naughty,' said Chattie, picking up one of the kittens. 'But he told her to shut up, and we'd never been better looked after. Goodness, Harriet, you've gone all pink in the face.'

Trees rattled against her bedroom window. She looked at the yellow daffodils on the curtains round her bed and felt curiously happy. William was getting more gorgeous every day. She was getting fonder and fonder of Chattie and Jonah. Sevenoaks lay snoring across her feet. She felt her wounded heart gingerly; she was not yet deliriously happy but she was content.

'Happy Birthday to you,' sang a voice tunelessly,

'Happy Birthday, dear Harriet, Happy Birthday to you.'

And Chattie staggered in with a breakfast tray consisting of a bunch of wild daffodils, a brown boiled egg, toast and coffee.

'Oh how lovely!' said Harriet. 'Shall I take the coffee off?' She put it on the table beside her bed.

'Daddy's just finished feeding William,' said Chattie. 'And he's coming up with all your presents. Oh, why are you crying, Harriet?'

'Harriet's crying, Daddy,' she said to Cory, followed by Mrs Bottomley, as he came in and dumped William on the floor.

Cory saw Harriet's brimming eyes.

'She's entitled to do what she bloody well likes on her birthday,' he said. 'Get off the bed, Sevenoaks.'

'She'd better put on her dressing gown,' said Mrs Bottomley, looking at Harriet's see-through nightgown. 'Happy Birthday, love.'

Harriet couldn't believe her eyes when she opened her presents. Ambrose and Tadpole had given her a rust silk shirt. Sevenoaks was broke and had only given her a pencil sharpener. Chattie gave her a box of chocolates, several of which had already been eaten.

'I just had to test they were all right,' said Chattie.

There was also a maroon cineraria from Jonah, which he had chosen himself and bought with his own pocket money, and a vast cochineal pink mohair stole from Mrs Bottomley, which she'd knitted herself, because Harriet never wore enough clothes. Cory gave her a grey and black velvet blazer, and a pale grey angora dress.

'But they're beautiful,' she breathed. 'I've never seen anything so lovely.'

'Sick of seeing you in that old duffle coat,' said Cory.

'Daddy loves giving presents,' said Chattie, 'and he hasn't got Mummy to give them to any more.'

When she'd eaten her breakfast, she got up and went to look for Cory. She found him in his study flipping through the pages of the script he'd written yesterday.

Harriet cleared her throat.

'I just want to thank you for everything,' she said, blushing scarlet. 'For making me feel so happy here, and for all those heavenly presents. I really don't deserve either, what with Sevenoaks and all the messages I forget to pass on and all that.'

And, reaching up, she gave him a very quick kiss on the cheek and scuttled out of the room.

'Sexy,' said Chattie, from the passage.

As the hour for Arabella's party approached, Harriet grew more and more nervous. She'd been a disaster in the singles bar. What likelihood was there that she'd be any better with the hunting set? She must remember to say hounds instead of dogs.

She was sitting wrapped in a towel, putting her make-up on, when Chattie banged on her door.

'Come on. I want to show you something. Keep your eyes shut.'

'It can't be another present,' thought Harriet, feeling the thick carpet under her feet as Chattie led her towards the stairs, then turned sharp right into Jonah's bedroom. She shivered as a blast of icy air hit her.

'Don't look yet,' said Chattie pushing her forward, 'Now you can.'

Through the open window above the elm trees, at the bottom of the garden, Harriet could see a tiny cuticle of new silver moon.

'Now wish,' said Chattie. 'It doesn't work if you see it through glass. Wish for the thing you most want in your life. I've already wished for some bubble gum.'

Harriet, listening to the mournful cawing of the rooks, suddenly felt confused.

For the first time in months, she didn't automatically wish she could have Simon back. He was the fix, the first drink, that would trigger off the whole earth-shattering addiction all over again. She didn't want her life disrupted. Her thoughts flickered towards Cory for a second, then turned resolutely away. Please give William and me happiness and security whatever form it takes, she wished.

She turned round and found Cory standing in the doorway watching her. She couldn't read the expression on his face.

'I hope it's a sensible wish,' he said acidly. 'Like making your dear friend Sevenoaks less of a nuisance. He's just eaten the back off my only pair of dress shoes.'

He kicked Sevenoaks who slunk towards Harriet,

rolling his eyes and looking chastened at the front,
but waving his tail at the back.

Chattie flung her arms round him.

'He's so clever, Sevenoaks,' she said. 'He's eaten
your shoes because he doesn't want you to go out.'

'He's definitely an asset, Daddy,' said Jonah,
who'd just arrived for the weekend.

'He's a very silly asset,' said Cory.

'Ryder Cock Ross to Banbury Cross,' said Chattie.

The Ryder-Ross's house was large, Georgian and set
back from the road at the end of a long drive.

Women were clashing jaw bones, exchanging
scented kisses in the hall. One of them, in plunging
black and wearing so many diamonds she put the
chandeliers to shame, was Sammy's boss, Elizabeth.

When Harriet went upstairs to take off her coat,
the bed was smoothered in fur coats.

She was wearing the dress Cory had given her for
her birthday. She examined herself in Arabella's
long gilt mirror. It did suit her; it was demure, yet, in
the subtle way it hugged her figure, very seductive.
Oh please, she prayed as she went downstairs, make
someone talk to me, so I'm not a drag on Cory.

He was waiting for her in the hall – tall, thin,
remote, the pale, patrician face as expressionless as
marble.

As they entered the drawing room, everyone
turned and stared. A figure, squawking with delight,
came over to meet them. It was Arabella, wearing a
sort of horse blanket long skirt, a pink blouse, and
her hair drawn back from her forehead by a bow.

'Cory, darling, I thought you were never coming!'

She seized Harriet's arm in a vice-like grip. 'I'm going to introduce Nanny to some people her own age.'

Whisking Harriet into the next room, she took her over to meet a fat German girl, saying, 'Helga, this is Mr Erskine's nanny. Helga looks after my brother's children. I thought you might be able to compare notes.'

Harriet couldn't help giggling to herself. Nothing could have reduced her to servant status more quickly. It was not long, however, before two tall chinless wonders came over and started to tell her about the abortive hunting season they'd had.

Half-an-hour later they were still talking foxiana, and Harriet allowed her eyes to wander into the next room to where Cory was standing. Three women – the sort who should have been permanently eating wafer-thin mints on candlelit terraces – were vying for his attention.

He's an attractive man, thought Harriet, with a stab of jealousy. I wonder it never hit me before.

Suddenly he looked up, half smiled at her, and mouthed: 'All right?' She nodded, the tinge of jealousy gone.

'A brace of foxes were accounted for on Wednesday,' said the better-looking of the two chinless wonders. 'I say,' he said to Harriet, 'would you like to come and dance?'

He had long light brown hair, very blue eyes, and a pink and white complexion.

'Yes please,' said Harriet.

There was no-one else in the darkened room as they shambled round the floor to the Supremes, but he was much too straight to lunge at her during a first dance, thought Harriet with relief.

'We haven't really been introduced,' he said. 'My name's Billy Bentley. Haven't seen you before. You staying with Arabella?'

'I work for Cory Erskine,' said Harriet.

'That must be interesting,' he said. 'Frightfully clever bloke Cory, read so many books, very hard man to hounds too.'

He's certainly not very kind to Sevenoaks, thought Harriet.

'You ought to come out with us one day,' said Billy Bentley.

They shambled a few more times round the floor.

'Suppose I ought to get you a drink,' he said. 'But honestly you're so jolly pretty, I could go on dancing with you all night.'

Harriet felt quite light-headed with pleasure, but, as they came out of the room, Arabella drew her aside.

'Nanny,' she said, as Harriet crossed the room, 'could you give them a hand in the kitchen? They're a bit short-staffed.'

Cory was out of earshot so Harriet could do nothing but comply. As she came out of the kitchen, half an hour later, she heard a slightly blurred man's voice say, 'I see old Cory's surfaced at last. Looks better, doesn't he?'

'So he should, my dear.' A woman's voice, catty, amused, 'Pretty cool, I call it, bringing your mistress and passing her off as a nanny. Arabella says she's got a baby. I wonder if it's Cory's.'

Scarlet in the face, trembling with humiliation, Harriet carried the glasses into the dining room, straight into Cory.

'What the hell are you doing?'

She lowered her eyes in confusion. 'Arabella said they needed help in the kitchen.'

'Like hell they do. Put those glasses down at once. You're shaking. What's the matter?'

'Nothing, it's nothing,' snapped Harriet, her voice rising. 'I was just upset at being treated as a servant.' She fled upstairs on the pretext of doing her face.

Returning to the drawing room, still shaking, she was button-holed by a very good-looking man with greying blond hair and a dissipated face.

'Lolita! At last!' Harriet drew back. 'My name's Charles Mander,' he went on. 'You're not local are you?'

'Yes,' said Harriet, defiantly. 'I look after Cory Erskine's children.'

'How electrifying! Lucky Cory.' His eyes, alert with sudden interest, travelled slowly over her body, stripping off every inch of clothing.

'And have you met Noel yet?' Then he began to laugh. 'No, of course you haven't. She's not silly enough to let a pretty girl like you under her roof.'

'What do you mean?' said Harriet angrily.

Then Cory was by her side.

'Hullo, Charles.'

'Hullo, Cory, old boy. Long time no see.'

The greeting was amicable enough, but Harriet could tell that the two men hated each other.

'I've just met your charming little – er – friend. I congratulate you, Cory. Such a comfort on these long winter nights.'

Cory gave a cigarette to Harriet, selected one himself and lit them both before he replied, 'You always did have your mind below your navel, Charles.'

Charles Mander started to laugh again. 'It reminds me of that song we used to sing in the nursery. How does it go? Something about "God bless Nanny, and make her good". I must say, I wouldn't mind making Nanny myself.'

There was a frozen pause.

'If I were a gentleman, Charles,' said Cory, in a voice that sent shivers down Harriet's spine, 'I'd knock you down. But it would only give you the satisfaction of being a public martyr.'

He turned, deliberately looking at a fat blonde woman lurching towards them.

'Your wife's drunk again,' he added quietly.

Cory and Harriet didn't speak until they were nearly home. Gone was the easy cameraderie of the past few weeks.

Then Cory said, 'I'm sorry about Charles Mander. There's no point in beating about the bush. He used to be a lover of Noel's, probably still is, so he can never resist bitching me up. I imagine you heard the same sort of remark as you came out of the kitchen.'

Harriet nodded.

'What did they say?'

Harriet's tongue seemed to be tied in knots. 'They said William was your child.'

'Charming,' said Cory. 'The hunting season's been so frightful they're very short on gossip. Doesn't bother me. But I should never have exposed you to that snake pit. I should have realized how vulnerable you are.'

'It was so lovely,' she muttered. 'Everything's spoilt now.'

'It needn't be,' he said as he turned the car into the drive.

Once inside, he followed her up to her room. Outside the door, she paused and stammered out her thanks for taking her to the party.

'I enjoyed taking you,' he said and, putting out a hand, smoothed back a loose strand of hair that had fallen over her eyes. 'I was watching you this evening. You had that lost wistful look of the moon when it suddenly appears during the day. I must say I've been wondering about you myself lately.'

Harriet looked up, startled. Cory's face was in shadow. Then suddenly they both jumped, as unmistakably down the passage came the sound of Sevenoaks drinking noisily out of the lavatory. The tension was broken. Harriet went off into peels of laughter.

'The enemy of promise,' said Cory. 'Go to bed little one, and don't worry.'

Harriet went to bed, but couldn't sleep. What had

Cory meant that he'd been wondering about her lately? It seemed her relationship with him was something so fragile, a candle that she had to protect with both hands because everyone was trying to blow it out.

Chapter Sixteen

She felt staggeringly untogether in the morning. She had a blinding headache. It was as much as she could do to feed William. Chattie, recognizing weakness, started playing up.

'We're going to the meet with Daddy,' she said. 'Can I wear my party dress?'

'No, you can't,' said Harriet.

'Well my red velvet dress then?'

'Trousers are much warmer.'

'I don't want to wear trousers. I'm not a boy.'

'Oh Chattie, please,' she said in despair.

'You'll wear them and bloody well like it,' said Cory, coming in tying a stock, his long legs encased in boots and tight white breeches.

Chattie tried a different approach.

'Can I have a two-wheeler with stabilizers?' she said.

'Only if you do what Harriet tells you. How do you feel?' he said to her.

'Frightful.'

'So do I,' said Cory. 'God knows what Arabella gave us to drink. Some fruity little paint stripper, I should imagine. One could almost hear the enamel dropping off one's teeth.'

'Why do you go on wearing a dinner jacket, Daddy,' said Chattie, 'if it always makes you feel sick in the morning?'

Harriet suspected he'd gone on drinking long after she'd gone to bed.

'Can Harriet come to the meet with us?' said Jonah.

'Oh please yes,' said Chattie.

'It's too much of a hassle with William and things,' said Harriet.

Cory, a cigarette hanging out of the corner of his mouth, was filling up a hip-flask with brandy.

'You can leave William with Mrs Bottomley,' he said. 'Do you good to get some fresh air. There's a button missing from my coat. Can you sew it on?'

'Are you taking Python?' said Harriet.

'Yes,' said Cory. 'As a second horse. I'd like to see how she makes out.'

The horses went to the meet by box. Cory drove Harriet, Jonah, Chattie and the dogs by car.

The mist had rolled back from the hills to reveal a beautiful mild day. The ivy was putting out shining pale leaves; young nettles were thrusting through the green spring grass. Catkins shook in the breeze, the bracken burned the same rusty red as the curling leaves that still clung to the oak trees. The wet roads glittered and the stone walls gave off an almost incandescent whiteness in the sunlight.

'I'm hot,' said Chattie. 'I could have worn my party dress.'

'Chattie I've told you a hundred times,' said Harriet.

'No you didn't, you only told me twice.'

'Don't be rude,' said Cory.

There was a pause.

'It's raining, it's pouring,' sang Chattie. 'The old man's snoring. He went to bed and bumped his head, and couldn't get up in the morning. The doctor came and flushed the chain and out flew an aeroplane.'

Both children collapsed in giggles.

'The doctor came and flushed,' sang Chattie.

'Shut up,' said Cory.

'Ouch. Sevenoaks is treading on me.'

'Can we stop for some sweets? There's an absolutely brilliant sweet shop in Gargrave,' said Jonah.

Gradually they caught up with riders hacking to the meet. Soon there was a steady stream of cars and horse boxes.

Cory parked on the side of the road.

'You can bring Tadpole,' he said, locking Sevenoaks in the car. 'I'm not risking that delinquent getting loose.'

'We must give him a bit of window,' said Harriet, winding it down.

Cory went off to find his horse box. Harriet took Chattie and Jonah and walked along to the village where the meet was being held. Little grey cottages lined a triangular village green. A stream choked its way through pussy willows and hazel trees. The churchyard was full of daffodils in bud.

Riders everywhere were gossiping and saddling

up. There was a marvellous smell of trodden grass and hot, sweating horses. Anxious whinnyings came from the horse boxes. Hunt terriers yapped from the backs of cars.

There was Arabella looking considerably the worse for wear, Harriet was glad to notice, impatiently slapping her boots with her whip and looking round for her horse. And there was Billy Bentley, looking far more glamorous than he had last night, in a red coat, his long mousy hair curling under his black velvet cap, sitting on a huge dapple grey which was already leaping about as though the ground was red hot under its feet. Next to him, taking a swig out of his hip-flask, eyeing the girls, supervising the unboxing of a magnificent chestnut in a dark green rug, was Charles Mander.

Harriet tried to slide past them, but she had not counted on Chattie, who rushed up and said, 'Hullo, Charles.'

He turned. 'Hullo Chattie,' he said. 'How are you?'

'Fine,' said Chattie. 'Why don't you come and see us any more? He always used to come and bring us presents when Mummy lived with us,' she added to Harriet.

'Hullo, pretty Nanny,' said Charles.

Harriet tried to look straight through him, but only managed to look sulky.

'I'm five now,' said Chattie. 'I used to be four.'

'I used to be four too,' said Charles.

'My daddy's twenty-one,' said Chattie.

'I wish my children put out propaganda like that,' said Charles, laughing.

'I'm getting a two-wheeler soon with stabilizers,' said Chattie.

'I could do with some stabilizers myself,' said Charles.

He walked over to Harriet, the dissipated gin-soaked blue eyes looking almost gentle.

'Look, I've got rather a hazy recollection of what happened last night, but I've a feeling I bitched you up. I'm sorry. I can never resist taking the mickey out of Cory. He's so damn supercilious.'

'He *is* my boss,' said Harriet.

'Thank Christ he's not mine, but I didn't mean to take it out on you.'

Harriet stared at him, not knowing what to say.

She was rescued by a voice behind her saying, 'Hullo Harriet.' It was the haw haw tones of Billy Bentley. She was flattered he remembered her. 'You disappeared very fast last night,' he said. 'Saw Charles chatting you up and then you bolted. Can't say I blame you. Enough to put anyone orf.'

He brayed with laughter. He should just sit on his horse and look glamorous, thought Harriet.

'I suppose I better get mounted,' said Charles. 'We're friends now, are we?' he added to Harriet.

'Yes, as long as you're not foul to Mr Erskine,' she said.

He shrugged his shoulders. 'That's old history. Perhaps you'd have dinner with me one evening, and I'll tell you all about it.'

'I say, hands orf, Charles,' said Billy Bentley. 'You're married. Leave the field free for us single blokes.'

His horse suddenly bucked and lashed out warningly at a nearby chestnut.

'This bugger's had too much corn,' he said. 'I wish we could get going.'

Charles Mander settled himself onto his horse. An earnest-looking grey-haired woman sidled up to him and pressed an anti-fox-hunting pamphlet into his hand.

'Thank you so much,' he said to her politely and, getting out his lighter, set fire to it and dropped it flaming at her feet. She jumped away and disappeared, shaking her fist, into the crowd.

'Bloody hunt saboteurs,' he said, riding off towards the pub. 'I'm going to get my flask topped up.'

Billy Bentley hung about, looking down at Harriet, trying to control his restless horse.

'Going to the hunt ball?' he asked.

'No, I'm not.'

'Going away?'

'No, I'm just not going.'

'What a shame,' said Billy, suddenly turning pink. 'I say, I liked talking to you last night. Wonder if you'd come out one evening?'

'I'd love to, but it's a bit difficult,' said Harriet, turning pink too. 'I've got this baby, my own I mean, not Jonah or Chattie.'

'Doesn't matter a scrap,' said Billy. 'Bring the little chap with you if you like. Still got our old nanny at home; got nothing to do; love to look after him.'

Harriet was touched and wanted to tell him so,

but next moment the whipper-in arrived with the hounds, who looked curiously naked without collars, tails waving frantically.

'They haven't been fed for two days,' said an anti-fox-hunting youth who was waving a poster saying, 'Hounds off our wild life'.

Grooms were sweeping rugs off sweating, shuddering horses; riders were mounting and jogging off in a noisy glittering cavalcade, with a yelp of voices and a jingle of bits.

Cory rode up on Python, black coat gleaming, eyes popping, letting out snorts of hysterical excitement at all the activity around her.

'I'll ring you this evening,' said Billy. 'Morning, Cory. That's new, very nice too.'

'Kit found her in Ireland,' said Cory. 'Had a couple of days on her with the Kildare.'

'Up to his weight, was she?' said Billy. 'Bloody good. Put her in for the point-to-point, will you?'

'I thought I might.'

'Cory darling!' It was Elizabeth Pemberton, wearing rather too much make-up, but looking stunning in a black coat, and the tightest white breeches. She caught sight of Harriet and nodded to her dismissively.

'You are coming with us on Friday, aren't you?' she said to Cory.

There was a pause, his eyes flickered towards Harriet, then away.

'Yes I'd like to,' he said.

'I think we'll be about twenty-four for dinner,' she said.

Big bloody deal, thought Harriet.

The Master was blowing his horn up the road. Next moment Arabella rolled up on a thoroughly over-excited bay, which barged round, nearly sending Harriet and the children for six.

As the hunt rode down into the valley, the pigeons rose like smoke from the newly ploughed fields.

'Let's follow them,' said Harriet.

But when they got back to the car, she gave a gasp of horror. The back seat was empty; Sevenoaks had gone; he must have wriggled out of the window. She had terrifying visions of him chasing sheep, running under the horses' feet, or getting onto the motorway.

'We must look for him,' she said, getting into the car and driving off in the direction of the hunt, which had disappeared into the wood. Then followed a desperately frustrating half-hour bucketing along the narrow country lanes, having to pull into side-roads every time an oncoming car approached, nearly crashing several times because she was so busy scouring the fields for Sevenoaks.

The hunt were having an equally frustrating time; hounds were not picking up any scent. Riders stood around on the edge of the wood, fidgeting. Then suddenly an old bitch hound gave tongue, and the chorus of hounds swelled, and the whole hillside was echoing. Pa pa pa pa went the melancholy, plaintive note of the horn, and the next moment the hunt came spilling across the road. There was a clash as stirrups hit each other, a snorting of horses, and they were jumping over the wall on the opposite side of the road. From the top of the hill Harriet watched them streaming across the field. There was Cory blown like a beech leaf in his red coat, standing up in his stirrups now to see what was on the other side of a large wall. The next moment Python had cleared it by inches. Hounds were splaying out by a small wood at the bottom of the valley, then suddenly they turned and came thundering back in Harriet's direction.

'There's the fox,' screamed Chattie, and gave the most ear-splitting view halloo.

Ten seconds later the hounds came flowing past her. Suddenly in the middle Harriet recognized a familiar figure, dirty grey, pink tongue hanging out, galloping joyously.

'Oh look, there's Sevenoaks,' screamed the children.

'Come here,' bellowed Harriet.

For a second he looked in her direction and gave her a naughty, flickering, rolling look, then trundled on in the centre of the pack which swept in a liver, black and white wave over the hill.

All the pent-up emotion of the last twenty-four hours welled up in Harriet. She sat down on the bank and laughed until she cried.

Her elation was short-lived. The hunt was soon miles away. She must get back to William. She drove home feeling depressed – not merely because of the day's catastrophic developments. She tried to analyse why, as she got the children a late lunch, and fed William. Perhaps I'm just tired, she thought.

*   *   *

'I just landed on one of your hotels, and you didn't even notice,' said Jonah.

'Oh God, how much do you owe me?' said Harriet.

'£1,000,' said Jonah. 'It was jolly honest of me to tell you.'

'Jolly honest,' answered Harriet, wishing he hadn't.

'Here's £1,000,' said Jonah. 'Now we can go on for another half-hour.'

Harriet was dying for him to beat her. Worried about Sevenoaks, she was finding it impossible to concentrate. There was no way she could win now; she wanted to get the game over as quickly as possible.

Fortunately Sammy arrived at that moment, bringing Georgie and Timothy, the Pembertons' elder child, who was a friend of Jonah's, so all four children disappeared to the attic.

Sammy and Harriet went back into the nursery where William was rolling around on the rug.

'How was Arabella's party last night?' said Sammy.

Harriet gave her an expurgated edition of what had happened.

'It was hideously embarrassing, but Cory was so sweet about it afterwards.'

'I think Charles Mander's rather attractive,' said Sammy. 'He's reputed to beat his wife. He's known round here as Rotation of Riding Crops.' She shrieked with laughter. 'Fancy old Arabella shoving you off to do the washing up.'

'She'd be quite attractive,' mused Harriet, 'if she didn't push so hard.'

'Must be getting desperate. I wonder how old she is. About thirty I should think. I hope I die before I'm thirty. It sounds so old.'

'Forty must be worse,' said Harriet. 'Mrs Bottomley must be over fifty.'

They brooded silently over this horror.

'Cory's thirty-four,' said Sammy. 'It doesn't seem too bad for a man; but, just think, when you were born he was fourteen, getting all clammy-handed and heavy breathing over girls at parties.'

Harriet thought she'd rather not.

'Elizabeth and Michael didn't have much fun last night either,' said Sammy. 'There weren't any alkaseltzers in the house. We'd run out, but Michael came down in the night and had sixteen junior aspirins.'

'What's happening on Friday?' said Harriet.

'The Hunt Ball,' said Sammy. 'Everyone gets absolutely smashed and blows hunting horns, and rushes upstairs and fornicates in cordoned-off bedrooms.'

She picked up a cushion and peered round it at William, making him go off into fits of giggles.

Harriet was sorting out a pile of washing.

'Who else is going to Elizabeth's party?' she asked casually.

Sammy looked at her slyly. 'You mean who's she asked for Cory?'

Harriet went pink.

'I just wondered if any of the people I met last night are going to be there.'

'She's invited another of her glamorous, neurotic,

172

divorced girlfriends called Melanie Brooks for Cory.
I saw the letter Elizabeth wrote her:

'"Darling Melanie, So pleased you can make it.
Try and catch an earlier train, as it's a bit of a rush
on Friday night and you want to look your best
because I've lined up a gorgeous man for you, a
disconsolate husband whose wife's just left him, but
very fascinating."'

Harriet winced.

'Don't worry,' said Sammy. 'She's ancient. At
least thirty, and her legs are awful.'

'But those'll be covered by a long dress at a ball,'
said Harriet gloomily.

The telephone rang. To Harriet's surprise it was
Billy Bentley.

'Hullo,' she said. 'Have you finished already?'

'My horse went lame; not badly; he'll be all right
after a few days' rest.'

'Did you have a good day?'

'Slightly chaotic actually. The Hunt saboteurs fed
in an enormous black and grey dog which completely disrupted the pack. They ran right across the
motorway – no-one was hurt, thank God – and
ended up in a council estate, cornering a ginger cat
in an outside lavatory.'

'Oh goodness! Is the cat all right?'

'Got away, thank God,' said Billy. 'Or it'd be all
over the papers.'

'And the big grey and black dog?'

'Well we whipped it out of the pack and Cory very
kindly took care of it. He gave a man on the council
estate a fiver to bring it back to your house. He's

going to hold it as hostage until the Antis claim it. It's completely wild.'

Harriet thought she would explode trying not to laugh.

'After that we had a terrific run. Look, are you doing anything on Friday?'

'No, at least I don't think so. My night off.'

'Like to come out?'

'All right.' Damn it, if Cory was going to go gallivanting with gorgeous divorcées, she wasn't going to get in his way.

'It's the Hunt Ball. You won't mind that, will you?' said Billy.

'Oh,' Harriet gave a yelp of alarm.

'We'll eat at home first. I'll come and pick you up about eight.'

'I haven't got anything to wear.'

'You'd look smashing in nothing,' he brayed nervously. 'See you Friday and bring William. Nanny's looking forward to seeing him.'

Harriet replaced the receiver very slowly.

'You lucky, lucky thing,' said Sammy.

'I'm sure Cory won't like it. He'll think I'm trying to cramp his style,' said Harriet. 'But Billy was so sweet about William.'

'Oh they're used to illegits in that family. Billy's sister's had two at least. Half of their ancestors have been born on the wrong side of the duvet. Now throw that photograph of Simon away,' she went on, 'and make a fresh start. Billy's lovely and stinking rich, and faint heart never won fair chinless wonder.'

174

'I've got nothing to wear,' said Harriet.

'I've got just the thing,' said Sammy. 'A fantastically long slinky orange dress I bought last year, in the hope that I might lose weight and get into it. I didn't, but it would look sensational on you.'

The noises above became wilder.

'I'd better go and turn the hot water up,' said Harriet. 'Cory'll go spare if he doesn't get a decent bath when he gets home.'

She couldn't bring herself to tell Cory she was going to the Hunt Ball. She washed and starched his dress shirt and brought the red tail coat with grey facings back from the cleaners and tried on Sammy's orange dress which became her absurdly well. But as the day grew nearer she put off telling him, because he was too abstracted to bother, or because he was in such a good mood and she didn't want to spoil it, or in a bad mood which she didn't want to make any worse.

On the pretext of buying Chattie tights, she went into Skipton and found a flame-coloured boa to cover up some of the lack of dress. She failed, on the other hand, to find a bra to wear under it.

'Go without,' said Sammy. 'Live a little.'

'I'll fall out when I dance – if anyone asks me to.'

She spent the day of the ball surreptitiously getting herself ready, as she knew with putting the children to bed there wouldn't be much time later. She painted her nails and washed her hair, and put on a headscarf so it dried smooth. She was peeling chips for the children's tea when Cory came into the kitchen, carrying a couple of shirts.

'Don't do any more work, Daddy,' said Chattie, seizing his hand.

He opened the washing-machine door and was just about to throw the shirts in, when instead he drew out an old bunch of daffodils:

'Planning to wash these?'

'Oh dear, I'm getting so vague. I meant to put them down the waste disposal,' said Harriet.

'I suppose you also mean to put those chips down the waste disposal and the peelings into the pan?' he said. 'And why are you wearing a headscarf? Are you feeling all right?'

'Fine. Do you want a cup of tea?' said Harriet nervously.

'I want something stronger,' said Cory, pouring himself a large whisky.

'You ought to eat something,' said Harriet.

'I know, but I'll be eating again in an hour or two.

He cut a slice of pork from the joint, covered it in chili pickle, put it between two slices of bread and settled down with the evening paper. His eating habits drove her to despair.

Chattie scrambled onto his knee.

'Are you going out tonight?'

'Yes.'

'To the Ball? Will you take me?'

'No.'

'Are you going to dance with Harriet?' she went on, ignoring Harriet's agonized signals. 'She's going to wear an orange dress which shows all her bosoms.'

'Don't talk rubbish,' said Cory.

'She is,' said Chattie. 'Sammy lent it to her.'

He turned to Harriet.

'Is this true?' he said sharply.

She nodded, blushing, grating cheese so frenziedly over the cauliflower that she cut one of her fingers.

'Who's taking you?'

'Billy Bentley,' she said, sucking her finger.

'Didn't know you knew him.'

'I met him at Arabella's party, and at the meet.'

'I see. Who's looking after William and the children?'

'Well it is my night off, and Mrs Bottomley said she'd babysit, but if that's difficult Billy says their old nanny can look after William.'

'Billy seems to have displayed more initiative than usual,' said Cory. 'Where are you having dinner?'

'With his parents.'

'You'll be poisoned before you get to the ball. They've got the worst cook in the West Riding.'

And he stalked out of the room, leaving the half-eaten pork sandwich and the glass of whisky. Harriet wondered if she should go after him and apologize. But what was there to apologize for, except she hadn't told him? It was entirely up to her what she did on her evenings off. Perhaps he didn't like downstairs mixing with his upstairs friends. Oh, why had she agreed to go?

She was getting ready, sitting in front of her looking glass, just wearing a pair of pants, when there was a knock on the door. She grabbed a towel; it was Cory. His dark hair sleeked down,

177

wearing his red tail coat with the grey facings and black trousers.

'You do look nice,' she stammered. Privately she thought he looked stunning.

Cory shrugged. 'I'll have champagne poured over it before the night's out. Can you cut the nails on my right hand?'

As she bent over his hand, her hair in Carmen rollers tied up with a scarf, keeping the towel up with her elbows, her hand shook so much, she was frightened she'd cut him.

'You can leave William here,' he said. 'I've cleared it with Mrs Bottomley.'

'You're sure you don't mind?'

'Been monopolizing you too much myself lately. Do you good to get out.'

'Yes,' she said, trying to sound more enthusiastic.

He glanced round the room. 'The light's terrible in here. Go and make up in Noel's room. I must go. I'm invited for eight. If any of the young bloods start pestering you, give me a shout.'

The mirrors in Noel's room showed her from every angle. It's like a Hollywood set, she thought, all those pink roses and ruffles. It's a mistress's room not a wife's, and quite wrong expecting Cory to sleep in it, like putting a wolfhound in a diamante studded collar and a tartan coat. And how extraordinary to have so many photographs of oneself looking down from the walls: Noel sunbathing topless, Noel receiving a screen award, Noel arriving at a première smothered in ermine, Noel laughing, with Chattie, Jonah and Tadpole gazing up adoringly. That one hurt Harriet most of all. Trust Tadpole to suck up, she thought. Sevenoaks would be more discriminating.

She gazed in the mirror. She looked small and defenceless. She'd been rubbing olive oil into her eyelashes for at least a week now, and they didn't seem any longer. If only she could be a thousandth as beautiful as Noel tonight. The orange dress slithered over her head – it really was low; she took out the rollers and brushed her hair until it shone and stood back, for once pleased with her appearance.

She took the hair out of her brush, opened the window and threw it out; it promptly blew back again. Time was running out. Hastily she loaded up her evening bag, breaking her comb to get it inside. Pinching some of Noel's loose powder to fill the little gold compact her parents had given her for her sixteenth birthday she wondered when she would ever see them again. Her sudden overwhelming wave of homesickness was only interrupted by the doorbell.

Chapter Seventeen

Dinner was much less alarming than she expected. Billy's parents were friendly in a bluff horsey sort of way, and even though there were twenty for dinner – mostly hunting types – they were much less glamorous and bitchy than the people at Arabella's party. There was only one really pretty woman there, a Mrs Willoughby who had red hair and sparkling green eyes like a little cat.

Harriet sat between the joint-master and Billy's Uncle Bertie, who squeezed her thigh absent-mindedly and flirted with her in a gentle way.

The food, as Cory predicted, was disgusting. Fortunately a Jack Russell with beseeching eyes sat under the table and wolfed all her fish. The second course, Coq au Vin, was full of soot and quite inedible. Harriet toyed with hers for a bit then, when a maid came round with a large bowl full of bones, thankfully threw her chicken pieces in too. It was only when the maid moved on to Billy's Uncle Bertie on Harriet's right, who immediately picked up Harriet's bits and put them on his plate, that she realized with horror that the maid was handing round second helpings.

She also put up another black after dinner when the women were drinking coffee. 'Have you lived here long?' she said to Billy's mother, during a pause.

'Well quite a long time,' said Mrs Bentley.

'About five hundred years,' whispered Mrs Willoughby, out of the corner of her mouth.

Fortunately the wine had been orbiting the table pretty fast at dinner and everyone laughed.

Nice car, thought Harriet, as Billy's Ferrari roared along the narrow roads. She snuggled down under the fur rug. Perhaps it was its coating of dog hairs that made it so warm.

'Do you ride?' said Billy.

'No. I'm afraid I don't. I get taken for one occasionally,' said Harriet.

'You'd look super on a horse. I could teach you very quickly.'

'Do you really think you could?'

'We've got an old pony of my sister's. It taught us all to ride. It's as quiet as anything. Soon get you going on that.'

She'd soon be talking about running martingales with Arabella!

Billy swung the car between a huge pair of gates. Sneering lions reared up on pillars on either side; the curtains flickered in the lodge window as they went by. Ahead the big house was blazing with lights; floodlighting illuminated the blond walls. Drink had done nothing to still the butterflies in Harriet's stomach.

The car park was a quagmire from the recent rain.

'Up to my fucking hocks in mud,' bellowed a hunting lady in disgust, holding her dress above muscly knees. The wind plastered Harriet's feather boa against her lipstick.

She left her coat on a huge four-poster, its rose pink brocade tattered with age. In the distance she could hear the sensual throb of the music. It was almost eleven; the ball was in full swing. Pale-shouldered women crowded in front of the gilt-framed looking glass, putting on scarlet lipstick and slapping powder over flushed-from-dinner faces.

The frayed banners hanging from the walls shivered in the heat; a pair of huge, blue chandeliers hung from the ceiling. On the landing a group of women laughed loudly. Elizabeth Pemberton in hyacinth blue was one of them. As Harriet went downstairs, clutching the curved banisters for support, she breathed in the sweet heady scent of a huge tub of pink hyacinths.

Billy was standing looking distinguished under some antlers. 'You're easily the prettiest girl in the room,' he said, taking her hand. Beyond lay the ballroom brilliantly lit. On tables round the walls champagne was plunged into ice buckets. The Master's wife, heavily corsetted, stood in the door distributing largesse. The band had stopped; couples were drifting off the floor. There was Arabella her face looking glamorously suntanned for once against a floating white dress; and Charles Mander

182

leaving his hand lingeringly on the bare back of a fast-looking beauty. She couldn't see Cory anywhere.

Harriet was instantly conscious that Billy was regarded as somebody. Seeing her with him lots of people who'd ignored her at Arabella's party said 'Hullo,' and were obviously trying to remember where they'd seen her before. Billy found their table and the rest of the dinner party near the band, and after knocking back a few more glasses of champagne, asked Harriet to dance.

Surreptitiously Harriet was still searching everywhere for Cory. Then, as they reached the far end of the ballroom, suddenly she saw him and felt an absolute explosion of jealousy. He was talking to a beautiful, slightly ravaged looking woman with greeny gold hair, slanting eyes, high cheekbones and a beautiful green silk dress worn off one shoulder. That must be Melanie. She had the kind of mystery and sophistication that made Harriet feel as raw as a broken egg.

'Hullo Harriet,' said Elizabeth, who was sitting at the same table. 'Sammy's dress *does* suit you. Harriet's terrifyingly thick with my nanny,' she added to the ferret-faced man in a red coat sitting beside her. 'One shudders to think what they tell each other about us.'

Cory looked up suddenly and noticed them.

'Hullo, Cory,' shouted Billy, waggling his arms and legs so vigorously in time to the music that his mousy locks fell over his pink forehead. 'I'm taking good care of her,' he brayed with laughter.

'I'm sure you are, Billy,' said Cory, giving them both a rather wintry smile. He turned back to Melanie.

Harriet felt a great stab of disappointment. Suddenly she knew all the scenting and curling and orange dress had been directed at Cory, and he'd hardly glanced at her.

The ball grew more raucous. Young men were trying to lob ice cubes down the front of girls' dresses. In the kitchen a group were engaged in feeding a long string of cocktail sausages down the waste disposal, with shrieks of laughter. Harriet had danced with nearly everyone in the party, and drunk nearly a bottle of champagne, which only deepened her despair. Billy was doing his duty dance with his aunt. Mrs Willoughby was as usual dancing out of her party. Everyone else was on the floor, except Harriet and two men in red coats who sat with their backs to her discussing a day out with the Quorn. Harriet tried to put on an animated 'I-am-just-waiting-for-my-partner-to-return' sort of face. She was terrified Cory would see her being a wallflower. Billy's mother stopped at the table and whispered to one of the men in a red coat. He turned and looked at Harriet. 'Of course,' he said, in a long-suffering voice. 'May I have the pleasure of this dance?'

Harriet was so humiliated, she got all hot and flustered and said sorry each time he tripped over her feet. He never apologized at all. There was Cory dancing again with the beautiful Melanie. Oh God, don't let him fancy her too much.

The ball became wilder; upstairs the cordoned-off

bedrooms were heaving with occupants. After a trip to the ladies, Harriet saw Mrs Willoughby emerge from a side room, patting her hair, with Elizabeth Pemberton's husband, Michael. During a break between dances, a drunk poured a whole bottle of champagne over his wife, and then, picking up another, started to water the rest of his party. Two men in dinner jackets carried him bellowing out of the ballroom, his legs wriggling like a sheep about to be dipped.

Harriet was well on her way down a second bottle. She felt very above ground now and cannoned into several chairs when Billy asked her to dance.

'I've got you under my skin,' played the band.

I've got you under my lack of chin, thought Harriet and giggled, as Billy pressed her to his chest. Cory was dancing with Melanie yet again, her face pale and dreamy against his scarlet coat. They looked so beautiful together, quite separate from anyone else in the room. Harriet felt the music and longing eating into her soul.

'He will not always say, what you would have him say, but now and then he'll say something wonderful,' played the band.

Harriet and Billy were passing Cory and Melanie now. Harriet looked up, and suddenly her eyes met Cory's and she found she couldn't tear them away. On and on they stared at each other, as the colour mounted in her cheeks.

Billy looked down at her, as though he could feel the current.

'Hey,' he said, 'are you still with me?'

'I'd like a drink,' muttered Harriet. She felt jolted and uneasy; her heart was thumping. She was just gulping down a second glass, when a soft voice said, 'Would you spare a dance for an old fogey?'

She turned expectantly. It was Charles Mander, his face flushed, his cheeks veined with red. It was twenty to two, only a few minutes and they'd all be posthorn galloping. Suddenly she wanted to dance so badly with Cory, she nearly wept.

The next minute she was being mauled to bits on the floor. The tempo was very slow now and Charles was breathing down her neck, peering down the front of her dress, one warm hand wandering over her back and neck, the other which was holding her hand, nudging continually at her breast.

How could Noel have ever fancied him, thought Harriet. The music stopped.

'Not letting you go so easily,' said Charles.

'I must get back to my party,' said Harriet desperately and, wriggling away, went slap into Cory.

'My turn, I think, Charles,' he said.

And, joyfully, she melted into his arms. She was conscious of his height and strength, and in spite of being very drunk now, she tried to make herself as light as possible.

'Have you had a nice time?' he said.

She nodded, not trusting herself to speak.

He's my boss, she thought, and he loves Noel; but she felt herself curling round him like bindweed, lust leaping in her like a salmon.

Suddenly the contact of his body became unbearable; she lost her step. The music stopped to desultory clapping; several young men were galloping about the floor, kicking up their legs and uttering hunting cries. Across the room she saw Elizabeth Pemberton beckon imperiously to Billy and nod in their direction. Cory, however, held firmly onto her hand; perhaps after all he wanted her to stay. The band started up again. Reprieve, reprieve! Harriet's self-control went to the winds. She put both her arms round Cory's neck and smiled up at him.

'I've been wanting to dance with you all evening,' she said.

He laughed. 'You're pissed out of your mind.'

'Am I really?' she giggled, nestling against him. 'I've enjoyed myself.'

'Clinging to Charles Mander like a limpet?' said Cory.

'You mustn't have a hang-up about him,' said Harriet.

'I have not,' said Cory, extremely tartly.

'He's attractive, but not a millionth millionth as attractive as you.'

Melanie danced by with Michael Pemberton, trying to catch Cory's eye with a do-you-need-rescuing expression on her face.

Harriet glanced at her.

'She's not the answer for you either,' she said.

Cory raised his eyebrows.

'Since when did I give you permission to dictate my sex life?'

'Only tonight. I could supervise the whole world's sex life tonight. Sammy says she doesn't look nearly as hot first thing in the morning, and she'd got awful legs, and she asked Sammy to put a hot water bottle in her bed tonight, so she can't be expecting to give you her all this evening.'

'The nanny mafia,' sighed Cory. 'You spend far too much time gossiping to Sammy.'

'Sammy says Melanie's marriage broke up because she didn't like sex. Anyway she's too old for you.'

'She's four years younger than me.'

'I know. But she's too old inside. You need someone young and silly to stop you looking so sad.'

Her foot caught in her hem, and she stumbled and fell against him. His grip tightened on her; he laid his cheek against her hair.

'You talk a lot of nonsense,' he said. 'And you're going to feel terrible in the morning.'

'It's not morning yet,' said Harriet dreamily. 'It was the nightingale and not the lark that pierced the fearful hollows of thine ear.'

Suddenly there was a tantivy of hunting horns and view halloos, the sober fox trot tempo quickened, and broke into D'Ye Ken John Peel.

'Oh Christ,' said Cory, as a whooping line came thundering towards them.

What a noise of galloping feet! Harriet could feel the boards heaving as they rushed round the floor, one cavalry charge after another gathering up couples still trying to dance like fish in a net. With Cory protecting her from the scrimmage, Harriet was loving every minute, her cheeks flushed, dark hair flying.

Round and round they went until she was quite breathless. Suddenly they all slithered to a halt, stopped like statues, while the band played God Save the Queen. Just in front of them Charles Mander was patting Mrs Willoughby's bottom while Mrs Mander snored peacefully in a chair with her mouth open. Harriet found her fingers curling in and out of Cory's, and looking up saw Elizabeth Pemberton glaring in their direction.

The band stopped. A fat woman executed a pirouette and collapsed on the floor with cackles of laughter.

Harriet watched fascinated.

'At least I'm not as drunk as her.'

'Nor are you going to be allowed to be,' said Cory firmly. Picking up Harriet's bag which was lying on the table, he extracted the cloakroom ticket and handed it to Mrs Willoughby who was on her way upstairs.

'Annie, be an angel and get Harriet's coat while you're up there. She's much too slewed to find anything.'

Billy Bentley arrived, braying nervously.

'We got lorst,' he said.

'This child has had far too much to drink,' said Cory sternly.

''Fraid she hash; entirely my fault; take her home at onshe.'

'You're as bad as she is,' said Cory, dropping his cigarette into a discarded plate of fruit salad. 'Neither of you is in a fit state. Give her a ring in the morning, but for God's sake get someone to drive you home.'

'Or you might go slap into a tree along the Fair-mile,' said Harriet and laughed.

Elizabeth came up to them. 'You're coming back for a drink, aren't you, Cory?'

Cory said he had to take Harriet home.

'Billy can take her,' said Elizabeth.

'Far too drunk.'

'Michael can run her back then.'

Harriet frantically pressed Cory's hand.

'He's too drunk too,' he said. 'It's late, and she *is* my responsibility.'

'I am, I am,' agreed Harriet, beaming.

'Thanks, Annie,' said Cory taking her coat from Mrs Willoughby. 'I feel I ought to tip you.'

'I'd much rather have a kiss,' said Mrs Willoughby, her eyes gleaming. 'You and Harriet,' she shot a sly glance at Elizabeth, 'must both come to dinner.'

Harriet had never seen anyone so cross as Elizabeth Pemberton.

Outside the rain had stopped; the clouds had rolled back like a blind on a clear starry night.

'Damn,' said Cory, going up to his car. 'I've left the lights on; the battery's flat.'

'As flat as Elizabeth Pemberton's chest,' said Harriet. Really she was behaving very badly; she must get a grip on herself.

'Having trouble?' It was Harry Mytton, one of the red-faced stalwarts in the Bentleys' party. Out of the corner of her eye, Harriet saw Elizabeth and her party bearing down on them.

'Quick,' she whispered.

'Battery's flat,' said Cory. 'Can you give us a

190

lift? The garage can come and get it in the morning.'

Harriet leapt into the car as quick as a dog thinking it might be left behind. She found she was sitting
on two riding crops and a dog lead. There was a
sticker for the Aylesford point-to-point in the back
window.

As the headlights lit up the bracken and the
trailing traveller's joy, she was achingly conscious of
Cory sitting beside her in the back. Mrs Mytton
discussed one of the drunks in their party.

'Kept a pack in some unlikely place like Hasle-
mere,' said Harry Mytton. The huge stars seemed to
be crowding in on them as they drove along the
winding road. Harriet kept being thrown against
Cory.

'Annie Willoughby's a damned attractive woman,'
said Harry Mytton, 'magnificent woman across
country you know.'

'She can even keep potted plants alive,' said Mrs
Mytton.

Another corner, another lurch across the back of
the car. This time Harriet didn't bother to move
away, nuzzling up to Cory like a puppy. Her head
kept flopping forward. In the end Cory turned her
over, so she lay with her head in his lap, and stroked
her gently behind the ears, almost as he might have
petted Tadpole or one of the children.

Looking up she could see the lean line of his jaw,
above the white tie. Behind his head, out of the back
window, Orion glittered in a sooty, black sky. Now
he disappeared, now he appeared again as the car
swung round the bends.

'What did Orion do?' she said sleepily.

'He was a mighty hunter who died of a scorpion sting,' said Cory. 'After boasting he'd rid the world of wild beasts. Then Zeus put him in the sky.'

'Who was that, Cory?' said Harry Mytton. 'Didn't he used to hunt with the York and Ainsty?'

Cory's lips twitched. Harriet started to giggle. He put his hand over her mouth. She started to kiss it. He shook his head, smoothing her hair back from her forehead.

Orion was moving back and forth again. Following his progress, Harriet suddenly began to feel very odd. She shut her eyes. Everything went round and round. She sat bolt upright.

'What's the matter?' asked Cory.

'I feel sick.'

'Serves you bloody well right.' Cory wound down the window, and shoved her head out. Icy blasts of cold made her feel better, but it was a relief when Harry Mytton turned into the Wilderness drive.

The owls were hooting in the garden. Mrs Bottomley's thermos of cocoa was waiting for them in the kitchen. Cory unscrewed it and poured it down the sink.

'Don't want to upset the old girl,' he said.

Harriet fled upstairs, put on more scent and cleaned her teeth. Then, thinking Cory might smell the toothpaste and think she was trying too hard, rinsed her mouth out again. Then she turned off her electric blanket.

'Careful, Harriet, careful,' said her reflection in

the mirror. 'This kind of behaviour got you into trouble before.'

Down in the drawing room Cory had taken off his coat and tie and stood in front of a dying fire nursing a glass of whisky.

Harriet curled up on the sofa, watching the light from one lamp fall on the bowed heads of a pot of white cyclamen.

The telephone rang. Cory picked it up.

'No, it's very kind, Elizabeth, but I'm absolutely knackered. Thank you for a tremendous evening.' There was a pause. 'As to that, I don't think it's any of your bloody business. Goodnight.' And he dropped the receiver back on the hook.

'Interfering bitch,' he said.

Harriet giggled. 'I bet she said, "That child's been hurt enough".'

Cory looked startled, then he laughed. 'That's exactly what she did say.'

For a minute he looked out over the silent valley, then he drew the curtains, stubbed out his cigarette and came towards her. Then he held out his arms, and she went into them like a bird out of the storm. As he kissed her she could feel the current of excitement coursing over her. God, this is absolute dynamite, she thought, as her hands crept around his neck, her fingers twining into the thick black hair.

Suddenly the telephone rang.

'Leave it,' said Cory, his hold tightening.

'It might be important,' murmured Harriet.

'Can't be.'

'I'll get it. It might wake Mrs Bottomley and

193

we don't want that,' said Harriet, giggling. 'I'll say you're in a meeting.'

She picked up the receiver. She could hear the pips.

'It's long distance for you from America.'

'I expect it's MGM about the treatment,' he said, taking the receiver from her.

Suddenly the colour drained from his face. Some-one must have died. She could see the knuckles white where his hand clutched the receiver. The conversation was very brief. Harriet collapsed onto the sofa. She had a premonition that some-thing very terrible was about to happen to her. She looked at Cory and suddenly had a vision of pulling a wounded man up to the edge of a cliff, then finally letting him go so his body circled round and round as he splattered on the rocks below. Cory put down the receiver and reached automatically for a cigarette.

'That was Noel,' he said. 'She's finished filming and she's flying back to England tomorrow. She and Ronnie Acland are coming North next week. She wants to see the children so they're coming over for lunch on Wednesday.'

'But she can't,' gasped Harriet. 'It'll crucify you. She can't go round playing fast and loose with other people's lives.'

Cory glared at her, his face grey. He seemed to have aged ten years. The last hour might never have happened.

'They're her children as much as mine,' he snapped.

194

Harriet stepped back as though he'd hit her, giving a whimper of anguish.

'And don't stare at me with those great eyes of yours,' he said brutally. 'If Noel and I choose to behave in a civilized manner, it's nothing to do with you. You'd better go to bed.'

Harriet heard the cocks crowing. She looked at the photograph by the bed. She couldn't even be loyal to Simon's memory. Cory was a different generation; his world was in ruins; he merely regarded her as a diversion, because he was a bit tight and she was available.

Her mind raced round seeking comfort, but she found none. She saw her dishevelled clothes in the bedroom, the unstopped make-up, the cellophane pack which had contained her new tights. She remembered the excitement with which she'd dressed. She'd been so sure, she'd even turned off her electric blanket. She crept between the sheets and shivered until dawn.

Chapter Eighteen

As Wednesday approached Cory grew more and more impossible, snapping at Mrs Bottomley, the children and, most of all, at Harriet.

On Tuesday night he was going to a dinner in Leeds and asked Harriet to iron a white dress shirt for him. She took considerable pains over it but, unfortunately, Ambrose, who had been looking for mice in the coal hole, walked all over it when she wasn't looking.

Cory hit the roof. 'Can't you ever concentrate on one thing for more than five minutes?'

Harriet lost her temper. She had been cooking all day for tomorrow's lunch and she had a headache.

'If you didn't make people so nervous, they might stop making a hash of things.'

'Go on!' he said glaring at her.

'I don't mind you shouting at me. But I don't see why you should take it out on Mrs Bottomley and the children. It's not their fault your rotten wife's turning up tomorrow.'

Oh, God, she thought, as his face twisted with rage. I've really put my foot in it now.

'It would be as well if you remembered whose house this is, and who pays your salary!' he said, stalking out of the room.

Half-an-hour later she heard the front door bang and his car drive off with a whirring sound of gravel.

Gibbering with rage, Harriet ate a large piece of walnut cake, and then another piece, and was just embarking on a third, when she heard a step and nearly jumped out of her skin as two hands grabbed her round the waist and a familiar voice said, 'Guess who?'

Leaping away, choking over the walnut cake, she swung round and looked up through streaming eyes into a handsome, decadent face. There was something familiar about the dark eyes, which were now narrowed to slits with laughter.

'Hullo, darling,' he said. 'I'm Kit Erskine.'

'Goodness, you surprised me.'

'Oh, I'm full of surprises. Where's Cory?'

'Out, gone to Leeds.'

'That's good. We're alone at last.'

'Mrs Bottomley's upstairs,' said Harriet hastily, backing away.

'How is old Botters?'

'On the scurry – sweeping under carpets. Mrs Erskine and Ronnie Acland are coming to lunch tomorrow, so there's a lot to do.'

Kit whistled. 'They are? What a carve-up. That cake looks good.' He cut himself a large piece. 'I'm starving. Where shall we have dinner?'

'I can't,' said Harriet. 'I've got to . . .'

'Wash your hair,' said Kit. 'Don't worry. You can give Noel a good ten years.'

At that moment Mrs Bottomley walked in with a feather duster.

'Master Kit!' she squeaked. 'Whatever are you doing here?'

'Botters! Darling!' He gathered her up as though she were light as a feather, and carried her round the room.

'Put me down, Master Kit!' she protested, half laughing, her legs going like a centipede.

The kitchen was large, but with Kit's arrival, it seemed to shrink. He polished off three double whiskies and most of the walnut cake, and exchanged gossip with Mrs Bottomley, but all the time his eyes were wandering lazily over Harriet.

She tried to decorate a pudding for tomorrow, but found, in her nervousness, she was decorating far more of the table.

Kit picked up a handful of crystallized violets and scattered them higgledy-piggledy on the top of the mousse.

'It's got to look nice for Mrs Erskine,' wailed Harriet.

'No-one bothers about her,' said Kit. 'You should have the courage of your confections.'

'How's Cory?' he asked Mrs Bottomley.

'I've never known him as bad as this,' said Mrs Bottomley disapprovingly. 'I made that walnut cake this morning. You know it's his favourite and he wouldn't touch it. Like a bear with a sore head. Ever since he heard she was bringing that Ronald

Acland. What's he like? He looks a smart fellow.'

'Ronnie Acland? Well, he calls himself an actor but, frankly, I wouldn't have him on my side playing charades. But his father is dying, which means any moment dear Ronnie will become Lord Acland, and that's what Noel finds attractive. She's spent all her life waiting for Lord Right to come along.'

Harriet giggled. You couldn't help liking Kit. Kit sensed weakness. 'I say Botters . . .'

'Don't call me that. It's rude.'

'Will you babysit so I can take Harriet out to dinner?'

Mrs Bottomley looked dubious. 'She needs a break. Mr Cory's been nagging her terrible but he won't like you both swanning off the moment his back's turned.'

'He won't know. I'll get her back early. Please, darling Botters?'

'Well, if I weren't fumigating with Mr Cory, I wouldn't do it.'

Kit took Harriet to a small dimly-lit club where they both talked and drank a great deal.

Kit shook his head. 'So Noel's really coming tomorrow. I suppose Botters told you Noel and I once had a walk-out.'

'It sounded more like a stay-in to me,' said Harriet.

Kit grinned. 'So the kitten had claws, after all. The odd thing is that Cory's never held it against me. "How can I blame you," he said to me afterwards, "when I'm incapable of resisting her myself".'

'Oh poor Cory,' said Harriet. 'Why doesn't he find someone else? He's so attractive.'

'He's bewitched,' said Kit. 'He's burnt himself out in the idiotic hope that one day, after a year, maybe five years, ten years, a lifetime, he'll suddenly crack the rock, and conquer that shallow, dried-up heart.'

'I hate her,' Kit went on savagely, 'for her damn narcissism, and yet when you first meet her she's so dazzling, you can't see anything else. It's like looking straight into the sun. Anyway.' He stretched his legs so one of them brushed against Harriet's. 'Enough of other people's worries. What about yours? What made you keep the baby? Hung up on the father are you?'

'Yes – I suppose I still am.' She flaming well wasn't going to tell him anything about Cory.

Kit took her hand. 'I'm realistic about love. What's the point of eating your heart out for someone who doesn't love you? The answer is to find an adequate substitute.'

'Yes?' said Harriet, taking her hand away 'And where do I find that?'

'Right here, darling. What could be more adequate than me?'

Harriet looked at him. Yes, he was adequate all right. Everything about him, the deep, expensive voice, the sexy eyes, the mocking mouth, the thick blond hair, the broad, flat shoulders, the long muscular thighs, one of which was rubbing against hers again.

'I think we'd better go home,' said Harriet.

He stopped the car halfway up the drive and switched off the engine. Suddenly he reached forward and took hold of the ribbon tying back her hair.

'Don't touch me,' she spat, springing away.

'My, but you're jumpy,' he said, pulling off the ribbon, so her hair rippled down thickly over her shoulders.

'That's better,' he said. 'You must stop hiding the fact that you're a very attractive girl.'

'I don't want to attract men,' she said in a frozen voice.

'Listen, darling, you've had a bad knock, but it's like falling off a horse. The longer you take to ride again, the more difficult you're going to find it.'

Bending his head, he kissed her very gently on the lips.

'There,' he said, as though he were soothing a frightened animal. 'Not so bad, was it?'

Not bad at all, thought Harriet. Very pleasant, in fact. And when he kissed her again, she kissed him back.

'God,' he whispered, 'we're going to be great together.'

He opened his fur coat and pulled her inside, so she could feel the length of his hard muscular body against her.

Oh dear, oh dear, she thought. Here I go again. I mustn't be so loose.

'Come on,' he said softly. 'Relax, I'm not silly enough to let you get pregnant again.'

Pregnant. If he had jabbed a branding iron on her back, nothing could have brought her to her senses more quickly. Panic stricken, she wrenched herself away from him, opened the car door, and tore up the drive.

'Hey, wait a minute!' She heard Kit laughing behind her. 'Take it easy, darling. Don't be in such a hurry to get me into bed.'

Panting, she pushed open the front door, and fled into the house, slap into Cory.

'Harriet! Thank God you're back. Are you all right?'

Her hands shot to her face, rubbing mascara from beneath her eyes, smoothing her hair, tucking in her shirt.

'I'm fine,' she stammered. 'I've been having a drink with Kit.'

'You've been out with Kit?' The voice changed, became so brutally icy that Harriet drew back as though she'd been struck. For a second she saw the blaze of contempt in his eyes, as he took in her dishevelled condition, then the shutters came down, and his face resumed its normal deadpan expression.

'I might have guessed you'd run true to type,' he said. 'William's been yelling his guts out for the past hour. If you can't have a more responsible attitude towards the children, you'd better pack your bags and get out in the morning!'

For a minute Harriet gazed at Cory appalled. Then she jumped as a voice behind her said, 'Do I hear the sound of high words?' and Kit wandered through the front door, straightening his tie, and ostentatiously wiping lipstick off his face.

'Hullo, Cory,' he went on. 'You look a bit peaky, my dear. What you need is a few late nights.'

Harriet didn't wait for Cory's reply. She fled upstairs, scalded by remorse and humiliation. Surely he couldn't sack her for something so trivial.

She found William scarlet in the face, his eyes piggy from crying for so long.

'I'm sorry, darling, so sorry,' she whispered, as she picked him up and cuddled him. Gradually his sobs subsided and, as she waited for his bottle to heat up, she shivered with terror at the thought of the future – bleak, salary-less, with no Chattie and Jonah, no Cory even when he was being nice. In just a few weeks, she thought miserably, I've come to regard this rambling house as home.

As she gave William his bottle, however, there was a knock on the door. It was Cory.

'Don't get up,' he said, looking at William. 'Is he all right?'

'He's fine,' stammered Harriet. 'I'm sorry about going out.'

'It wasn't a very good idea going out with Kit. He's only interested in easy lays – and that's the last thing you need.'

Harriet hung her head. 'Then you don't hate me?'

Cory smiled faintly. 'When my horses do stupid wilful things, I beat the hell out of them. It doesn't mean I love them any the less.'

'Then you w-won't send me away?'

Cory shook his head. 'The children would be desolated. Anyway, it's me who ought to apologize, I've behaved like a bastard the past few days.'

He picked up Simon's photograph by Harriet's bed.

'I've been so bound up in my own private hell. I've been impervious to anyone else's. Poor little Harriet.' He touched her cheek gently with his hand. 'Do you still miss him so much?'

Harriet flushed.

'Yes . . . no, I don't know. Why don't you tell your wife not to come tomorrow? It's not too late,' she blurted out.

'I've got to see her and Ronnie Acland together some time,' he said, going towards the door.

In the doorway, he paused and turned. 'And please tie your hair back again when Noel comes tomorrow. You look far too pretty like that, and I don't want her to start cross-petitioning.'

The moment he'd gone, Harriet, carrying a protesting William, raced to the mirror. He'd called her pretty. Cory had actually called her far too pretty! He'd never paid her a compliment before. She put her hand to her face where Cory had touched it, and just for a second wondered what it would be like to be loved by him, to see the haughty, inscrutable face, miraculously softened, to hear the detached voice, for once passionate and tender. Then the great shadowy owl of shame at her own presumption swooped down to overwhelm her.

Even so, after she had put William to bed, she washed her hair, and was just drying it, when a note was thrust under the door.

On it was written ten times in huge childish scrawl: 'I must not try and seduce Harriet.' Then the

204

writer had reverted to normal handwriting. 'Darling Harriet, Cory wants me to write this line a thousand times, but my hand is aching and I want to go to bed. So please forgive me. Love, Kit.'

Harriet giggled. You couldn't be angry with Kit for long.

Chapter Nineteen

Noel and Ronnie Acland arrived at least an hour late the next day, by which time the children were frenzied with frustrated excitement, and Harriet had run upstairs at least a dozen times, to re-tie her ribbon and powder her nose.

But when she saw the figure smothered in squashy blond furs getting out of a large Rolls-Royce, she realized that her efforts had been to no avail. For Noel Balfour was undoubtedly the most beautiful woman she had ever seen. She had a gold, breath-taking, erupting beauty, and she swooped down on the family with a rasping cry of love like a bird of paradise.

'Cory, darling, you've lost far too much weight! Chattie, baby, what a beautiful dress! Jonah, my angel, how tall and handsome you've grown!'

When Harriet had recovered from the shock, she made out that Noel's face was thin and oval, her skin of a thick magnolia creaminess, her eyes tawny, clear and restless, and the impression of gold came from her marvellous mane of hair. She was tall – almost as tall as Cory – but her body was as supple as silk. Underneath her furs, she wore a saffron wool dress which clung to every curve.

As soon as she had hugged the children, she turned her dazzling smile on Harriet. 'We're horribly, horribly late. There's no excuse. Well, let's all go and have an enormous drink,' she said, putting her arm through Harriet's. 'I can't tell you how relieved I am you're looking after the children – I've heard such marvellous reports about you. After lunch I want to come and see your little baby, and you must tell me all about yourself.'

Harriet, expecting indifference, hauteur, antagonism, was completely disarmed by such friendliness. In the drawing room, they found Ronnie Acland talking to Cory about shooting.

Harriet was further surprised to find herself liking Ronnie Acland, who was a tall, handsome, rather florid man in tweeds, with a loud voice and excellent teeth. He seemed to be smiling all the time, probably from embarrassment.

Cory had completely regained his sang-froid. He gave the impression of being slightly bored by this intrusion. Not once did the aloof, unsmiling face betray the turmoil that must have been raging within.

God, he's cool, thought Harriet in admiration. I could never behave like that if I suddenly had to face Simon.

Noel took her drink from Cory, running a caressing finger along his hand as she did so, and then wandered round the room moving ornaments and straightening pictures.

'When did this fire start smoking?' she asked Cory, kicking a log with a blond suede shoe.

At that moment, Kit wandered in, wearing obscenely tight strawberry pink trousers.

For a moment Noel stiffened. She hadn't bargained on Kit.

'Whatever are you doing here?' she said, trying to keep the hostility out of her voice.

Kit stared at her insolently for a minute, then yawned so hard that Harriet thought he was going to dislocate his jaw.

'I'm visiting my brother Cory – your husband, if you remember. And laying siege to this steaming girl,' he said, putting an arm round Harriet's shoulders and kissing her on the cheek. 'But you've put that bloody bow back on again,' he added.

And once again he pulled off the ribbon that tied back Harriet's hair, letting it spill in a dark cloud over her shoulders. Leaving her scarlet with confusion, he turned and smiled at Ronnie Acland.

'We haven't met,' he said amiably, 'but I gather you're going to be Mr Noel Balfour Number Two. Or is it Three? I can never keep track.'

Harriet escaped to the kitchen to find Mrs Bottomley red-faced over the duck.

'Whew, it's tense in there,' she said. 'Do you think I have to have lunch with them?'

'Yes,' said Mrs Bottomley. 'Mr E'll expect you to keep an eye on the children. She's very hot on manners, Mrs E.'

'Oh God,' said Harriet. 'By the way, I put some more salt in the soup.'

'So did I,' said Mrs Bottomley.

*   *   *

Lunch for Harriet was a nightmare. Beneath the idle chatter, the tinkle of glasses, the exclamations of pleasure over the food, the ultra-civilized behaviour, lay the jungle.

She was amazed that these people could act as though nothing was the matter, that they could discuss friends, swap gossip, with such apparent amicability.

Noel never stopped talking – the rich, husky voice flowing on and on, about Paris and parties given in her honour and the film she'd been shooting in Africa, and what the man at Cartier's had said about the ring Ronnie had bought her.

Kit, having downed three large dry Martinis on an empty stomach before lunch, was thoroughly enjoying himself.

'Marvellous soup,' he said to Harriet. 'I always think there are two things a woman should do instinctively. And one of them's cooking!'

Noel took a mouthful and immediately asked for a glass of water.

'That's a soup spoon, not a trowel,' she said sharply to Chattie. 'Why do my children always eat as though they were gardening? I suppose it's the influence of television.'

'What a clever woman you'd have been, Noel, if you'd have been to University,' said Kit.

'I hear you hunt a lot,' said Ronnie hastily to Cory, before Noel could think up a crushing reply.

Her beautiful tawny eyes had taken on a dangerous smouldering look, which increased as Ronnie and Cory got into a discussion about different packs. She obviously didn't like to be out of the limelight for a second. When the duck arrived, she took a mouthful and this time immediately asked for the salt and then rained pepper down onto her plate.

Next moment a diversion was caused by the arrival of Sevenoaks, straight from the stream at the bottom of the garden. He greeted Harriet rapturously and then bounded up to Noel. She drew away from him in horror.

'Where did that dreadful beast come from? Look at the mess he's making on the carpet.'

'It's Harriet's dog,' said Cory.

'He needs a bath,' snapped Noel.

'He needs a psychiatrist,' said Cory.

'Is there any orange salad?' Noel asked Harriet, after Sevenoaks had been forcibly removed.

'Quit upstaging, Noel!' said Kit sharply.

Noel glared at him, pushed the food to the side of her plate and lit a cigarette.

'Did I tell you I spent a week in Israel last month?' she said to Cory. 'I've never seen anything like the wild flowers around the Sea of Galilee. And I actually saw the place they fed the five thousand.'

'If you'd spurned your fish and loaves the way you've treated Harriet's much more miraculous duck you'd have been excommunicated, darling,' said Kit.

'It's a pity you're not staying longer, Mummy. You won't see Daddy riding in the point-to-point,' said Chattie.

Noel turned her tawny eyes on Cory.

'But, darling, that's wonderful!' she said. 'You're racing again, after all this time! Might you win?'

Cory shook his head. 'Not a chance. She's only a baby, and it's her first race.'

Noel's eyes lit up. 'Do you remember that race you won the day we got home from our honeymoon? Goodness, how excited we were, and how we celebrated.'

'And what appalling hangovers we had the next day,' said Cory dryly.

'Harriet had a hangover this morning,' said Chattie. 'And she always does when Daddy takes her out, too.'

Noel's face hardened. She looked from Cory to Harriet.

'Come on, Cory, open another bottle,' said Kit. 'The drink's flowing like concrete.'

'What was that marvellous Beaujolais we had when we dined with Jackie Onassis, the night the Aga Khan was there?' Noel asked Ronnie.

'Pick up those names, darling,' drawled Kit, 'you're not impressing anyone.'

Noel flushed angrily. Ronnie turned to Chattie. 'And what are you going to do when you grow up?' he asked.

Chattie beamed at him. 'I'm not going to get married,' she said. 'I might make a habit of it, like Mummy.'

Kit and Ronnie shouted with laughter. Even Cory grinned.

'Ronnie's a fine one to laugh,' said Noel angrily. 'He's had three wives already!'

'His own or other people's?' said Kit.

Harriet felt depression descending on her. She got

up to remove the plates and bring in the pudding. Kit followed her into the kitchen.

'Marvellous party,' he said.

Harriet said nothing.

'Oh, darling, relax, enjoy it. Noel's putting on a command performance.'

'And what about Cory?' said Harriet savagely, clattering plates into the sink.

'You mustn't ever forget that Cory's a writer,' said Kit. 'It's all grist to his mill. This entire lunch will appear in a screen play one day.'

Back in the dining room, Ronnie Acland was doing his best to keep the conversation going.

'How's the latest script?' he asked Cory.

'It's not,' said Cory.

'I enjoyed your last book,' said Kit, refilling everyone's glasses. 'I came across it in a girlfriend's bedroom, and stayed up all afternoon reading it.'

Cory smiled.

'Harriet makes bloody lovely puddings,' said Chattie dreamily, making rivers of cream in her chocolate mousse. 'If you're going to marry Ronnie, Mummy, why can't Daddy marry Harriet?'

There was a frozen pause, then Kit began to laugh. Harriet knocked her wine glass over.

Cory calmly dipped his napkin in the water jug and started sponging the red stain.

'I don't know where you're intending to stay tonight,' he said to Ronnie Acland, 'but a very good hotel's just opened at Bolton Abbey,' and launched into a dissertation on its merits.

Suddenly, there was a faint wail from upstairs.

'Oh, there's William crying,' said Harriet thankfully, leaping to her feet.

Upstairs, Harriet pressed her burning face against the bedroom window. How could Chattie have said that! In front of Noel, too!

Just as she finished feeding William, there was a knock on the door. To her amazement it was Noel.

'I thought I'd leave the men to their port,' she said. 'What a gorgeous baby. May I hold him?'

'He's very tricky with strangers' said Harriet dubiously.

But Noel had already gathered William up in her arms, and had soon reduced him to fits of uncontrollable giggles, tickling him and giving him butterfly kisses with her long, long eyelashes.

How beautiful she is, thought Harriet enviously.

Suddenly Noel stopped tickling William and turned her huge eyes on Harriet. 'Tell me truthfully – how *is* Cory? Did he mind my coming today?'

Harriet was caught off guard.

'Yes he did. Particularly with you bringing Mr Acland.'

'Oh I know I shouldn't have done that,' said Noel. 'But Cory's so off-hand with me these days and, somehow, I felt I wanted to jolt him. I expect you think I'm wicked, but you've no idea how difficult it was being married ten years to a man who's married to his typewriter. And yet, you know, I don't really find other men lastingly attractive,' Noel went on. 'Every affair I've had has really been an attempt to shake Cory into loving me more.'

'But he adores you!' said Harriet amazed.

'Maybe he does in his fashion – but that didn't stop him switching off for hours on end when he was married to me, bashing out those bloody scripts. And he's horribly arrogant. All the Erskine family are the same. You must admit he's tricky to live with.'

She looked at William who snuggled his head against her.

'I wish they were all as easy to cope with as you,' she sighed. 'If only I could be certain I was doing the right thing, divorcing Cory and marrying Ronnie. What do you think I should do?'

'I don't know,' muttered Harriet. She shouldn't talk to me like this, she thought desperately. I don't want to discuss Cory with her.

But Noel hadn't finished turning the screw. 'Do you really think Cory does love me and nobody else?'

Harriet thought for a minute. 'Yes, I do. I think he's being torn to pieces.'

Noel put William down and, smirking slightly, wandered over to Harriet's dressing table. For a minute she examined herself in the mirror, then her eyes lighted on Simon's photograph.

'My, he's pretty. Good God, it's Simon!' She looked at William and, in a flash, put two and two together. 'He's your baby's father?'

Harriet nodded, unable to speak.

'But I know him!' said Noel. 'Very well. He's doing brilliantly. There's even talk of him doing a film with me this summer. And he's this baby's father? Well! Does he know?'

'I wrote to him,' said Harriet.

'Well, he can't have got the letter. He adores children. He's always saying he wants at least ten of his own.'

Harriet's eyes filled with tears. 'Tell me how he is,' she said.

Later, Kit went to sleep on the sofa. Noel and Ronnie took the children out to tea up the valley, Cory shut himself in his study, and Harriet was thankful to be left with the washing-up and her own tangled emotions.

When Noel returned she went into Cory's study, but after a few minutes came out looking like a thundercloud and went upstairs to change. She and Ronnie were going out to dinner.

Eight-thirty found Ronnie pacing up and down the drawing room. 'I don't know if Erskine had this trouble with her,' he said to Kit and Harriet, 'but Noel's incapable of getting anywhere on time. Rather embarrassing. We're dining with friends of my father's. Shouldn't keep that generation waiting.'

Kit was eating potato crisps. 'My advice,' he said, 'is to treat her as you would a nasty boy of ten.'

Cory came in and poured himself a drink. He looked absolutely exhausted.

'How's the script going?' asked Kit.

Cory shrugged his shoulders.

'So so. I spent today crossing out most of what I wrote yesterday. I suppose it's good for the wrist.'

'What's good for the wrist?' came a mocking voice, and Noel walked in.

Harriet heard Cory's sharp intake of breath. Ronnie choked over his cigar.

'Christ!' said Kit.

Noel was wearing a transparent black dress. Only her hips were concealed by a thin layer of ostrich feathers. The rest of her body, including the magnificent breasts, gleamed pearly white through the thin, black material. Her blonde hair was piled up on top of her head, diamonds glittering round her throat, in her ears, on her wrists. She looked staggering.

Kit was the first to recover.

'You look just like a picture I saw outside Raymond's Revue Bar the other day. I didn't know you'd gone into cabaret,' he said.

Ronnie Acland looked dazed. 'Very simple friends of my father's we're going to see, Noel, darling. Is it quite the thing, do you think?' Noel just shrugged.

Kit poured himself another drink. 'I shouldn't worry, Ronnie,' he said. 'That generation expect actresses to look unbelievably tarty.'

Noel's lips tightened. 'Go and fetch my coat, would you, Ronnie?'

She turned to Cory, who was still standing as if turned to stone.

'What do you think of me, my darling?' she said softly.

Cory walked over and stood in front of her, looking her over very slowly. His hands were clenched, a muscle was leaping in his cheek. Only the ticking of the grandfather clock broke the intolerable silence. Then he put out his hand. 'Goodbye, Noel,' he said.

'You don't really mean that,' she said slowly, her yellow eyes blazing.

'Yes, I do, I do, I do,' he said wearily, as though he was trying to convince himself.

'Come on, darling,' said Ronnie Acland, bustling in and knocking over a small table in his haste to get something more substantial round Noel's body. We're embarrassingly late as it is.'

In the hall, Jonah's face was putty-coloured, the tears kept well back. Chattie, in a scarlet dressing gown, had no such reserve. 'Please don't go, Mummy!' she cried, flinging her arms round Noel's legs and bursting into tears.

'I must go,' said Noel, detaching herself gently. 'Careful, or you'll ladder my tights.'

'Oh, Mummy, Mummy,' whispered the choked little voice. 'I can't bear it. When will you come back?'

'I can't say, bebé. You must make the best of it.'

She didn't say another word to Cory, but as she climbed into the huge Rolls-Royce, she turned to Harriet. 'Goodbye, I'll certainly tell Simon I've seen you.'

Chattie began to howl in earnest as soon as Noel had gone.

'Hush darling,' said Harriet, picking her up. 'You'll see her again soon.'

Cory went into his study and slammed the door behind him.

I wish I could comfort him as easily as Chattie, thought Harriet.

Kit left soon after Noel. He handed her his

telephone number and address in London. 'If you get into any difficulties, ring me. I'm worried about Cory, but you're a warm, lovely girl and I've a feeling you're going to be the one to get hurt the most.'

Cory refused any supper, and Harriet, feeling exhausted, went to bed early, but found she couldn't sleep. She tried to work out exactly what she felt about Simon. But he seemed to have become a shadowy figure, and her thoughts kept straying back to Cory, and the hell he must be going through.

Oh, why can't I fall for straightforward men who fall in love with me, she thought miserably.

About midnight, the storm broke. Lightning brighter than day, followed immediately by great poundings of thunder. Wandering down the landing to see if the children were all right, Harriet heard the sound of crying coming from Jonah's room. She went in and turned on the light.

'It's only thunder, darling,' she said taking him in her arms. He was such a reserved child that it took several minutes before she discovered it wasn't the storm that was upsetting him. He was sick with misery about Noel and Cory.

'I know it's beastly,' said Harriet. 'Of course, it doesn't matter a scrap about crying. Everyone cries about things like this, and you've been terribly brave up till now.'

Jonah gave a sniff. 'You think so?'

'Yes, I do. You're like your father. He's very brave, too.'

'Then why does my mother want to marry that awful man? What's my father done wrong that my mother doesn't like him any more?'

'He hasn't done anything wrong. People just stop loving people sometimes. Like you cooling off people you've been very friendly with the term before at school, and now you can't see what you saw in them.'

Jonah looked dubious. 'Is it the same?'

'In a way. It happened to me with William's father. I loved him so much, but he still stopped loving me. But not because I'd done anything wrong.'

'*You* won't go away, will you?' said Jonah.

Harriet shook her head.

'Perhaps you could marry Daddy, like Chattie suggested,' he added hopefully.

'He doesn't want to, and the same thing would probably happen all over again. People should only marry people they love.'

A shadow fell across the bed. Harriet looked up in embarrassment to see Cory standing there.

'Hullo,' said Jonah.

'I'll go and get some hot chocolate to make you sleep,' said Harriet, fleeing from the room. When she got back upstairs, Jonah was nearly asleep.

'Don't go,' he muttered drowsily. 'Both stay, Harriet's not very happy either, Daddy. I think you should look after her.'

Harriet suddenly felt the tears trickling down her cheeks. She sat down on the bed, and turned her face away so Jonah shouldn't see her. Then she felt Cory's hand, warm and dry, over hers.

She didn't move, breathlessly aware of how close he was to her. And she was filled with a brazen, shameless longing to be closer still. She looked away, dumb and stricken, afraid that he might read the lust in her eyes.

'He's asleep,' said Cory.

Harriet got clumsily to her feet and, without speaking, went out of the room. Cory caught up with her outside his bedroom, put his hand on her shoulder and pulled her round to face him. The light from the bedroom lit up his face, and Harriet noticed how old and tired he looked suddenly.

Oh, poor, poor Cory, she thought.

'It's so bloody for you,' she said in a choked voice.

'And for you, too,' he said gently and, quite naturally he pulled her into his arms.

'Don't cry, little Harriet.'

She melted.

'Don't cry,' he went on. 'It's crazy to go on like this, when we both need each other. Come on, little one. You'll see, I'll make everything all right for you.'

And Harriet knew with a sudden, blinding intensity of grief how much she loved him.

But I can't take it again, she told herself in panic. It's no good falling again for a man who doesn't love me, who this time, is absolutely mad about someone else.

For a second she trembled violently in his arms, then she moved away.

'It's no good,' she gasped, 'you can't just take me like aspirin to deaden your pain for a few hours. It'll come back worse than ever afterwards.'

'Not always. Sometimes you wake up and find the pain's gone altogether.'

But she bolted down the passage to her room, and cried until dawn, because she realized she'd failed him when he needed her most, and that being Cory he'd never lower his guard again.

Chapter Twenty

The atmosphere in the house was so highly charged that it was almost a relief when Cory got a cable next day from MGM to fly out to the States at once. Tadpole drooped when he saw the suitcases coming out, and went and sat in one of them looking utterly miserable. Harriet knew how he felt. At least Cory was unlikely to be gone more than a fortnight, as he wanted to get back in time to ride Python in the point-to-point.

Once he'd gone, Harriet missed him terribly. She had got so used to having him around, to turn to for help and advice; she felt completely lost. For the millionth time, she kicked herself for rejecting him.

Chattie soon cheered up after Noel had left. Cory had finally relented and bought her a bicycle, and all her energies were employed in learning to ride it. Jonah on the other hand seemed very pulled down; he refused to eat, and complained of headaches.

The day after he left was Mrs Bottomley's day off.

'I must put something in the *Craven Herald*,' she said, walking into the kitchen in her purple turban and musquash coat.

'Whatever for?' said Harriet listlessly.

'It's ten years now since Mr Bottomley passed on,' said Mrs Bottomley solemnly. 'I always put something in the *In Memoriam* column. It seems fitting.'

'Of course,' thought Harriet. 'Loving remembrances to dear Gran, who certainly wasn't an also ran, from Dad and Mum and all the family.'

'Mr Cory usually writes it for me,' grumbled Mrs Bottomley, 'but he went off in such a hurry.'

'Is Mr Bottomley staying in God's spare room now?' inquired Chattie, who was very interested in death.

'I expect so,' said Harriet hastily.

'Lucky thing. He'll have biscuits in a tin by his bed. Do you think one has to clean one's teeth in heaven?'

'Perhaps you could put in the same verse you used last year,' said Harriet.

'Folk would notice,' said Mrs Bottomley, 'I'll have to think up something myself. Cheerio everyone,' and, humming Rock of Ages, she set out for the bus stop.

Harriet picked up a pile of ironing and went upstairs. She'd have to get William up in a minute. Suddenly she heard a terrible moaning from Jonah's room. Dropping the ironing and rushing in, she found him lying on the bed, white faced, clutching his head.

'I've got these terrible, terrible pains,' he moaned.

Harriet took his temperature. It was 103, he was pouring with sweat.

The doctor came at lunchtime and said there was a lot of 'flu about, and prescribed antibiotics.

'Sponge him down if he gets too hot. He should be better tomorrow.'

Jonah, in fact, seemed better by the afternoon. His headache had gone and he was hungry. He wolfed all the boiled chicken, mashed potato and ice-cream Harriet brought him.

'You wouldn't, no I'm sure you wouldn't,' he said as she took the tray away.

'What?' said Harriet.

'Play a game of Monopoly.'

'Sevenoaks has eaten Old Kent Road and May-fair.'

'I'll make some new cards,' said Jonah. 'Can we play for 10p?'

Then, just as they were about to start playing, Jonah was violently sick. By the time Harriet had cleaned up and changed the sheets, he was much worse; his temperature had shot up to 106, he was burning hot and screaming about the pain in his head.

At that moment William chose to wake up from his afternoon rest, and Chattie, as usual wandering round without shoes, stubbed her toe on the corner of Jonah's bed, and burst into noisy sobs.

'Oh please be quiet, all of you,' screamed Harriet, her nerves already in shreds.

She rushed downstairs to ring the doctor. Dr Burnett was on his rounds, said the recording machine; if she left a message they would get in touch with her as soon as possible. She tried Dr Rowbotham and got the same answer. It was such a lovely day, they were probably both out playing golf.

She waited half-an-hour; no-one rang back. William was bellowing to be fed. Chattie charged about trying to be helpful and getting in the way. Sevenoaks, having decided it was time for a walk, lay across the landing moaning piteously. Jonah was thrashing on the bed now groaning in anguish, chattering, deliriously, about coachmen and the horses not being ready in time.

In despair Harriet rang Elizabeth Pemberton. She could hear bridge party noises in the background. She could imagine them all stuffing themselves with chocolate cake, and tearing everyone to shreds.

'Yes,' said Elizabeth unhelpfully.

'Cory's gone to the States. Mrs Bottomley's out. I think Jonah's very ill. He's complaining of pains in his head. I can't get hold of Dr Rowbotham or Dr Burnett. Can you suggest anyone else?'

'I'll have a think,' said Elizabeth. 'I'm awfully tied up at the moment, Harriet.'

'Bugger you,' she was saying, thought Harriet.

'Try Dr Melhuish in Gargrave,' said Elizabeth. 'He's old-fashioned but very reliable. Ring back later if you need any help.'

Dr Melhuish was also on his rounds. She could hear Jonah screaming with pain. Harriet took a deep breath and dialled 999.

'I'm stuck in the house with a baby and two children, and the boy's seriously ill. I think he's got brain damage or something. Please can you help?'

She was trying so hard not to cry, she had great trouble telling them the address.

'Don't worry, luv,' came the reassuring Yorkshire accent, 'we'll be over in a minute.'

She was just getting down Jonah's suitcase, trying to dress William, comfort Chattie and not fall over Sevenoaks, when the telephone rang again.

It was Sammy.

'What's happening?'

'Jonah's ill. I've rung for an ambulance.'

'Good for you. I'll come straight over. We'll take Chattie and William. Yes, of course we can. We'll manage. You must go with Jonah.'

'What will Elizabeth say?'

'She can stuff herself,' said Sammy. 'She won't be looking after them anyway. Keep smiling. I'll be right over.'

Harriet charged round gathering up pyjamas, toothpaste, an old teddy bear, Jonah's favourite *Just William* book. She wanted to write a note to Mrs Bottomley, but she couldn't find a biro. Cory always whipped them all to write with.

Sammy arrived with the ambulance, her round face full of concern.

'I got away as soon as I could, the unfeeling bitch and her bridge parties. I'll sort out the bottles, the nappies, and Mrs Bottomley. Don't you worry about a thing.'

Two ambulance men, who had camp voices and left-of-centre partings, came down the stairs with Jonah on a stretcher.

He was quieter now. Sammy smiled down at his white pain-racked face.

'Poor old love, you do look poorly. Never mind, the

nurses'll make you better. I'll bring you a present tomorrow.'

'Can I sleep in the same bed as Georgie?' said Chattie.

'How old is Cory?' said the doctor at the hospital.

'Thirty-four,' said Harriet.

The doctor raised his eyebrows.

'Oh I'm sorry. Cory's only his first name. We call him Jonah. He's eight.'

The doctor underlined the word Jonah with a fountain pen and went on to ask her a lot of questions – when did Jonah first sit up and walk? Had he had all his injections? – none of which she could answer.

Then they were taken down endless passages into a room with one bed. Everything was covered in cellophane; the nurses came in in masks.

'Just a precaution until we find out what it is,' said one of the nurses.

It was a nice little room. On the blind was painted a village street with dogs and cats and people buying from a market stall. The church clock stood at three o'clock; a chimney sweep was cleaning an immaculate chimney; children looked out of the window. Harriet gazed mindlessly at it as she waited for the results of Jonah's lumbar puncture.

Thoughts of typhoid, smallpox, polio chased themselves relentlessly round her head. Oh God, don't let him die.

Jonah's blond hair was dark with sweat but he seemed calmer. Harriet bent over him, sponging his forehead.

'Your tits are too low in that blouse,' he said with a weak grin.

'I didn't have time to put on a bra,' said Harriet.

Half an hour later, the nurses took off their gowns and masks. Much later a specialist arrived. He was a tall man with untidy grey hair, scurf all over his collar, who stank of body odour.

'We think it's early meningitis,' he said. 'We've found far too many white corpuscles in the fluid, but that's not too much to worry about unless there's a growth. But I think you should notify the boy's parents.'

Then followed the hassle of trying to find where Cory was in America.

Harriet tried very hard not to show Jonah how panicky she felt. The only thing that sustained her was the thought of talking to Cory on the telephone. Never had she needed him so badly.

She was frustrated, however, at every turn. Cory's agent in London had closed his office for the weekend and couldn't be found at home. She hadn't enough money to dial the number Cory left her in New York. Noel's agent said she'd gone to Paris for the weekend, was due back on Tuesday but had left no forwarding address. A queue of large swollen ladies in quilted dressing gowns from the Maternity Ward were waiting to use the telephone and starting to mutter. In desperation she rung Elizabeth Pemberton, who promised rather unwillingly to see what she could do. Afterwards Harriet had a word with Chattie. Her heart was wrung listening to the choked little voice:

'Elizabeth asked me if I used a dry brush or a wet brush to do my teeth. I wasn't thinking. I said dry. It was horrid. Everyone's gone away, Daddy, Mummy, Jonah, you. I do miss you, Harriet.'

As the night nurses came in Jonah grew increasingly worse; his temperature shot up to 106 again. He couldn't keep any of the antibiotics down. He kept asking for water, but every time he drank he was violently sick. Soon he became delirious, crying for Noel, for Cory, shouting out about the black coachman who was coming to get him. Harriet kept hoping he'd gone to sleep, then his eyes would open and he'd groan. On other occasions he'd drop off, then wake up, be all right for a few seconds, and the pain would take over.

Harriet clung on to his hot dry hand and wondered how she'd get through the night.

Chapter Twenty-one

The noise of the floor-polisher was like sandpaper on her brain; the bleep of a doctor's walkie-talkie made her jump out of her skin. After twenty-four hours in hospital with no sleep, she seemed to have Jonah's head – even the slightest sound, running water, the air conditioner, seemed to be magnified a thousand-fold.

Jonah was no better. He had kept nothing down. In between bouts of delirium he complained of a stiff neck.

'No-one's trying to make me better,' he groaned. 'You're all trying to kill me.'

Harriet was very near to breaking. She had been unable to locate Cory or Noel. She had not slept at all, and she had taken against the new day nurse, Sister Maddox, who was a snooty, good-looking redhead with a school prefect manner. I've got twenty-five other children to see to in this ward, so don't waste my time, she seemed to say.

'We've seen much worse than Jonah, I can tell you,' she said briskly as she checked his pulse.

'Dying, dying, dying,' intoned Jonah like a Dalek.

'Now pull yourself together, young man,' she said.

'We're trying to make you better.'

She looked out through the glass partition at a group that was coming down the passage. Hastily she patted her hair and straightened her belt. Harriet understood why when the Houseman Dr Williams entered. He was by any standards good-looking: tall, dark, with classical features, and cold grey eyes behind thick horn-rimmed spectacles. Sister Maddox became the picture of fluttering deference as he examined Jonah and looked at the temperature charts.

He glanced at Harriet without interest, making her acutely aware of her shiny unmade-up face, sweat-stained shirt and dirty hair.

'Hasn't kept anything down,' he said. 'Probably have to put up a drip soon.'

'Can't he have anything to stop the pain?' protested Harriet.

'Not till we can locate what's causing it,' said Dr Williams in a bored voice. 'He'll have to sweat it out.'

Harriet followed him into the passage. 'He's not going to die, is he?' she said in a trembling voice. 'I mean, how ill is he?'

'Well, he's seriously ill,' said Dr Williams, 'but he's not on the danger list yet.'

Harriet went off and cried in the lavatory. Sister Maddox was talking to Dr Williams as she came out.

'I'll see you at eight o'clock then, Ruth,' he was saying.

'Handsome, isn't he?' said a junior nurse.

Yes, thought Harriet, and he knows it.

*   *   *

When she got back, Jonah was awake and screaming with pain.

'Everyone's gone away. You left me, you left me. Where's Daddy? I want to *see* him.'

Suddenly she had a brain wave. She would ring Kit. The next time Jonah fell asleep, she went and called him. He took so long to answer she nearly rang off.

'Were you in bed?' she said.

'Naturally,' said Kit. 'It's lunchtime!'

She told him about Jonah's meningitis and that she still couldn't raise Noel or Cory. She tried to be calm, but hysteria kept breaking through her voice.

'I wouldn't bother about Noel, darling; she's not likely to be of help to anyone, but I'll get hold of Cory for you, don't worry. If I can't find him by tomorrow, I'll drive up myself. Jonah'll pull through. The Erskines are a pretty tough bunch.'

Another day and night limped by. Jonah woke at 1.30 in the morning screaming for Noel. Harriet felt her self-control snapping as the nurse trotted out the same platitudes about having to get worse before he got better.

He woke again at five and at seven. Another day to get through, thought Harriet, as the sun filtered in through the blind. It seemed like midnight. She must know every inch of that village scene now. She was weak with exhaustion; her eyes were red and felt as though they were full of gravel. Neuralgia travelled round her head, one moment headache, then tooth-ache, then earache.

It was impossible to keep Jonah quiet. Reading aloud was too loud, sponging his head was too painful.

'Where's the doctor, where's the doctor?' he screamed.

'He'll be here soon,' said Harriet soothingly, but the very word 'soon' had become meaningless. Mrs Bottomley popped in to see him, and went away looking shattered.

'Poor little lamb, lying between death and life,' she said telephoning Sammy when she got home. 'Still where there's life . . .'

She brought Harriet a change of clothes – a tweed skirt, which Harriet hated, a brown jersey that sagged round the waist, and a cream shirt that had no buttons.

Might as well stay in jeans, thought Harriet.

Eventually at mid-day Dr Williams rolled up, yawning and rubbing his eyes. Too much Sister Maddox, thought Harriet.

'You've got to do something,' she pleaded in desperation. 'I don't think he can take much more.'

Jonah started to scream out about the pain killing him.

'Hush, darling,' said Harriet. 'The doctor's here.'

'And you can shut up,' said Jonah, turning round and bashing her in the face with his hand, 'Shut up! Shut up! You're all trying to kill me.'

'He's losing faith in all of you,' said Harriet with a sob.

Dr Williams drew her outside.

'The child is getting too demanding,' he said. 'He's playing you up and you're overreacting. He senses your panic and it panics him too. I suppose his parents will turn up eventually. How long is it since you ate?'

'I don't know,' said Harriet.

'Well, go downstairs and have something.'

Down in the canteen, Harriet spread marmalade on toast the consistency of a flannel. All round her nurses were gossiping and chattering about their lives. They all ought to be upstairs making Jonah better. Sister Maddox and Dr Williams obviously felt she was hopeless and hysterical and were trying to keep her away from Jonah. She mustn't get paranoiac. She mustn't build up a hatred.

Upstairs she found Jonah having his temperature taken, the thermometer sticking out of his mouth like a cigar. With his slitty eyes and his hair brushed off his forehead, he suddenly looked very like Cory. Oh, I love him, I love him, she thought.

As the afternoon wore on he grew more and more incoherent, and difficult to quiet, now semi-conscious, now screaming with pain.

'Daddy, Daddy, I want Daddy. I don't want you, I want Mummy,' he shouted. 'Why can't I have a Mummy? Everyone else at school does.' He struggled free from the blankets. 'I want Daddy.'

'You shall have him very soon. Kit's finding him.'

'I want him *now*.'

Oh so do I, thought Harriet.

She hoped Jonah was falling asleep, but just as she tried to move away, she found him gazing at her in horror, trying to bring her face into focus.

'Harriet! Oh it's you. Don't leave me!'

'Of course I won't.'

'I'm so thirsty.' The hands clutching her were hot, dry and emaciated.

'This isn't my room. Why am I here? I want to go home.'

Dr Williams came back in around six. He looked even more bored.

'We're going to put up a drip now. He can't take anything orally and obviously isn't responding to treatment.'

A junior nurse popped her head round the door.

'There's a Kit Erskine on the telephone for you in Sister's office,' she said to Harriet.

'Darling Harriet, are you all right?' said Kit. 'I gather from the nurse Jonah's not too bright. Don't worry, I got a message through to Cory. He's on location, but he's flying back tonight. He should be with you tomorrow afternoon. I've left a message for Superbitch too. All that rubbish about a weekend in Paris was absolute crap. She's been frantically losing weight at a health farm, so she may descend on you too, I'm afraid.'

Harriet didn't care about Noel. That Cory was coming back was all she could think about.

The drip was up when she got back, a great bag of liquid seeping into Jonah's arm. He was delirious most of the time now, his cheeks hectically flushed, his pulse racing. In the end they had to strap his arm down, as the needle kept slipping and blood came racing back down the tube.

Sammy arrived next with Chattie. 'It's long past her bedtime but she wanted to come.' Sammy brought Jonah a book about Tarzan, Chattie a balloon she'd bought out of her own pocket money.

'William's fine,' said Sammy. 'Chattie and I've been looking after him, haven't we?' Harriet felt guilty yet relieved they hadn't brought him; her well-springs of affection seemed to have dried up. 'Elizabeth's been the last straw,' Sammy went on, 'telling all her friends how she'd taken the baby and Chattie in to help Cory out.'

Chattie seemed quite cheerful, but she hugged Harriet very tightly. 'Can I see Jonah?'

'Yes, of course,' said Harriet, 'but whisper and don't worry if he's not quite himself.'

Unfortunately, just as Chattie was walking into the room, the balloon popped. Jonah woke up with a start and, not recognizing any of them, started raving incoherently about monsters coming to get him.

'I'll stay with him,' said Sammy. 'You take Chattie down to the canteen for an ice-cream.'

Chattie charmed everyone, her long blonde hair swinging as she skipped about the canteen talking to all the nurses. Then suddenly she clung to Harriet, her eyes filling with tears.

'He's not going to die, is he?'

'Of course he isn't,' said Harriet, hugging her, but feeling inside a sickening lack of conviction.

'I heard Mrs Bottomley telling Sammy it could go either way. What does that mean?'

'Nothing really,' said Harriet.

'If he died he'd go to heaven wouldn't he?' said Chattie.

'Of course he would,' said Harriet, 'but he's not going to.'

'Then I'll never see him again,' said Chattie, 'because I'm so naughty, I'll go straight to hell.' She broke into noisy sobs.

Harriet cuddled her, trying to keep control of herself. 'Darling, of course you'll go to heaven.'

'I don't really believe in heaven anyway,' sobbed Chattie. 'I've been up in the sky in an aeroplane, and I didn't see it.'

Harriet sat biting her nails watching two very young nurses fiddling with the Heath Robinson equipment constituting the drip. Bubbles were streaming down the tube, as they tapped away and the needle kept slipping out of the proper place. Jonah lay in a rare moment of consciousness, the tears pouring down his cheeks.

Harriet turned to the nurses, her control snapping. 'Why the bloody hell,' she snapped, 'can't one of you make it work?'

As a result, Dr Williams gave her a talking-to.

'We're going to give you a mogadon tonight,' he said. 'We know you feel responsible with both the parents away, but you *must* pull yourself together. You only upset him by screaming at the nurses; they're doing their best.'

'But why can't he have proper pain killers and sedatives? If he felt you were doing something to make him better, I know he'd relax and stop fighting you.'

'Jonah's a very brave child, Miss Poole,' said Dr Williams coldly. 'It's you who can't take the pain, not him.'

'He's very very ill isn't he?' said Harriet. She had heard the nurses talking about the intensive care unit.

'He's certainly not a well child,' said Dr Williams, 'but where there's life there's hope.'

By midnight Jonah had gone into a coma. Harriet had pretended to take her mogadon, but had thrown it down the lavatory. She sat hour after hour fighting exhaustion and despair, listening to his heavy breathing, holding his hand and praying. Through the glass panel, she could see the black night nurse moving round the wards, adjusting blankets, checking pulses. In a minute she'd be coming into Harriet's room to change the drip. This time tomorrow Cory would be here. How could she face him if anything happened to Jonah? She put her head in her hands and wept.

She must have fallen asleep. When she woke up it was nearly light. Jonah lay motionless in bed. For a terrifying moment, Harriet thought he was dead. She felt his forehead; it was cold; he was still breathing faintly.

Getting to her feet, she ran into the passage to the sister's office.

'Jonah, he's breathing so quietly now,' she stammered. 'He looks so peaceful, as though he was d-dying.'

The black nurse got up and took Harriet's arm. 'I'll come and see.' She felt his pulse, and took his temperature. She turned to Harriet, a great white toothy smile splitting her face.

'I think he's over the crisis,' she said. 'He's breathing quite normally and his pulse rate's coming down.'

Harriet turned away, her shoulders shaking.

'There, there,' said the nurse. 'I'll get you a cup of tea, then you can get some sleep.'

Harriet didn't trust doctors and nurses; she knew they lied. For all she knew Jonah was still in danger. She sat by his bed until breakfast time, as plastic bag after plastic bag dripped into his arm, listening to the heavy breathing getting slower and more even, the restless movements growing quieter.

Sister Maddox came on at eight, looking as ice-cool and elegant as ever.

'Good morning. How's the patient?' she said briskly. 'I expect you had a nice sleep with that mogadon. I envy you. I didn't get to bed till four o'clock.'

She picked up Jonah's chart. His temperature and pulse ratings were right down.

'Well, that is better,' she said. 'I hope you appreciate Dr Williams a bit more now.'

'Jonah hasn't come round yet,' said Harriet sulkily. She knew she was being ungracious.

'He's getting a much-needed rest,' said Sister Maddox. 'I wouldn't fuss him any more if I were you. I'd go and have some breakfast.'

Instead Harriet tried to concentrate on an old copy of *Reader's Digest*. It pays to improve your ward power, she said to herself. She felt absolutely all in. She hardly recognized her grey face in the mirror. She wished she could wash her hair and have a bath before Cory came, but she was too scared to leave Jonah until she knew he was out of danger.

The specialist arrived at eleven and didn't appear altogether happy. 'He's not out of the woods yet,' he said. 'Let me know when he regains consciousness.'

Back came the panic, the terrifying fears. Oh don't let him die, prayed Harriet.

Quarter of an hour later came Dr Williams, even more unreceptive than usual, as Harriet bombarded him with questions about Jonah's condition.

'But he is going to get better, isn't he?' she said in desperation.

'Really, Miss Poole,' said Sister Maddox, 'Dr Williams has got a hundred and one other people to look after.'

'I'm sorry,' insisted Harriet, 'but Jonah's father's due after lunch and he'll want to know exactly what the score is.'

'Oh, he rang ten minutes ago,' said Sister Maddox.

Harriet went white. 'What did he say? Why didn't you let me speak to him?'

'You were in the loo or making a cup of coffee,' said Sister Maddox. 'I didn't think it was that important.'

'But you could have got me. You must have known I'd want to talk to him.'

'And you must realize that Sister Maddox has

better things to do than acting as a switchboard for all the patients' relations. You must realize Jonah isn't the only child in the hospital,' snapped Dr Williams.

'But he's the only child here belonging to me,' shouted Harriet.

'Have I come to the right place,' said a deep throbbing vice. They all turned round. There in the doorway making the perfect stage entrance smothered in a huge black fur hat stood Noel Balfour.

'Oh yes, I have,' she said seeing Jonah, and walked quickly towards the bed.

'Oh my precious, precious darling,' she said with a break in her voice.

And suddenly exactly on cue, Jonah stirred, sighed and opened his eyes, for a moment he looked at Noel incredulously.

'Mummy,' he croaked weakly.

Harriet felt once more the explosion of jealousy as Jonah's pale face lit up.

'Mummy, is it really you?'

'Yes, it is, my darling. What a dreadful, dreadful time you've had.' She brushed the dank blond hair back from his forehead.

'My arm's sore,' muttered Jonah.

'I know, darling,' said Noel, 'it's that horrid drip, but it's making you so much better every minute, so I know you'll be brave about it. Because these kind nurses and doctors have been working so hard to make you well.'

'I feel better,' said Jonah, 'but my head's still sore,' and, sighing, he drifted back to sleep. Noel

241

bent and kissed him on the forehead, aware that she made a most touching sight. Hardly a dry eye in the room, thought Harriet. Everyone was gaping in admiration.

Noel stood up and looked round. Pulling off her fur hat and running a careless hand through her blonde hair, so that it fell perfectly into shape, she smiled with dazzling wistfulness at the nurses, then turned her headlamp stare on Dr Williams who was blushing like a schoolgirl.

She held out a hand. 'My name's Noel Balfour,' she said, as if everyone didn't know it.

'We didn't know you were his mother,' said Sister Maddox, looking rather shaken.

'I don't expect Harriet thought it important,' said Noel. 'Not when Jonah's life was at stake. How is my son, Doctor?'

'Well it's been touch and go, but it looks as though he'll pull through now.'

'How long has he been here?'

'Four days now.'

'*Four days!* Why wasn't I told before?' Noel collapsed on a chair, and got out a cigarette with a trembling hand, letting her fur coat fall open to display her magnificent bosom.

Dr Williams leapt forward with a lighter.

'We tried to find you,' protested Harriet. 'They said you were in Paris, but they didn't know where.'

'It was the studio trying to protect me,' said Noel. 'I escaped to Paris to learn a part. And you've been all by yourself, poor Harriet. What you must have been through! I'm sure she's been wonderful.'

Dr Williams gave a chilly smile. 'Miss Poole takes her responsibility as a nanny very seriously.'

Noel, instantly detecting tension, looked from one to the other.

'Where's Cory?' she asked Harriet.

'He's on his way back from the States,' said Harriet.

'He rang to say he'd be here this afternoon,' added Sister Maddox.

'Oh thank God,' said Noel, 'thank God we can give him good news. Let me sit with him for a bit, Harriet,' she went on. 'Go and have a cup of tea and get some rest. You look so tired.'

Dropping with fatigue, black-ringed beneath the eyes, greasy-haired, and wearing the wrong length skirt, Harriet was only too well aware of the contrast she must make to Noel.

As she went listlessly down to the canteen she knew she'd been outmanoeuvred. No doubt at this moment Dr Williams was telling Noel how stroppy she'd been with the nurses, and what a bad influence she was on Jonah. And this afternoon Cory would be back, and the first thing he'd find was Noel looking stunning by the bedside. Suddenly she felt twitchy and threatened.

Chapter Twenty-two

Noel, like all charming people, was totally dependent on the approval and admiration of others. When she sensed disapproval, she merely moved on to fresh conquests. She only liked to live in the sunshine. Her effect on the hospital was dramatic. Suddenly every doctor and nurse in the building seemed to find an excuse to pop in and check Jonah's condition. The passage outside was like Paddington Station.

'The poor little lad took a turn for the better the moment his mother arrived,' Harriet heard one nurse saying to another as they added ice-cream scoops of potato to the roast lamb on the supper trays.

'Isn't she lovely, and so natural?' said the other. ' "Nurse you must be so tired," she said, "Thank you for saving my baby's life." Which is more than the complaints we got from that . . .' They stopped abruptly when they saw Harriet.

'Did you see her shoes?' said one.

'Weren't they lovely? And her hair. And did you see the way her face lit up when she heard her husband was coming? Such a shame they're splitting up. She's obviously still in love with him. Perhaps this'll bring them together again.'

The most dramatic change was in Dr Williams's behaviour. Usually one couldn't see him for dust the moment he'd done his rounds, but now Noel was ensconced, he was looking in every five minutes. Harriet knew he was off duty that day at three o'clock, but he was still hanging around at five. The compelling, cold, surgical grey eyes were quite moony now, the bored voice husky and caressing. Harriet even caught a waft of aftershave.

He was very concerned that Noel hadn't had any lunch. But there was no suggestion that she might go down to the canteen for a cup of tea, Irish stew and carrots. A quarter of an hour later, smoked salmon sandwiches and iced white wine appeared.

'Isn't he wonderful?' Noel said to Harriet. 'So considerate and so concerned about Jonah.'

'It's only since you've been here,' said Harriet sulkily. 'He's been a pig up till now.'

One of the day nurses popped her head round the door.

'I was just going off duty, Miss Balfour. I wondered if I could have your autograph.'

'Tell me your name,' said Noel, taking the piece of paper.

'Nurse Rankin,' said the nurse.

'No. I know you're Nurse Rankin. I mean your christian name.'

Nurse Rankin giggled. 'Actually it's Dorothy. But everyone calls me Dotty.'

'To Dotty with great pleasure, love and gratitude,'

wrote Noel in her huge scrawl. 'I think Dotty's a lovely name. Imagine what it was like being christened Noel. People were always making jokes about the first Noel.'

'I've seen all your pictures,' said Nurse Rankin, a slave to sudden passion. 'I think you're absolutely wonderful.'

'And I can never thank you enough for what you've done for my little boy.'

Lay it on with a trowel, thought Harriet in disgust.

'Everything all right?' It was Dr Williams popping in again.

'Absolutely marvellous,' said Noel, turning her startling tawny eyes on him. 'You are a saint, David.'

David now, thought Harriet. He was looking exactly like Sevenoaks when Mytton's bitch was on heat.

'I haven't managed all the sandwiches,' said Noel, 'I'm feeling too upset to eat, but the wine is delicious. Won't you have some?'

'Not when I'm on duty,' he said, 'but I'd love one later.'

Harriet's only comfort was that Sister Maddox was looking absolutely furious.

When Noel heard that Chattie and William were staying at the Pembertons', she went off and had a long telephone conversation with Elizabeth.

When she returned her attitude was distinctly less friendly towards Harriet. Oh God, I bet Elizabeth mentioned something about my being wrapped round Cory at the Hunt Ball, thought Harriet.

Noel's main preoccupation now seemed to be to get her out of the hospital before Cory came back.

'I really don't feel we can dump William and Chattie on Elizabeth any longer,' she said, 'particularly when William's teething and keeping them up every night. I think you should go and collect them, and take them home.'

'Sammy really doesn't mind looking after them,' said Harriet. 'I would like to stay here with Jonah, just another night.'

'Are you quite sure you're the best person?' said Noel gently. 'People here seem to think you're rather – well – overemotional.'

'I l-love him,' stammered Harriet. 'I was worried.'

'I quite realize that, but you must remember you're well, only . . .'

'The nanny.' Harriet felt herself going very red in the face.

'Exactly,' said Noel, pouring herself another glass of wine. 'And it's your duty to go home and look after Chattie and William, so I'd like you to pack your things at once, and my driver will take you home, and you can collect the children on the way.'

'But Mr Erskine left me in charge of the children. I'm sure he'd want me to stay.'

Noel lost her temper.

'I've been married to Cory for ten years. I think I know him slightly better than you. The thing he'll like best when he arrives is to find me here with Jonah.'

Harriet was beaten. She went next door and began to gather up her things. She heard Jonah waking up

247

again and complaining that his head ached, and could he have some iced water. Noel poked her head through the door.

'Could you just pop down and get me some ice,' she said.

Running the tray under the tap to get out the ice cubes, Harriet suddenly thought she'd burst if she didn't see Cory. I hate Noel, I hate her, I hate her.

Then soon she heard a quick step in the passage and there was Cory walking past. Her heart lurched. She tried to call out to him, but her voice stuck in her throat. She went out into the passage. It required the greatest control of her life not to run after him.

As it was, she reached the door in time to see Noel leaping to her feet. The next moment Cory had taken her in his arms and was comforting her as she sobbed with great restraint, but not enough to spoil her make-up. I can't bear it, thought Harriet, her nails digging into her hands.

She saw Cory let Noel go, and move forward to speak to Jonah. She tiptoed forward trying to hear what he was saying.

But Sister Maddox was too quick for her. The faster Noel transferred her attentions to Cory and got her claws out of Dr Williams the better.

'I think the family would all like a little time on their own,' she said firmly. 'The porter downstairs has just rung up to say the car's waiting for you.'

Harriet went into the side room, and mindlessly put the rest of her things into the canvas bag Mrs Bottomley had brought.

Then she heard Jonah say, 'Where's Harriet?' And Cory saying, 'Yes, where is she?'

'I'm here,' said Harriet, pushing open the door.

Cory was sitting on the bed holding Jonah's hand. Harriet expected him to be pale and drawn. But he was tanned dark brown by the Los Angeles sun. Never had he seemed more handsome – or more beyond her reach. He looked up quickly, full of concern. 'My God, what you must have been through! I'm sorry I wasn't here.'

'I'm so glad you've come now,' she muttered, fighting back the tears.

'All I can say is thank you,' he said. 'Sit down. You look absolutely knackered. Are you up to telling me something about it?'

'My driver's waiting to take her home, Cory,' said Noel in icy tones. 'She's been here for four days. She needs a break. And she's going to collect Chattie and William. Elizabeth's looking after them but we can't leave them with her for ever.'

Cory didn't turn round.

Jonah, still drowsy, suddenly said, 'Where's Mummy?'

'Here darling,' said Noel, going towards the bed.

'Where's Harriet?' muttered Jonah.

'She's going home, darling.'

'No,' said Jonah, sitting bolt upright, suddenly hysterical, 'I don't want her to go home. I want her to stay. I want Harriet! I want Harriet!'

'But *I'm* here,' snapped Noel, her lips tightening.

'But you won't stay,' he screamed in desperation.

249

'You only say you'll stay, then you go. Harriet stays all the time.'

He started to cry.

Cory took him by the shoulders, and gently eased him back on the pillow. 'It's all right, old boy. Harriet's not going anywhere.'

He turned to Noel. 'I took the precaution of getting Kit to find us a temporary nanny. She came up in the plane with me. She took the taxi home. She's going to look after William and Chattie. I thought as you'd seen the whole thing through you'd probably want to stay with Jonah,' he added to Harriet.

'Oh, yes please,' she whispered.

'But Cory,' began Noel. 'Can we have a brief word?'

Harriet retreated into the side room shutting the door. She was shaking like a leaf. No doubt Noel was telling Cory what a disaster she'd been with all the nurses and doctors. She caught the word 'hysterical' several times, and then Noel was saying in acid tones, 'She complained about Dr Williams, but honestly he couldn't have been kinder, popping in every five minutes, solicitude and kindness itself. She's obviously the sort of girl that gets people's backs up.'

Harriet couldn't hear Cory's reply. She collapsed on the bed, holding her clenched fists against her forehead in a desperate attempt to gain control.

A minute later Cory came in, shut the door behind him and sat down on the bed. Her whole body was shaken with sobs.

'It's all right, little one,' he said gently, stroking her hair. 'I know what you've been through.'

'And I know I'm bad for Jonah at the moment,' she sobbed. 'I'm overreacting, but I love him so much, and I thought he was going to die, and no-one would take any notice, and they wouldn't give him any pain killers, and bloody Dr Williams was so bored with the whole case it wasn't true. And then she, I mean Noel, turns up this morning, and suddenly everyone rolls up, and starts paying attention to the case, and giving Jonah VIP treatment, and he's been getting better all day. I know I should be h-happy. I prayed to God, if he m-made Jonah better, I'd never be unhappy again. I c-can't think why I'm so miserable.'

'I can,' said Cory, his hand over hers. 'You're absolutely played out. What I want you to do now, is not to argue, but to go and have a bath and wash your hair, have a little gentle supper, and then go to bed and have a decent night's sleep. Then you'll be fresh to look after him in the morning.'

'But he gets such frightful nightmares. You think he's better, and suddenly he gets worse. Will someone sit with him tonight?'

'I will,' said Cory.

He went back into Jonah's room.

'Well,' said Noel icily. 'Have you finished consoling her?'

'For the time being,' answered Cory in a level voice. 'She must have been through hell and back. I'm absolutely appalled by her appearance.'

'She's obviously one of these people who go to pieces in a crisis,' said Noel.

Cory was about to reply when Noel added quickly, 'Where can one eat round here?'

'There's a good restaurant in Skipton,' said Cory.

'As soon as Jonah's asleep, I thought we might go there. In fact I've asked Dr Williams to join us. He's charming, and I thought he could give you the low-down on Jonah.'

'No thanks,' said Cory. 'I didn't come four thousand miles to go out to dinner.'

Jonah in fact made very good progress and was out in five days. Harriet hardly recognized the nursery and the children's rooms when she got home, they were so tidy. All the playing cards and jigsaw puzzles had been sorted out, the children's clothes lay in serried ranks, beautifully ironed in the drawers. William's nappies were all fluffy and as white as snow, even the old table in the nursery coated with generations of poster paints, gripfix, pentel, and coca-cola, had been scrubbed and was now gleaming like a furniture polish ad. Miss Hanbury, the temporary nanny, was a miracle, and Noel took every opportunity to point out the fact.

Noel stayed at the Wilderness and only left at the end of a week because she had to be in London to go on the Parkinson Show. It was one of the worst weeks of Harriet's life. William was teething and, like Cherubim and Seraphim, continually did cry, which gave Noel plenty of excuse for more bitchiness. Jonah, having had undivided attention for so long, displayed all the despotism and capriciousness of the convalescent. Chattie, from lack of attention, was very jealous and playing up. She was only just stopped from giving two of Noel's minks to a woman collecting jumble, and one afternoon Harriet came into the kitchen and found her and Sevenoaks both looking sick and extremely sheepish. They had consumed a whole tin of Good Boy Dog Choc Drops between them.

Chattie burst into tears when Harriet ticked her off. 'I was only trying to turn Sevenoaks into a Good Boy,' she wailed.

The worst part was having Noel about the place, looking gorgeous, getting in the way, and interfering with the running of the house.

'I can't call my kitchen my castle any more,' grumbled Mrs Bottomley.

Nor did the telephone ever stop ringing. It was either Noel's agent, or the people on the Parkinson Show, or the *Yorkshire Post* wanting to interview her, or Ronnie Acland, or Dr Williams. Then, if people weren't ringing her, she was making long distance telephone calls herself, or getting Harriet to run errands for her, or wash her shirts, or sew on her buttons. Then there were the interminable discussions about her choosing the right thing to wear on Parkinson.

When one has passed through a time of great anxiety, relief and happiness do not immediately follow. Harriet found herself subject to fits of depression, inclined to be crotchety. She told herself she was very run down. She was fed up with seeing

Noel's peach-coloured silk underwear on the line, of smelling her wafts of scent everywhere.

Dr Williams called every day, which Harriet was sure was quite unorthodox. Looking out of the window, while making beds one day, Harriet saw Noel sitting girlishly on the old swing under the walnut tree, with Dr Williams pushing her, totally infatuated. The next moment she was called inside for a ten-minute drool with Ronnie Acland. Wedging her options open, thought Harriet.

One lunchtime, Dr Williams rang up, and after a brief conversation Noel disappeared in Cory's car. She returned five hours later, flushed and radiant, and came into the kitchen to regale Mrs Bottomley and Harriet with a long spiel about the impossibility of finding the right pair of shoes in Leeds for her television appearance.

'Did you try Schofields?' said Mrs Bottomley.

'I tried everywhere. I must have visited twenty shoe shops,' sighed Noel.

At that moment, Sevenoaks wandered over to her big bag which lay open on a chair, and before she could stop him, plunged his face inside and drew out a pair of frilly peach-coloured pants.

'I'm surprised you didn't find anything at Dolcis,' said Mrs Bottomley.

Harriet had to go out of the room to stop herself from laughing. She would have given anything to have told Cory.

She suspected, however, that Dr Williams and Ronnie were pure dalliance, and Noel's big guns were aimed at getting Cory back. Cory avoided opportunities to be alone with her and slept in the spare room. He buried himself in a load of work he'd brought back from America, and in getting Python ready for the point-to-point on Saturday. Occasionally Harriet saw his eyes resting on Noel, but she could not read their meaning. How did that beauty affect him now? He was kind to Harriet, but detached, as though his mind was somewhere beyond her reach. One thing she was certain of. If Noel came back, she would be straight out of a job. It made her very uneasy.

On the last evening before Noel went South, she and Cory stayed up talking. Harriet, coming down to get some Ribena for William, heard raised voices. The door was ajar and she stopped to listen:

'You've been content to leave the children entirely to me,' Cory was saying. 'Now you have the effrontery to say you want them back.'

'Ronnie and I have a house in France now as well as one in London,' said Noel. 'They'd be proper bases for the children to live. Be honest, Cory, children need a mother. A man can't really bring up children on his own.'

'I haven't managed too badly so far,' snapped Cory. 'You know perfectly well there is only one set of terms on which I'm prepared for you to have the children and as you're quite incapable of complying with them, there's no point in discussing it.'

He means her coming back to him and chucking all the others, thought Harriet miserably.

'How do you know I'm incapable of complying with them?' said Noel huskily.

The next moment the door shut.

Harriet fled upstairs. It's going to happen, she thought in anguish. But five minutes later she heard Cory come upstairs and the spare-room door open and shut. It was as though a great spear had been drawn out of her side.

Chapter Twenty-three

Harriet never forgot the day of the point-to-point –
the bookies shouting, the county in their well-cut
tweeds, the children sucking toffee apples, the
crowds pressing around the paddock and the finish-
ing post, the circling horses with their glossy coats.

She stood in the paddock trying to hold on to an
impossibly over-excited Chattie – poor Jonah hadn't
been allowed out – watching Python being saddled
up. The black mare's coat rippling blue in the sunshine.

Cory came over to them. He was wearing a pink
and grey striped shirt, and carrying a pink and grey
cap. They had hardly spoken since Noel left. He
picked up her hand and gave her his watch.

'Look after it for me,' he said, curling her fingers
over it.

'Good luck,' she whispered.

'Good luck, Daddy,' said Chattie.

They watched him feel Python's girths, clap a
hand on the ebony quarters, put a foot in the stirrup
and he was up, riding slowly round the paddock.

Two men beside Harriet in the crowd were discussing them.

'Grand looking beast. Bit young, bit light, though.'

'Erskine can ride her.'

'Oh it's Erskine is it? That's worth a fiver each way.'

Harriet's heart swelled with pride. Oh, please let him win. He needs this small, unimportant victory so much to cheer him up.

There were nine horses in the race. Acceptance, the favourite, a tall rangy bay, had been heavily backed to win. Harriet and Chattie climbed to the top of the hill, so they could see nearly all the way round the course and also hear the commentator. Harriet was so nervous she could hardly bear to watch.

At last they were off. For the first time round, Python was lying sixth for most of the way, but as the field started to jump the fences for the second time, she slowly began moving up.

'And now they've only got eight fences to jump,' said the commentator. 'And it's still Snow Moss from Acceptance, then Lazy Lucy and Tragedy Queen. Python is going very well and making ground all the time. Now they're coming up to the seventh from home and it's still Acceptance and Snow Moss. But Acceptance jumped that crooked and someone's down. I can't see exactly who it is . . . yes, it's Python! Python's down, I'm afraid.'

The crowd gave a groan. Harriet felt an agonizing pain shoot through her. But she was only conscious of fear – that Cory might be hurt, badly hurt.

Chattie started to cry.

'He'll be all right,' said Harriet in a shaking voice.

The microphone crackled. 'I'm sorry,' said the commentator. 'I made a mistake. It wasn't Python, it was Lazy Lucy who fell at the last fence – they've got similar colours. Python's there and still making ground.'

Tears pricked Harriet's eyes. Relief streamed over her.

As if in a dream, she watched Cory's figure crouched over the little black mare, coaxing her, urging her on. Slowly the distance between him and the leaders shortened. Only one more fence to go, and then Snow Moss had fallen, and it was only a tiring Acceptance between Cory and victory.

'Come on,' shrieked Harriet. And now Python was drawing level. For a split second, it looked as though Acceptance was going to hold on, then Python drew ahead by a nose as they passed the post.

How Harriet and Chattie hugged each other!

'I've won 50p,' screamed Chattie.

Everyone cheered as Cory rode in. For once, a broad grin was spread across the impassive features, as he patted the sweating mare.

'Oh, clever, clever Daddy!' screeched Chattie.

Cory's eyes met Harriet's. 'Well,' he said, 'we did it.'

He dismounted and then, Harriet never remembered afterwards how it happened, a golden figure smothered in furs suddenly pushed her way through the crowd, and flung her arms round Cory's neck. It was Noel.

'Oh, darling, darling,' she cried. 'I'm so proud of you.'

'Mummy! Whatever are you doing here?' said Chattie.

'I'm not going to marry Ronnie,' cried Noel. 'I've come back, back to Daddy. We're all going to be one happy family again.'

Suddenly the paddock seemed to be full of photographers.

'This is the most wonderful day of my life,' said Noel, smiling at them radiantly.

Cory's face was quite expressionless.

In a daze, Harriet watched Chattie pulling at Noel's coat.

'Mummy, Mummy! Did you bring me a present?'

'Yes, of course I did, darling.' She turned round to Harriet with a mocking smile on her beautiful face. 'I even brought a little *cadeau* for Harriet.'

Harriet looked round and gave a gasp. She hadn't noticed the slender, elegant figure in the black fur coat and dark glasses.

'Hullo, Harriet, darling,' said Simon.

'Simon! Oh, my God,' whispered Harriet. 'What are you doing here?' Her hand flew to her cheek. Then Chattie gave a shriek. 'Look at Harriet! She's hurt herself.'

Looking down, Harriet realized that blood was pouring from her hand. Then the horrified faces in front of her started going round and round, and she lost consciousness.

*   *   *

Darkness, sickness, throbbing pain engulfed her. The sound of different voices drummed in her ears.

A wail from Chattie: 'She's not dying, is she?'

Noel's voice, steel-tipped with irritation: 'Of course not, she's only fainted.'

Cory's voice like gravel, harsh with anxiety: 'Get back all of you! Can't you see she needs more air?'

Another voice, tender, caressing, languid. Could it really be Simon's?

'Everything's going to be all right, darling, I'm with you now.'

Then great whirling clouds of darkness coming down again, then slowly clearing and, suddenly, she opened her eyes and saw a face looking down at her, pale against the sable coat, a face she was only used to seeing in dreams, or disappearing in nightmares.

'Oh, Simon,' she croaked weakly, 'is it really you?'

'Hullo, baby. Yes, it's me, but you mustn't try to talk.'

'I'm not dreaming, am I?'

He smiled, but there were tears in his eyes 'Not dreaming. Feel.' He touched her cheek with his hand but, as she turned her head to kiss it, he said, 'Lie still.'

'Where am I?'

'In a draughty ambulance. A bossy old fag's been bandaging up your hand. You cut it breaking the glass on Cory's watch in your pocket. Must have been the shock of seeing me. Flattering, I suppose, that I still have that effect on you.'

That wasn't quite right, but Harriet was too dazed to work out why.

'Where's Cory? And the children and everyone?'

'Stop worrying about other people,' he said sooth-ingly.

'Oh, Simon, you do look lovely,' she sighed.

It was exactly the right thing to have said. He smiled and dipped a lavender silk handkerchief in a mug of water beside her, and gently began to sponge the blood from the side of her face.

'When you're feeling up to it, I'm going to drive you to the hospital to have some stitches put in your hand.'

Harriet watched him light a cigarette and insert it carefully in a dark blue cigarette holder.

'Simon, Noel didn't force you to come up here?'

He looked mortified. 'Oh, darling! Do you think I'm that much of a bastard? Borzoi and I broke up just after I saw you last. I've been trying to trace you ever since. No-one knew where you were – your old boss, your landlady, even your parents. I didn't know a thing about the baby until Noel rang me this morning. I was completely poleaxed – half knocked out at finding you, half horror at what you'd been through.'

He took her hands. 'From now on I'm going to make the decisions, and I'm never going to let you go again.'

At that moment, Cory came into the ambulance, and Harriet was furious to find herself snatching her hands away. He was wearing a battered sheepskin coat over his pink and grey silk shirt, and had to stoop in order to avoid banging his head.

'Hullo, how are you?' How austere it sounded, after Simon's gushing tenderness.

She struggled to sit up. 'I'm all right. I'm sorry about your watch.'

'Doesn't matter at all, you only smashed the glass.'

'I'm so pleased you w-won the race.'

He smiled briefly. 'Bloody good, wasn't it? When you're feeling stronger, I'll run you over to the hospital.'

'I'm taking her to the hospital,' said Simon in his languid voice, tipping ash from his cigarette on to the floor just by Cory's feet. The gesture was curiously insolent. 'And then I thought we'd drive back to your place. I'm quite anxious to see my son.'

Then Noel came into the ambulance. 'I'm giving Harriet the weekend off, Cory,' she said. 'It won't do Mrs Bottomley any harm to do some work for a change. She can easily take care of the children and William.'

'Don't be ridiculous!' snapped Cory. 'Harriet's lost a lot of blood. She's going stright home to bed after she's been to hospital.'

'Cory,' said Noel patiently, 'these children haven't seen each other for absolutely ages. They ought to be on their own together.'

'Rubbish,' said Cory brusquely. 'They've got nothing to say to each other. It was all over years ago.'

Harriet took no pleasure that these people were fighting over her. She felt a bit like a hostess with no drink in the house, invaded by a crowd of people. The mixture of heavy scent, antiseptic and French cigarettes was making her dizzy. Noel's cold yellow eyes were boring into her.

'I think I'd better go with Simon,' she said.

Harriet only remembered isolated incidents about the rest of the day. 'I've booked in at a hotel down the valley,' Simon said as he drove her back from the hospital. He put his hand on her thigh. 'I hadn't realized how much I'd want you. I've never met anyone who took to sex like you did.'

Harriet felt overwhelmed by a great weariness. She was in no mood for a sexual marathon.

Neither was Simon's meeting with William the success she had hoped. William, woken from sleep, was red-faced and bad-tempered. Simon, after initial cooings and ravings, had no idea what to do with him. Holding him at arm's length, like a bomb about to explode, fearful he might be sick over the beautiful fur coat, he handed him back to Harriet almost immediately.

She had fantasized about them meeting for so long, the joy, the incredulity, it was bound to be an anticlimax. Simon couldn't be expected to be as good with babies as Cory.

She tried to shake off her depression as she threw clothes into a small suitcase, but she was gripped with the same feeling of menace she'd always had when packing to go back to school. She felt rather ashamed that she put in three novels she wanted to read and the remains of the sleeping pills Cory had made her get from the doctor. Sevenoaks and Tadpole sat around looking miserable at the sight of suitcases.

'I'll see you both tomorrow,' she said hopefully.

Just as she was combing her hair in front of the mirror, Cory walked in without knocking.

'You're mad to go off with Simon,' he said harshly, speaking directly to her haggard reflection. 'He's a spoilt, corrupt little boy with no guts and no backbone. He's ditched you once, he'll ditch you again.'

Harriet put her head in her hands.

'Don't bully me,' she said in real anguish. 'I'm in such a muddle.'

'I'm sorry,' he said in a much gentler voice, putting his hands on her shoulders. 'But just because he's William's father, you mustn't feel you ought to marry him.'

For a second, Harriet leant against him, then she stood up.

'I've got to talk to Simon, and try to sort out what I feel.'

For a minute they stared at each other. Then he buttoned her coat up as if she was a little girl.

'Be careful,' he said.

Later, she remembered being impressed by the cool way Simon had written Mr and Mrs Villiers in the hotel visitors' book, as though he'd done it a hundred times before. He'd booked them into a luxury three-room suite.

He was at his most winning too, remorseful at his previous conduct, gazing into her eyes, telling her how beautiful she had become, beguiling her with bitchy stories about film stars he had met, speaking of his future with her and William. All perfect; yet

Harriet had the feeling she'd got onto the wrong bus and was desperately hurtling in a direction she didn't want to go.

He had changed too. He had all the sheen and glitter of the star now. When he talked to her, she felt he was playing to an audience.

'I want to know everything that's happened to you since we split up,' he said.

But when she started telling him, despite the intent look on his face, she knew his thoughts were miles away, so she changed the subjet. 'It's wonderful you've done so well, Simon.'

He spread his hands out. 'Just luck, really. I had mild success with a couple of television plays I did, and I made this film abroad; just a small part, but everyone's raving about the rushes. And in May I'm going to make a film with Noel, with a really meaty part in it. She's been terribly kind.'

Harriet wondered what form Noel's kindness had taken.

'You haven't been having an affair with her?' she asked idly.

'Dar-ling! Be reasonable. She's old enough to be my mother.'

'She could hardly be your mother when she was ten.'

'I wouldn't even put that past her! Anyway, I don't go for these busty, earth mother types – I like my women slim. You've got the most gorgeous figure since you lost all that weight.'

Harriet smiled, but she found her thoughts wandering back to Cory and how he and Noel were getting on at this moment, and then she realized it hadn't been the shock of seeing Simon that had made her cut her hand, it must have been the sharp, ignored pain that shot through her when she thought Cory's horse had fallen in the race.

Simon was still talking about his new film. Concentrate on his beauty, she kept telling herself. He's far better looking than Cory. The champagne was beginning to make her feel sick.

He got to his feet and came towards her with that sudden seductive smile that he could use as a weapon or a caress. The brilliant blue-green eyes wandered over her body – hard eyes now, endlessly craving distraction. She felt mesmerized like a small bird before a snake.

'Darling,' he murmured. 'It's stupid to try and communicate with words. Let's go to bed.'

And he pulled her into his arms and kissed her, but it wasn't the same as before – no turning of the entrails, no weakness at the knees, no black turgid drowning tide of passion.

For a minute she remembered the evening when Cory had kissed her, and she shivered as she re-lived the swooning, helpless ecstasy.

'No,' she cried wriggling away. 'I don't want to now. You must give me more time.'

Simon's face darkened. 'What's the matter? Gone off me since the old days?'

'I don't feel well,' she whispered. 'Would you mind if I lay down for a few minutes?'

Now he was all contrition. 'Darling, why didn't you tell me?'

Later she was lying in the dark, her head thrashing from side to side in an agony of indecision, when the telephone rang. She heard Simon lift the receiver. Then there was a pause as he shut the bedroom door.

In some blind hope that it might be Cory ringing, she picked up the extension by her bed. Then she stiffened as she heard Noel's voice: 'How's it all going, precious?'

Then Simon's voice, petulant. 'All right, but she's not going to be the pushover you predicted.'

'Well, you've got plenty of time. If you can't have her eating out of your hands in twenty-four hours, you're not the man you were last night.'

Simon laughed and growled wolfishly. 'Good, wasn't it? But then it's always good with you. You – er – spur me on to greater endeavour.'

'Well, close your eyes and pretend it's me.'

'God that it was! I do miss you, darling. You won't get so hooked on Cory again so that you'll forget me, will you?'

'Darling,' Noel's deep voice was like a sedative. 'I wouldn't have angled you that part so I could spend all that time with you this summer, if I hadn't been a tiny bit smitten, now would I?'

'I suppose not.'

'What do you think of your son and heir?'

'Oh, pretty horrific. But then I'm not mad about babies. I thought you said he looked just like me.'

Noel started to laugh. Harriet put down the receiver and went into the bathroom and was violently sick. Then she stood trembling, leaning against the bathroom door, icy cold and sweating, wondering what the hell to do next.

She washed her face and went into the sitting room. Simon was lounging across the armchair.

'Hello, beauty,' he said amiably. 'You look as though you've seen a ghost.'

'I've been listening in on the extension. I heard all your conversation with Noel.'

Simon sighed. 'Oh dear, you shouldn't have done that. Surely you know by now that eavesdroppers never . . . ?'

'Simon,' she interrupted furiously. 'Stop it! Stop it! Why can't you be serious for once? How long have you been in love with Noel?'

'I'm not in love with her.'

'Well, how many times have you slept with her?'

'Once, twice. What the hell does it matter? I don't love her. It's you I love.'

'You couldn't love me, the way you were talking to her.'

'Oh, darling, haven't you heard the expression "sleeping your way to the top"? Well, I want that film part, and if it means chatting up an old prima-donna like Noel that's OK by me.'

Harriet stared at him appalled.

'And you were prepared to try and make a go of it with me, while still carrying on an affair with Noel? I don't understand you, Simon.'

He looked at her for a minute, mocking, his head on one side, his hands in his pockets.

'Well, then, I can't help you, can I?'

Then he started to laugh. 'Oh come on, darling, see the funny side of it.'

Harriet shook her head. 'I don't think it's funny. I want to go home.'

It was a clear night, the stars shone electrically blue, the moon came over the crags and reflected milkily in the river. As he drove, Simon turned to look at Harriet.

'You're making a mistake going back, darling. Noel fights very dirty – and, however much Cory likes you as a plaything, he'll kick you out the moment she wants it.'

When they arrived at the house, Harriet let herself in and met Noel coming out of the drawing room.

'Hullo, darlings,' she said. 'Had a lovers' tiff already?'

Harriet took a deep breath. 'I overheard your conversation with Simon on the telephone. I want to see Cory at once.'

Not a flicker of an eyelid did Noel betray her surprise. 'My dear, he's not here. He went out half-an-hour ago. I don't know when he'll be back. I think we'd better have a little chat together. Simon, angel, would you excuse us a minute?'

Shepherding Harriet into the drawing room, she shut the door behind them.

Harriet sat down on the sofa. Her knees wouldn't stop trembling. Noel started pouring herself a drink.

'How can I make you understand,' she began, 'that I really love Cory? I admit I behaved badly in the past. But now it's different. I know he's the only person for me, and I'll do anything to get him back.'

'Like bringing your latest lover up here to lure me away and offering him the bait of a big film part?'

Noel banged the whisky bottle down on the metal tray.

'Oh, God!' she shouted. 'Grow up! I know you're nuts about Cory, but he doesn't give a damn about your stupid passion. I tried to let you out easily by getting Simon up here. He's ambitious as hell, that boy. He needed a bit of incentive. But if you honestly think I'm intending to have a prolonged affair with him and give him the lead in my next film, you need your head examined!'

She spoke as though Simon was a nasty mark on a new dress that the dry cleaners would have no trouble removing.

Harriet ran a dry tongue over her lips. 'I know Cory loves you, but he also likes me here looking after the children.'

'Darling,' Noel's eyes were huge now and strangely gentle. 'I did want to let you down easily. I admit I was the tiniest bit jealous of you. The children are wild about you, and so was Kit; and even Cory, who's notoriously hard to please, regarded you with something close to approval. But I got a letter from him this morning, which really convinced me I've got nothing to worry about.'

She opened her bag and took out a sheet of thick azure writing-paper and handed it to Harriet. The black, almost illegible writing was unmistakable.

'Oh, darling,' she read. 'I'm totally destroyed.

Ever since you left yesterday, I know that it's impossible for me to live without you any longer. I give in. Please, please come back, on any terms. I don't care. The thought that you could feel jealous of that zombie who looks after the children would be ludicrous, if it weren't tragic that something so trivial could keep us apart. I've got no complaints about her work, but she'll leave tomorrow if it means your coming back any sooner.'

If you walk into a torture chamber and ask to be tortured, Harriet reflected, you can't complain of the pain. Very carefully she folded Cory's letter and put it on the table, and sat still for a minute.

'And you'd like me to go now?' she said numbly.

Noel nodded. 'I think it would be better in every way. There's no need to say goodbye to the children. It'll only upset them. They need a mother and, from now on, I shall stay at home and look after them.'

'May I leave a letter for Cory telling him I'm going?'

'Of course you may,' said Noel kindly.

Before Harriet left, Noel gave her a cheque for £100. 'We wouldn't want you to starve.'

Harriet wished she were in a position to refuse.

Chapter Twenty-four

Harriet sat watching the smouldering log fire. She had been home with her parents a week now, and all was forgiven. But the peace and resignation she craved had not come. If it hadn't been for William, she would never have had the strength to go on living. What's going to happen to me? she thought in panic. I can't lump a broken heart around for the rest of my life.

None of the loose ends seemed to tie up either. Why had Cory come to her bedroom that last evening and tried to persuade her not to go off with Simon? Why hadn't he been home when she and Simon had returned later? One would have thought he'd be so delirious to have Noel back he'd never have left her side.

But as the days passed, it became increasingly obvious that she couldn't go on without news of him, until she knew that he and the children were all right. And what about Sevenoaks? She had put a PS on her letter asking Cory to look after him till she found a job where she could keep him. But how long would it be before Noel persuaded Cory that Sevenoaks was too much of a nuisance? But how could she find out how things were going? If she rang Mrs Bottomley Noel might easily answer the telephone. Then she remembered Kit. Of course. He would certainly have news of Cory. The number was permanently engaged when she rang. He must have taken the telephone off the hook.

'I'm going up to London,' she said to her mother, as she went into the kitchen. 'I'll take William with me.'

Upstairs she glared at her worn reflection in the mirror. 'I'm almost beyond redemption,' she sighed sadly. But she brushed her hair until it shone, put on the grey dress Cory had given her, and tried, without much success, to paint the circles out from under her eyes.

Kit's studio was in Islington. There was no answer when Harriet rang the bell. He must be out, she thought despairingly. It was nearly half past four and the milk hadn't been taken in. She rang again. Still no answer. Heavy-hearted, she started down the steps when the door opened and Kit, a golden giant, dishevelled and naked to the waist, stood blinking down at her. Then he gave a bellow of rage like an apoplectic colonel, which sent her even further down the steps.

'Harriet!' he shouted. 'Where the bloody hell do you think you're going?'

He bounded down the stairs, grabbed her by the scruff of the neck and pulled her inside the house. Then slammed the door and leant his huge shoulders against it.

'You little bitch!' he swore at her. 'After all your cant about loyalty. God, you make me sick!'

'W-what's the m-matter?' she faltered.

William had started to howl. Harriet herself was close to tears, when a ravishingly pretty coloured girl wandered out of a bedroom, wearing a scanty orange towel.

'What is all this noise, Keet?' she said yawning.

'Tangie, darling,' said Kit, taking the howling child from Harriet and handing him to her. 'Take this sweet little baby away and keep him quiet for a minute or two.'

The coloured girl's eyes flashed.

'Oh, no,' said Kit hastily, 'he's not mine, scout's honour! Nothing to do with me. Nor is she either, thank God. She's got herself mixed up with my unfortunate brother, Cory.'

William looked dubiously up at the sleek black face, but he stopped crying.

'Give him back to me,' protested Harriet.

'Shut up!' snarled Kit and, propelling her into the nearest room, shut the door behind them.

'Well?' he said, towering above her like some avenging angel. 'What made you do it? Swanning off with lover boy without a word of explanation.'

'It wasn't like that!' protested Harriet.

'Go on then,' said Kit coldly. 'Amaze me.'

'I didn't go off with Simon, and I left a letter for Cory with Noel.'

'The great postmistress,' said Kit acidly. 'You're even more stupid than I thought.'

He got up and poured himself a drink. 'I suppose you'd better tell me the whole story.'

When she had finished, he said, 'Noel seems to have overreached herself this time. I told you never to believe a word she says. She must have torn your letter up and told Cory you'd done a bunk with Simon. He's still divorcing her. The case comes up next week.'

'It is?' Harriet whispered incredulously. 'But what about that letter from Cory Noel showed me, begging her to come back?'

'He probably wrote it years ago. She's always made a fuss about every nanny they had, and she hoards all her love letters. Did you notice the date?'

Harriet shook her head.

'Well then. I had dinner with Cory last night. He's in a pretty bad shape.'

'He's in London?' asked Harriet, turning red then white. 'Did he mention me?'

Kit conceded a grin. 'I've never known Cory really boring before. He's convinced he messed everything up by trying to pull you, then letting you go off with Simon.'

'Oh, God!' said Harriet with a sob. 'What am I going to do?'

Kit got to his feet. 'You'd better go round to his house at once and ask him to take you back.'

'I can't! What can I say to him?'

'I should tell him the truth – that you love him. I'll get you a taxi. Don't worry about William. We'll look after him for an hour or two.'

Chapter Twenty-five

In the taxi, she desperately tried to keep her hands steady as she re-did her face, spilling scent and foundation all over her bag. Now they were entering Chiltern Street; there was the familiar dark blue house. Oh wait, she wanted to say, I haven't put any mascara on. Then she thought, how silly to worry about mascara at a time like this!

She rang the bell and waited, hands clammy, throat dry, her heart pounding like surf. When Cory opened the door he seemed about to tell her to go to hell, then he realized who she was and just stared at her in amazement. She stared back unable to speak. For a moment, she thought he was going to take her in his arms, then he stood back to let her come in. They went upstairs to the room where he'd first interviewed her. He seemed to have grown taller and thinner, paler too – the haughty, inscrutable face heavily shadowed and tired. There was an embarrassed silence; then he said, 'Sit down. How are you?'

Harriet perched on the edge of one of the yellow silk armchairs. Her legs wouldn't hold her up any longer.

'I'm all right.'

'And William?'

'He's lovely.'

She refused when he offered her a cigarette, her hands were shaking too much.

'How's it going, you and Simon?' he asked in a matter-of-fact voice, as he concentrated on lighting his own cigarette.

'I'm not with Simon, I never have been – only for a couple of hours that Saturday night. I realized then we were completely washed-up. Didn't Noel give you my letter?'

He shook his head slowly. He didn't seem interested in explanations. 'Where are you now?'

'At home.'

'Made it up with your parents? That's good.'

'I came up to London to look for a job,' she lied.

'Why don't you come back?' He paused. 'The children are desolate without you.'

'And you?' she wanted to cry.

He was playing with a green glass paperweight on his desk. 'If you were to come back,' he said carefully, 'there wouldn't be any funny business. I shall be abroad for most of the rest of the year.'

'No!' she interrupted him with a violence that brought her to her feet, face-to-face with him. 'I couldn't come back on those terms.'

'I see,' he said in a flat voice.

She went over to the window and looked out at the young leaves of the plane tree, glinting white in the setting sun. Her throat felt like sand. She was trying to summon up courage to do the most difficult thing she'd ever done in her life.

'For someone who's too clever by three-quarters,' she said in a shaking voice, 'you're awfully dumb, where women are concerned. Don't you see, if I were living in the same house, and you were away all the time, and never laid a finger on me, I'd die of frustration?'

Cory looked up – the weary eyes suddenly alert.

'Don't you understand,' she went on slowly, 'that I only ran away because Noel said she was coming back to you, and I just couldn't take it?'

'Go on, go on,' he said, his face as white as hers.

'Don't you understand,' she sobbed, 'that I love you? Love you more than anything else in the world. And I can't live without you!'

She didn't need to say any more. He was across the room, the great arms she had been waiting for closed round her, and he was kissing her so fiercely she almost lost consciousness.

Then he said despairingly, 'Oh, darling Harriet. I love you. But it wouldn't work. I'm too old and tired and bitter for you.'

'You're not,' she jibbered. 'Just thinking about you turns me to jelly,' she went on. 'I've never been crazy over anyone as I am over you.'

Cory stared down at her, at the parted lips, the burning eyes, the flushed cheeks, the dishevelled hair.

'Hey,' he said wonderingly. 'You do love me, don't you? What the hell am I going to do about it?'

'You will do something, won't you?' she said

nuzzling against him, so he could feel the frantic beating of her heart.

'Be careful,' he said, trying to smile.

'What do you mean?'

'I'm beginning to feel as though I can be consoled,' and he kissed her forehead, and then her cheeks, salt with tears, and then her lips.

'Oh, darling,' he muttered. 'Don't give me time to be ashamed of what I'm doing. I'm going to keep you. What else can I do, when you're so adorable? But you don't know what you're in for. I shall make a bloody awful husband.'

Harriet leapt away in horror. 'I didn't mean that! You don't have to marry me.'

Cory smiled. 'You're not the only one who's allowed to dictate terms. You've just said you'll never come back to Yorkshire unless I devote every minute of the day to laying fingers on you.'

Harriet blushed. 'I never said that.'

'So if I take you, it's for good. For ever and ever.'

She was trembling now, really perturbed.

'But I forced you into it.'

He sat down and pulled her onto his knee.

'Sweetheart,' he said very gently. 'I know what a shy, reserved person you are, except when you get sloshed at Hunt Balls, and I know what it cost you to come here and tell me you loved me. But if you knew what it meant to me, for the first time in ten years, the miracle of hearing the girl I love tell me she loves me, and really mean it.

'It's strange,' he went on, pushing her hair back from her forehead. 'I can't even place the moment I started loving you. It's so mixed up with convincing myself I was acting for your own good – dragging you away from Billy, bawling you out for going out with Kit, because he was a wolf, trying to persuade you not to go off with Simon because he'd make you a rotten husband, but all the time I must have been eaten up with jealousy because I wanted you for myself. I got so used to being hung-up on Noel, I never believed I could love anyone else, and then you ran away and the house was like a morgue. I knew I ought to give you and Simon a chance, but after five days I couldn't stand it any longer, so I came South. And . . . look.'

He pulled a packet of cigarettes out of his pocket, on which was scribbled a telephone number.

'That's Simon's number,' said Harriet.

He nodded. 'I was going to ring up and try to persuade you to come back.'

And then Harriet realized that this awkward, difficult, beautiful man really did love her.

'Oh, I'm so happy,' she said, bursting into tears and flinging her arms round his neck. 'You're really over Noel?'

'Really, really. She's like measles – you don't catch her twice.'

Harriet giggled. 'That sounds more like Kit. Where is she now?'

'I don't know. Conserving her energies some-where for her appearance in the divorce courts next week.' His face hardened. 'I'm afraid it's going to be very nasty. She'll probably cite you.'

'I don't care,' and she began to kiss him.

*   *   *

'Are the children really all right?' she said later. 'God, I've missed them so much.'

'They've missed you – if I hadn't come down here, they were threatening to get on a train to London and fetch you themselves. We'll ring them up and give them the good news in a minute. Christ, it is good news.'

Only one thing was nagging Harriet. 'How's Sevenoaks?' she said.

'Well actually he's here,' said Cory. 'I thought he'd have withdrawal symptoms if we both abandoned him, so I brought him with me.'

'Oh, you *are* sweet. Can I see him?'

'Sure, he's in my bedroom, down the passage.'

He followed Harriet to the door, adding, 'He's greatly improved by the way. In your absence, I took the opportunity of teaching him a few manners. In actual fact he's quite trainable if one's firm. He sits and stays now, and comes when he's called. And at least I've stopped him climbing onto beds and chewing everything up.'

'That's amazing,' said Harriet, opening the bedroom door, and looking inside.

On the bed sprawled Sevenoaks, his shaggy grey head on the pillow, snoring loudly. Beside him, chewed to bits, lay the remains of a pair of suede shoes.

'Oh doesn't he look sweet lying there?' said Harriet.

Sevenoaks opened an eye, and suddenly saw Harriet.

'Stay,' thundered Cory. 'Stay.'

Sevenoaks took a flying leap through the air, and landing at Harriet's feet threw himself on her in ecstasy, nearly knocking her sideways, moaning with joy.

'Stay,' howled Cory.

Sevenoaks gave Cory an old-fashioned look and took no notice at all.

Harriet caught Cory's eye and went off into peals of laughter.

'Oh, darling,' she said, 'are you sure you really want to marry me? You won't get fed up?'

'Of course I will, but not for very long,' said Cory, pulling Sevenoaks off. 'I mean we're virtually married already. We've got three children and a problem dog between us. We've spent long evenings discussing their education and what we feel about life, you've cooked and washed and kept house for me. The only thing we haven't done is slept together, and I don't have any major hangups about that.'

'We've eaten all the gingerbread,' said Harriet ecstatically, 'and now we can enjoy the lovely, lovely gilt.'

'Exactly,' said Cory, and he began kissing her . . .

THE END

Fall in love all over again with seven stories from the pen of Jilly Cooper, 'The Jane Austen of our time' *Harpers & Queen*

EMILY
If Emily hadn't gone to Annie's party she would never have met and married the devastating Rory Balniel.
0 552 15249 8

BELLA
Bella was the most promising young actress in London. The dashingly handsome Ruper Henriques couldn't wait to marry her. But Bella had a secret in her past.
0 552 15250 1

IMOGEN
Imogen's holiday on the Riviera was a revelation – and so was she. A wild Yorkshire rose, a librarian, *and* a virgin, she was a prize worth winning.
0 552 15254 4

PRUDENCE
Prudence was overjoyed when her boyfriend invited her home to meet his family. But the rest of the family all seemed to be in love with the wrong people.
0 552 15256 0

HARRIET
Harriet was shattered when a brief affair left her a penniless, heartbroken single mother. She set off for Yorkshire to work as a nanny to the children of eccentric scriptwriter, Cory Erskine. But life in the country was anything but peaceful.
0 552 15251 X

OCTAVIA
When Octavia saw her school-friend's fabulous boyfriend she knew she just had to have him. But Gareth Llewellyn seemed determined to thwart her plans.
0 552 15252 8

LISA AND CO
Fourteen stories of great variety and undoubted class from an author who has endeared herself to millions of readers and bewitched them all.
0 552 15255 2

Is *your* collection complete?

CORGI BOOKS

Jilly Cooper's Rutshire Chronicles offer a heady blend of
skulduggery, sexual adventure and hilarious high jinks:

RIDERS
Takes the lid off international show jumping, a world in
which the brave horses are almost human, but the humans
frequently behave like animals.
0 552 15055 X

RIVALS
Into the cut-throat world of Corinium television comes Declan
O'Hara, a mega-star with two ravishing teenage daughters. Living
rather too closely across the valley is Rupert Campbell-Black,
divorced and as dissolute as ever.
0 552 15056 8

POLO
Follows the jet set world of the top polo players – to the *estancias*
of Argentina, to Palm Beach and Deauville, and on
to the royal polo fields of England and the glamorous
pitches of California.
0 552 15057 6

THE MAN WHO MADE HUSBANDS JEALOUS
Lysander couldn't pass a stray dog, an ill-treated horse, or a
neglected wife without rushing to the rescue. And with neglected
wives the rescue invariably led to ecstatic bonking, which didn't
please their erring husbands one bit.
0 552 15058 4

APPASSIONATA
When Abigail Rosen gets the chance to take over the Rutminster
Symphony Orchestra, she doesn't realize it is composed of the
wildest bunch of musicians ever to blow a horn or caress a fiddle.
0 552 15054 1

SCORE!
Sir Robert Rannaldini, the most successful but detested conductor
in the world, had two ambitions: to seduce the ravishing Tabitha
Campbell-Black, and to put his mark on musical history by
making the definitive film of Verdi's *Don Carlos*.
0 552 15059 2

CORGI BOOKS

PANDORA
by Jilly Cooper

No picture ever came more beautiful than Raphael's *Pandora*.
Discovered by a dashing young lieutenant, Raymond Belvedon, in
a Normandy Chateau in 1944, she had cast her spell over his
family – all artists and dealers – for fifty years. Hanging in a turret
of their lovely Cotswold house, Pandora witnessed Raymond's
tempestuous wife Galena both entertaining a string of lovers, and
giving birth to her four children: Jupiter, Alizarin, Jonathan and
superbrat Sienna. Then an exquisite stranger rolls up, claiming to
be a long-lost daughter of the family, setting the three Belvedon
brothers at each other's throats. Accompanying her is her fatally
glamorous boyfriend, whose very different agenda
includes an unhealthy interest in the Raphael.

During a fireworks party, the painting is stolen. The hunt to
retrieve it takes the reader on a thrilling journey to Vienna,
Geneva, Paris, New York and London. After a nail-biting court
case and a record-smashing Old Masters sale at Sotheby's,
passionate love triumphs and *Pandora* is
restored to her rightful home.

'Open the covers of Jilly Cooper's latest novel and you lift the lid
of a Pandora's box. From the pages flies a host of delicious and
deadly vices . . . Her sheer exuberance and energy are contagious'
The Times

'This is Jilly in top form with her most sparkling novel to date'
Evening Standard

'One reads her for her joie de vivre . . . and her razor-sharp sense
of humour. Oh, and the sex' *New Statesman*

'She's irresistible . . . she frees you from the daily drudge and
deposits you in an alternative universe where love, sex and
laughter rule' *Independent on Sunday*

'The whole thing is a riot – vastly superior to anything else in a
glossy cover' *Daily Telegraph*

'A wonderful, romantic spectacular of a novel' *Spectator*

0 552 14850 4

CORGI BOOKS

CLASS
by Jilly Cooper

The English have been and always will be, obsessed by class, even though they may not realize it. And Jilly Cooper has put an accurate, acerbic, and wickedly funny finger on the idiosyncracies of the English at home, whether it be in their castles, their nice villas in Weybridge, or in their high rise council flats. In *Class* we study the peculiar habits and mores of all classes – at play, at school, at work, during courtship and marriage rituals, even the way they dress, eat, and conduct their sex lives.

Here we have Harry and Caroline Stow-Crat who love their dogs more than each other, Gideon and Samantha Upward who drink too much and are always in respectable middle-class debt, and here, too, are the wonderful Nouveau Richards, whose luxury homes are in execrable taste but blissfully comfortable with chandeliers in the loo and a bidet on every bed.

'Witheringly funny, illuminated by astonishing brilliance'
Observer

'Enormously readable and very funny'
Cosmopolitan

0 552 14662 5

CORGI BOOKS

A LIST OF OTHER JILLY COOPER TITLES AVAILABLE FROM CORGI BOOKS AND BANTAM PRESS